CASCADE RENEGADES

Cover design by Kevin Breen
Book design by Russ Davis, Bravo Book Design

ISBN: 978-1-957607-42-9
Cataloging-in-Publication Data is available upon request

Manufactured in the United States of America

Published by
Latah Books, Spokane, Washington
www.latahbooks.com

The author may be contacted at yakimahunter@yahoo.com

Praise for THE LUKE MCCAIN SERIES

"Outdoors writer Rob Phillips produces yet another page-turner, further demonstrating his extensive, first-hand knowledge of central Washington State's backcountry and his mastery of the quick and compelling thrill ride of a suspenseful read....You don't have to read *Cascade Witness* in one sitting, but you'll want to."
–Adriana Janovich, Associate Editor of *Washington State Magazine* and author of *Unique Eats and Eateries of Spokane*

"Fast-paced and engaging, *Trapped in the Cascades* converges three separate storylines, each ripe with malicious intent and life-threatening repercussions. These are woven into a nail-biting finale with Luke McCain and his faithful companion, Jack, fighting off dangerous weather conditions and the ticking timer towards death if they are unsuccessful. A five-star read!"
–J.C. Fuller, author of *The Rockfish Island Mysteries*

"I had almost given up reading novels ... then I picked up *Creature of the Cascades*. Here is something you don't see every day. Rob Phillips writes real places into this page-turner, and he is not averse to taking risks with humor, suspense and wordplay. I was hooked from the first jump."
–Gary Lewis, TV host and author of *Fishing Central Oregon, Fishing Mount Hood Country*, and *John Nosler Going Ballistic*

"Rob Phillips takes you on another fun romp into the wilds of Washington State as Luke McCain works ... to figure out who or what is killing pets, livestock, and wild game in the South Cascades. Is it Sasquatch as some believe or is it something else?"
–John Kruse, host of *Northwestern Outdoors* and *America Outdoors Radio*

"*Cascade Manhunt* is the fifth book of Rob Phillips' Luke McCain series, and I believe it to be his best work . . . . As a retired Washington State undercover Fish and Wildlife detective, I found Rob's book to be spot-on. I simply couldn't put *Cascade Manhunt* down and am already thirsting for Rob's next book."

–Todd Vandivert, retired Washington State Fish and Wildlife detective and author of the Wildlife Justice series

"Poaching big game . . . check. A loveable yellow Lab . . . double check. Computer hackers from India . . . WHAT! That last item is the big checklist twist in outdoor writer Rob Phillips' latest novel, *Cascade Kidnapping*, the fourth in his Luke McCain series. As in all of Phillips' books, *Cascade Kidnapping* reinforces healthy respect for the outdoors and laws that protect it."

–Bob Crider, retired editor and publisher, *Yakima Herald-Republic*

"This is crime fiction at its finest–the perfect blend of a compelling mystery, a fabulous setting, the best dog ever, and a very likeable hero you won't forget."

–Christine Carbo, award-winning author of the Glacier Mystery Series

"*Cascade Vengeance* takes readers on a thrill ride through the dual worlds of drug dealing and big-game hunting deep in Washington's Cascade mountains. Rob Phillips uses his extensive knowledge of the region to tell the fast-moving tale . . . on the way to the story's harrowing and heartbreaking conclusion."

–Scott Graham, National Outdoor Book Award-winning author of *Mesa Verde Victim*

"*Cascade Vengeance*, the second book in the Luke McCain series, is another hang-onto-your-hat, nonstop action episode with Luke, a Washington State Fish and Wildlife officer, his FBI girlfriend Sara, and Jack, his loyal yellow Lab. I felt like I was riding shotgun in Luke's Ford pickup, bouncing along forest service roads where very bad guys might be lurking."

–Susan Richmond, owner of Inklings Bookshop

CASCADE RENEGADES

A LUKE MCCAIN
NOVEL

ROB PHILLIPS

Also by Rob Phillips

THE CASCADE KILLER

CASCADE VENGEANCE

CASCADE PREDATOR

CASCADE KIDNAPPING

CASCADE MANHUNT

CREATURE OF THE CASCADES

TRAPPED IN THE CASCADES

CASCADE WITNESS

A DOG LIFE WELL LIVED

CHAPTER 1

September 2004

The black and silver Chevy Silverado, pulling a twenty-foot horse trailer, slowly drove up the rough Forest Service road. It was just before four o'clock in the morning, and the headlights worked hard to light up the narrow road as it wound through giant black fir trees. The driver of the truck had been behind the wheel for nine hours, and he strained to keep his eyes, and the truck, on the road.

The driver and his partner had met a man pulling the horse trailer at a rest stop near Butte, Montana. The duo in the Chevy Silverado were paid twenty-two hundred dollars to transfer the trailer from the man's truck in the rest stop to their pickup. Then they were to drive the horse trailer, and the cargo within, to Washington State.

The two people in the Chevy pickup knew what was in the horse trailer, but they still wanted to take a look. So when they stopped for fuel in St. Regis, they walked back and looked inside.

Eight eyes, shining gold, stared back at them. Four from one heavy steel enclosure at the front of the trailer, and four more from an identical steel cage in the back of the trailer. The two people had seen wolves before, but never this close.

"This is so cool," the woman said to her partner as she looked at the adult wolves. "Our names will never be known, but we'll go down in history."

"Us and a few others," the man said.

The drive to Colville, Washington and then on north and west into the wilds of northeastern Washington had been uneventful. And now that they had reached their destination—a spot that had been marked on a map by the man who had handed them the envelope with the cash inside—they were ready to finish their task.

The man found a wide spot in the road and pulled off. He put on some leather gloves and went to the back of the horse trailer. The woman did the same.

"They'll be skittish," the man said. "But they won't attack. We'll just open the back doors, slide the cage door open, and stand back. They should just run out."

The woman nodded and went to one of the swing-away doors in the back of the horse trailer. When her partner lifted the lever to unlock the doors and started to swing his door one way, she did the same with the door on her side. Then the man unlatched the steel door on the first cage and slid it open. He stepped back and to the side of the trailer and waited.

Within fifteen seconds, both wolves jumped from the rear of the trailer and ran off into the trees.

With some effort, the man and woman slid the empty steel cage out of the trailer, and the man went in to open the door of the second cage. This was going to be trickier because he could be stuck inside the trailer with two wild gray wolves. The man who had paid them the money told him to jump up on the cage after opening the door to it, so that is what he did.

When the cage door was open, the smaller of the two wolves inside—a dark gray female—jumped out of the enclosure and flew out the door. But the second wolf, a larger male, much lighter than the female, with gray streaks along its back and tail, jumped out of the cage, stopped, and turned to look at the man.

The man froze. If the wolf decided to attack, there was nothing he could do. He was defenseless. A hundred things ran through his mind in that instant. He should have brought a club, or a pitchfork, or some kind of weapon into the trailer with him just in case something happened. The last thing he wanted to do was hurt or kill this beautiful animal, but he didn't really want to be mauled or killed by the wolf either.

After staring at the man, looking right into his eyes with the most beautiful but deadly cold eyes the man had ever seen, the wolf turned and followed the female out of the trailer.

It had all happened in seconds, but when the man retold the story to the very few confidants in their wolf recovery alliance, he said the big male stared at him for a full two minutes. His partner wanted to call bull but never did. She knew the truth, as did he, and it would be their secret.

When he climbed out of the trailer, both he and the woman shined their flashlights into the dark woods in the direction the wolves had run. The woman thought she caught the reflection of eyes in the black of the nighttime forest, but it happened so quickly she was never sure.

Although the two were never told the details of other releases that fall, or in the years that followed, they knew they had done their part to help bring the proud and noble gray wolf back to the wilds of Washington State after nearly being eradicated in the early 1900s.

* * *

Present Day

Rumors that wolves were secretly released into Washington State as early as the late 1990s have been tossed around for years. Some people claimed they knew when it happened, and who had done it, but the stories were just that, stories.

The Washington State Department of Fish and Wildlife's official stance on the subject is that no wolves were ever transplanted into the state. The current population of wolves, which is now made up of a few hundred individuals in over 42 packs around the state, migrated in on their own, the officials contend, from existing packs in Idaho and British Columbia.

Where the wolves came from, or how they arrived in Washington, is a moot point because they are here now. And as the number of wolves in the state continues to grow, the divide between those who are happy to see the predators back in the ecosystem, and those who aren't, also grows.

Eli Creech would just as soon see wolves exterminated for good. The third-generation rancher owned seventeen hundred acres of land in the region known as the Okanogan, in northcentral Washington, where he ran a hundred and twenty head of prime Black Angus beef cattle, along with a small herd of sheep.

Now in his late sixties, stooped slightly in the shoulders by hard work and age, Creech looked a bit like Jeff Bridges, with bushy eyebrows shading light brown eyes. His graying sandy hair covered the collar of his pearl-button western shirt, with long sleeves that he often had rolled up to his elbows.

Creech had been dealing with wolves for the past three decades, and he didn't give a damn about how the canines had arrived. Whether the animals were brought in by what he believed to be radical wolf lovers, or they flew in on gossamer wings, the wolves were a constant threat to his livestock and his livelihood.

Over thirty years, he figured he had lost nearly forty calves to wolves, and almost half of his sheep. In fact, if his wife, Anne

Marie, didn't like having the sheep so much, he would have sold them off a long time ago. The things were absolutely stupid around predators, often just tipping over like they had died of a heart attack when being pursued by whatever was after them that day. Cougars, coyotes, even golden eagles had preyed on Creech's sheep at one time or another.

But the wolves, they were a different problem altogether. While a cougar or a coyote will kill one sheep, a pack of wolves might come in and kill five or ten at a time. Sometimes, they would just leave without ever eating any of the dead animals.

"They kill just for the fun of killing," Creech said to Anne Marie after they lost seven sheep to a wolf attack one night. "The only good wolf is a dead wolf."

To help battle the loss of his sheep to predators, Creech brought in a pair of Great Pyrenees puppies. The white dogs grew up in and around the sheep and were their constant protectors. The large, long-haired canines virtually stopped the predation on the sheep, but they weren't much help protecting the cattle that, most of the year, were spread all over Creech's ranch.

One mid-summer day, after finding yet another wolf-killed calf, Creech declared war on the big canines. There was state and federal protection for the wolves, but he didn't care.

"The government is protecting the very thing that is threatening my way of life," Creech said one night at a meeting of like-minded farmers and ranchers. "Who is protecting me? Nobody! We need to do something about it."

Coincidence or not, a short time later, a dead wolf was discovered on National Forest Service land only thirty miles from Creech's ranch. The animal had been killed by a bullet from a high-powered rifle.

Law officials put out the word that a wolf had been poached, and two animal rights groups immediately put up five thousand dollars for information that would lead to the arrest and conviction of the poacher.

Six weeks later, there were no tips, no leads, no arrests.

A month later, Creech was working at his desk, trying to determine how many of his two-year-old steers he was going to take to the sale in a week, when he heard Anne Marie screaming from somewhere outside.

"What the hell?" Creech mumbled to himself as he grabbed his hat and the old .30-30 rifle that sat loaded and ready for action in the gun rack above the desk.

When he got to the front door, he saw Anne Marie running up the driveway from the mailbox, and she was still screaming.

"Wolves!" she shrieked. "Down in the corrals."

They had put a sickly calf in a small pen near the barn only the day before, and now, evidently, the wolves had come to try for an easy meal.

Anne Marie stopped running and yelling and was catching her breath as Creech ran by her. The big man was carrying an extra forty pounds, and although he had stopped smoking two decades before, his lungs were not capable of a long run. Still, he was determined to kill as many of the wolves as he could as they tried to get at his calf.

As Creech ran down the lane, Anne Marie watched. She saw him stop suddenly and start to raise the little rifle. Then, as if God himself had hit her husband on top of the head with a hammer, the big man collapsed, falling face-first into the gravel.

"NO!" Anne Marie screamed and ran toward Creech.

After much effort, she was able to roll him over. She could see his lips were already turning blue, and his eyes were wide open. Living on a ranch, she had seen many animals die. Their eyes told the story. She had seen death in hundreds of eyes, and she was looking at death now. She put her head down on her husband's chest and cried.

CHAPTER 2

Fall is always the busiest time for Washington State Department of Fish and Wildlife enforcement officers. The majority of the hunting seasons around the state open in September and October, and fishing is still going strong on many of the rivers and lakes in the region.

It was Luke McCain's favorite time of the year. As a twenty-four-year veteran officer with the WDFW, he had pretty much seen it all. If there was something he hadn't seen before, it was sure to pop up during September or October.

He had spent much of September checking on archery and muzzleloader hunters and worked several days on the Columbia River near Richland, checking salmon anglers.

One day during his patrols checking on bowhunters in early September, he heard the distinct sound of a rifle shot only a mile or so down the road. Luke was talking with a hunter who was all decked out in camouflage, including about four different green and brown colors of grease paint on his face, when the rifle cracked and echoed off the basalt rocks of the nearby ridges.

"I heard one shot from that way a little bit ago," the bowhunter said. "Maybe hunting grouse?"

"Grouse season isn't open yet," Luke said as he looked at the hunter's license. "Was the first shot you heard coming from that same direction?"

"Pretty much," the camo-faced man said.

Luke thanked the man, handed his license back to him, wished him good luck, and headed for his truck. Over the years, he had run across three different hunters who had killed a deer or elk with a rifle during bow season and then claimed to have shot it with their bow. He wondered if this was another one of those situations.

There were circumstances where a rifle could be used for big game hunting during September, including some very special tags for deer and elk where the lucky tag holder could hunt during any season with any weapon of their choice. Plus, hunters could shoot at coyotes any time of the year with a rifle. Hearing the shot still needed to be checked out.

Luke's hundred-pound yellow Lab, Jack, was riding along with him but had spent the last couple hours sleeping in cool, air-conditioned comfort on the back seat of the truck while Luke was out talking with hunters. Now, as they drove down the rough, dusty Forest Service road, the big dog stirred, sat up, and looked at Luke in the rearview mirror.

"What's up?" Luke said to Jack. As usual, the dog didn't answer. "I bet you need to get out to pee, don't you?"

On hearing that, Jack stood and wagged his tail, which beat out a rhythmic thud on the back of the seat.

"Alright," Luke said. "Let's get down here to see if we can figure out who was shooting, and we'll get out."

Somehow, Jack knew what Luke had just said and sat back down and looked out the rear driver's side passenger window.

They had only driven about a mile when Luke spotted an older Ford Explorer parked in a wide spot in the road. The Explorer was a faded gold color and looked like it might have about four hundred thousand miles on it.

As he slowed to check the SUV out, Luke saw two men dragging a mule deer buck down a trail toward the road. One of the two men was wearing a camouflage t-shirt and was carrying an older recurve bow. The other man wore a blue t-shirt with a drawing of Bigfoot on the front. Both men, who looked to be in their twenties or maybe early thirties, were rail-thin. The man in the camo shirt wore blue jeans and had on what looked to be yellow Timberland boots. The other guy, also in blue jeans, was wearing an old, dirty pair of Nike sneakers.

"Looks like you guys had some success?" Luke said to the men as he climbed out of the truck.

"We sure did," said camo shirt. The man had long blond hair sticking out in every direction from underneath a camo hat with a Bass Pro logo on the front.

Luke waited for the two men to drag the buck up on the road and then said, "Mind if I check it out?"

At a fit 227 pounds and almost six-foot-five inches tall, wearing a badge with a sidearm strapped to his belt, Luke made an imposing first impression on the people he met. He never wanted to come across as arrogant but tried to give off a self-assuredness that let people know that he was in charge. His daily workouts produced muscles that were obvious, even under long-sleeved shirts, which helped with keeping most situations under control.

"No, go ahead," camo shirt said proudly. "It's my first ever buck with a bow."

"That's great," Luke said as he looked at the deer. The buck was most likely two-and-a-half years old and had three points on one side, with only two on the other. Not very big, but it was legal.

"Congratulations," Luke said as he took a closer look at the body of the deer.

The buck had been field dressed, so Luke looked inside the body cavity. He could see a hole on each side of the buck, showing the cuts that a broadhead arrow might make.

Luke asked to see the men's hunting licenses as he looked at the tag affixed to the buck's right antler with black electrician's tape.

"I ain't got a hunting license," the man in the Bigfoot shirt said. He was about five-foot-ten, maybe a hundred and thirty pounds, with blue eyes and sandy brown hair sticking out from underneath a green John Deere hat.

Luke saw that the man wasn't carrying a bow or any other weapon, so it was certainly conceivable he wasn't hunting.

"How about a driver's license?" Luke asked the man.

"Ain't got it with me," he said. "I wasn't driving, so I left it at home."

"Okay," Luke said as he pulled his notebook out of his shirt pocket. "Tell me your name and give me your address and phone number."

"I ain't got a phone," the man said.

"You do have a name, though, right?" Luke asked, trying not to show the impatience that was starting to creep up. After seeing something weird about the arrow holes in the body cavity of the deer, he had his suspicions that these two weren't telling him the whole story. He had dealt with plenty of guys like these over the years and he wasn't ready to just send them on their way without further investigation.

The man in the John Deere hat said his name was Rafe Gibson, and he lived in Buena. Luke jotted the name and address Gibson gave him in his little notebook. He would run some priors on the guy when he had a minute.

"So, tell me the story," Luke said as he looked at camo shirt's license.

"We was just slowly walking along on the other side of that ridge," the man, whose name was Max Tucker, said with a head-bob back over his shoulder.

"Okay," Luke said.

"And we seen this buck feeding on a bush about a hundred yards away," Tucker said. "So we snuck up on him, and I shot him right in the side."

"Did he go down right away?" Luke asked.

"Well, no," Tucker said. "He ran up over the hill, and we went after him."

"What happened then?" Luke asked, wondering if they would come up with an explanation for the weird arrow hole inside the buck.

"We found some blood, and we started tracking him," Tucker said.

"Good blood?" Luke asked.

"Yessir," Tucker said. "Lots of it."

Before he asked about where they found the deer, Luke asked if he could look at the arrow Tucker had used to shoot the animal.

The man had an inexpensive version of a bow-mounted quiver attached to his bow with four arrows in it. When Luke asked to see the killing arrow, Tucker hesitated, then pulled it out and handed it to him.

Luke wasn't a bowhunter, but he knew plenty about the equipment archers used in hunting. The arrows Tucker used had aluminum shafts, and each aluminum shaft had a broadhead screwed into the business end. The broadhead was made up of three fixed, razor-sharp blades. There was blood on the broadhead Tucker handed to him and more blood on the arrow's shaft near the broadhead, but not nearly as much as there should be. A killing shot on a deer or elk would show blood at least halfway down the arrow shaft, if not all the way to the fletching if it had penetrated through to the other side.

Many times on deer, an arrow will pass through the animal, hitting lungs, heart, or liver on the way through, killing the animal fairly quickly. The blood on the arrow that Tucker handed to Luke showed it had only stuck into the deer about four inches.

Luke looked at the arrow, studied the blood, and then looked again inside the body cavity. He took the arrow and put the broadhead into the holes with the three cuts in it. The problem was, there was too much of a hole on the inside of the blade cuts. And, based on the angle of the cuts on each of the holes inside the deer, there was no way that arrow had passed that far into the deer's body based on the amount of blood visible on the shaft.

"Pretty good shot, huh?" Tucker said.

"I'll say," Luke said. "It's amazing what these arrows can do. About how far away was the buck when you shot him?"

The two men looked at each other, and then Tucker said, "Probably like forty yards or near there."

Tucker looked at Gibson, who said, "Yeah, it was right near forty yards."

"And what happened after you followed the buck over the hill?" Luke asked.

"Found him just layin' there deader than Jeff Davis," Gibson said.

Luke hadn't heard that one before. He figured Gibson must be a transplant from the deep South, and that was a saying the man had heard from his father or grandfather growing up.

"You fellas mind taking me to the spot where you found the deer?" Luke asked.

Gibson looked at Tucker for a long moment and then shrugged.

"Whatcha need to go back there for?" Tucker asked.

"I'm seeing some things that aren't quite adding up," Luke said. "I just want to get a clear picture of what happened where."

"We told ya what happened," Tucker said.

"Yes, you did, but I'd just like to see the spot for myself," Luke said. "Throw the buck into the back of my pickup for the time being, and let's go take a look."

The two men looked at each other one more time. Luke could tell they were not telling the whole story. And they were getting a little miffed.

"I'm going to bring my dog with us," Luke said as he walked back to the truck to let Jack out.

The men grabbed the buck by the antlers and pulled it over to Luke's truck. Luke dropped the tailgate, and the men tossed the buck into the back.

"Don't know why we can't just put it in the back of our rig," Tucker said.

"If everything checks out," Luke said as he let Jack out of the truck, "we'll load it into your rig, and you'll be on your way."

"You keep sayin' that like you don't believe us," Gibson said.

"Here's the deal," Luke said. "I'm wondering how the buck managed to live long enough to get shot by an arrow after it had been shot by a rifle?"

This time, the men didn't look at each other, but straight at Luke with obvious surprise.

"What?" Tucker exclaimed. "You seen the arrow. I shot this deer with that arrow."

"I'm not so sure you did," Luke said. "I believe you stuck the arrow into the bullet holes on the inside to make it look like it had penetrated through the deer. I heard a rifle shot right down here not long ago, and I talked to a witness who heard a second rifle shot here."

"I shot that buck with my bow," Tucker said. "And you can't prove otherwise."

Luke thought to himself, *We'll see about that*, then said aloud, "Take me to where the deer died."

CHAPTER 3

Eli Creech III didn't cry at his grandfather's funeral. The twenty-three-year-old had done his crying in private shortly after he received word from his father that the patriarch of the family had died of a massive coronary event while trying to protect his livestock from yet another wolf attack.

The younger Creech, who went by Trey, was built differently than his grandfather. Trey was taller, just over six feet, and was as thin as a cedar post. His brown hair was cut short, and his deep blue eyes glowed out of a suntanned face. The youngest Creech hated wolves before the death of his grandfather. Now he despised the animals, blaming the old man's death on the evil predators.

When the dust settled after his grandfather's funeral, Trey sat down with his father, and they discussed what else might be done to stop the wolves from preying on their livestock.

"We're doing everything we can," Trey's father said. "You know that. Short of going to war with the things, like your great-grandfather did back in the 1920s, there is nothing else we can do. And you know how the government feels about that. Shooting just one is a federal crime. I'm not willing to take that risk."

"I know," Trey said. "It just seems like desperate times call for desperate measures."

"We've been paid for the calves we could prove were killed by wolves," Eli Creech Jr. said. "And the state has been pretty good at taking out problem wolves. I think that's the best we can hope for right now."

As he listened to his father, Trey thought about his grandfather. He wasn't as passive as Trey's father. The old man had discussed putting together a group of vigilantes to take matters into their own hands. Now his grandfather was gone, and Trey could see his father wasn't interested in doing any more than what was being done now. Maybe it was time to see if he could get something going.

The next day, Trey started calling other ranchers in the region to see if they would want to meet to discuss the wolf situation. Many were not interested in meeting. They had discussed the wolf problem ad nauseam and believed, as Trey's father did, that everything that could be done was being done currently.

Still, several people showed up for the meeting, including a group of younger men, who, like Trey, were third- and fourth-generation ranchers. They met in the back room of a tavern in Tonasket.

The men ordered burgers and beers, and as they were finishing up their dinners, Trey stood and thanked the men for coming.

"As most of you know, my grandfather passed away a couple weeks ago of a heart attack," Trey said.

The men all nodded their heads, and some mumbled words like "tragic" and "sad."

"He was trying to protect a calf from yet another wolf attack," Trey continued.

Of course, the men already knew that.

"We all have had to deal with these critters," Trey said. "And many, like my father, believe the state is doing everything it can to protect our livestock."

Again, there were some murmurs from the group.

"My grandfather heard stories when he was a little boy about how his father and grandfather, my great-grandfather and great-great-grandfather, had eradicated the wolves from this area. He told me the stories. There was no pleasure in it, he said. It was just something they had to do to protect their livelihood."

Trey paused for a moment to let it sink in. He looked at the faces in the group.

"I'm of a mind to start doing things like our forefathers did," Trey said. "And I have a plan on how to get started."

* * *

A few weeks after Eli Creech's death and the meeting of the area ranchers, two dead wolves were found in Ferry County. The canines were two-year-old littermates from the Loup Loup Pack, and evidence on the wolves' bodies, by way of bullet holes in each, told authorities the wolves had been poached.

Ten days later, a nine-year-old female wolf, known to biologists as the matriarch of the Maverick Pack located northwest of Wenatchee, was found dead, another victim of a poacher's rifle.

Two weeks after that, the body of an adult male wolf was discovered not far from Goldendale, in Klickitat County. Upon the latest discovery of an obviously poached wolf, the U.S. Fish and Wildlife and the Washington State Department of Fish and Wildlife issued a joint press release regarding the discovery of the dead wolves. It read:

> *The U.S. Fish and Wildlife Service and the Washington Department of Fish and Wildlife are seeking information regarding the illegal killing of two federally listed endangered gray wolves: one in Klickitat County, Washington, and one in Chelan County,*

Washington. The USFWS is offering up to a $10,000 reward for any information that leads to an arrest, a criminal conviction, or civil penalty assessment per each case.

On September 20, WDFW staff investigated the poaching of a wolf in the central Cascade Mountains. The adult female wolf was discovered northwest of Wenatchee in Chelan County, Washington.

On September 26, WDFW staff investigated the death of an adult male gray wolf. This incident occurred east of the Klickitat River near U.S. Highway 142 and Goldendale, Klickitat County, Washington.

The press release didn't mention the two wolves killed near the Canadian border in Ferry County.

Over the next two weeks, seven more dead wolves were found in various parts of Eastern Washington. All but two were confirmed to have been killed by rifle fire. The remains of the other two wolves were so decomposed that no definite conclusions could be made about how the animals had died, but it was believed that they, too, died at the hands of poachers.

The wolf deaths and rewards kept piling up, and soon an inquisitive reporter from *The Seattle Times* started asking questions. After talking to officials with the U.S. Fish and Wildlife Service and the Washington State Department of Fish and Wildlife, along with two well-known wolf advocates, the reporter wrote an article that pointed to what he believed to be a conspiratorial plan by an unknown group of poachers who were working to systematically take out the wolves.

In his story, the reporter wrote: *This group of unknown renegades is taking the law into their own hands, with no regard whatsoever to the impact their actions are having on what many believe is one of the most important pieces of the ecosystem in Washington State. Their growing destruction of the wolves could undo a hundred years of work to bring these regal creatures back into the wilds of Washington where they belong.*

A copy of the article was emailed to Eli Creech Jr. who, after reading it, called his son. He had heard about the poached wolves and suspected his son might somehow be involved.

"I just read an article in the Seattle paper about the wolves that have been poached around here and south of us," Creech Jr. said. "I'm guessing you know something about all of this?"

"I've heard some things," Trey said. "But probably don't know much more than you do."

He wasn't really lying to his father; he just wasn't telling him all he knew. The fact was that after that first meeting in Tonasket, one of the ranch hands who worked with Trey was recruited to set up a site on the internet where all the members of the group could communicate with one another, posting wolf sightings and photos of wolves that had been killed.

"It's on the dark web," the ranch hand had said, and it would take some kind of a Microsoft genius to get into it. "Just don't ever use anyone's names, and we will be fine."

The young man also developed a cryptic signal that went out via a text thread to all eighteen members' phones. Whenever a wolf was killed by a member of the group, they would hit a three-digit code, and it would send the sound of one gong of the Liberty Bell to all the members.

"Send me the copy of the article," Trey said to his father. "I'd like to see it."

"I sure hope you aren't involved in this, Trey," his father said. "The people who are doing this will get caught sooner or later, and then there will be hell to pay."

His dad and his grandfather had been old school. They probably would have been caught if they had been involved. But Trey and the younger ranchers in the group were of the digital generation, and they could cover their tracks.

"I'm sure there will," Trey said. "But I have to say, it doesn't bother me a bit that someone has decided to do something about the wolves. Grandpa would be very happy to see what is happening if he was still here."

"Yes, he probably would be," Creech Jr. said. "But he'd be horrified if he were ever to find out that his only grandson has gone to federal prison for the better part of his life for killing an endangered species."

"You know they aren't endangered," Trey said. "They're hunting them for sport a hundred miles away in Idaho. There are more than enough wolves to go around."

His father didn't respond to that.

"They should have let the damn things go on the west side of the Cascades," Trey continued. "Then all those wolf-lovers around Seattle and Olympia would have to deal with them."

"They'll be on the other side of the mountains one of these days," Creech Jr. said.

"Not soon enough for me," Trey said. "When a pack of wolves attacks the family dog or drags down the kid's pet llama, then they'll know what we've been dealing with the past two decades."

His father didn't say anything to that, but Trey knew, deep down he was thinking the same thing.

As they were talking, Trey pulled the *Seattle Times* article up on his monitor from the email his father had just sent.

"Renegades, huh?" Trey said after a minute. "More like heroes to me. To me and the rest of the ranchers in Eastern Washington who are having to deal with the wolves."

While Creech Jr. ran the books, paid the bills, handled payroll, and did all the other financial management of the ranch, Trey was the boots-on-the-ground manager of their ranch. It was a job his father held when his grandfather ran the outfit. So Creech Jr. knew pretty much every tree and bush on their seventeen hundred acres.

"Where you headed tomorrow?" Creech Jr. asked his son, changing the subject.

"Me and Deke and Artie are going to fix some fence and check on that bunch of cattle up by Clear Creek," Trey said. "There was a lame steer that was cut and bleeding a bit the last time we were up there, tore its leg on a fence, I think. I doctored it up with some antiseptic salve and gave it a shot of penicillin, so I want to see how it's doing."

"Okay," Creech Jr. said. "Be careful."

"Will do," Trey said. "Tell Mom I love her."

"I will," his father said and then told his son to have a good night.

After they hung up, Trey thought about the call. He really wanted to tell his father what was happening with the syndicate regarding the wolves. Trey was sure his father suspected he was involved somehow but was unwilling to ask questions to find out the truth.

While Trey hadn't shot any of the wolves that had been killed since the group formed, he wouldn't think twice about shooting one if the opportunity came up. His concern was shooting one on Creech Ranch land. If he did shoot one on the family's property, there better be a darned good reason for doing so.

Later that night, as he was drifting off to sleep, Trey thought about the newspaper article his father had shared with him. He liked how the reporter had called them "Renegades." When he had some time, he would share the article with the rest of the group, and he would recommend that going forward they refer to their little syndicate as "The Renegades."

Chapter 4

Luke whistled for Jack, pointed up the trail, and told Tucker and Gibson to lead the way. The two thin men shrugged their shoulders, turned, and took off back up the trail they had used to drag the dead buck down to the road. Luke kept an eye on both men but especially watched Tucker, who was still carrying his recurve bow.

"This is stupid," Tucker said as they walked. "How could we shoot a deer with a rifle when we ain't got one? You saw us coming down the trail—we didn't have no rifle."

Luke didn't say anything, but as they walked, he watched both sides of the trail. Chances are, the men—probably Gibson—would have stashed the rifle not far off the trail. And close enough to the road so they could find it later, possibly in the dark of night.

Once they got to the top of the ridge, Luke told Jack to "hunt 'em up." He knew Jack had no idea what he wanted him to find, but Luke had seen the yellow dog find things other than birds before. If he smelled something unusual, like a knife or a rifle, he would at least go check it out. If he stopped and spent more than a few seconds in a spot, Luke would go see what had interested the dog.

"What's that dog doing?" Gibson asked.

"He's trained to look for weapons, like those dogs in the airport that look for drugs," Luke fibbed. "If there is a rifle stashed out here, he'll likely find it, so if you want to just take me to it, I'll consider being a little more lenient on you guys."

Again, the two men, who had stopped in the trail to watch as Jack quartered back and forth ahead of them, turned and looked at each other.

"That dog won't find nothin'," Tucker finally said, teeth clenched. "Will he, Rafe?"

"Nope," Gibson said. "There ain't nothin' to find."

But Luke could hear the uncertainty in Gibson's voice.

"Just tell me," Luke said to Gibson. "And I'll cut you loose. Mr. Tucker here will get the citation, and you'll be off with no fines."

"Max?" Gibson said to his friend in a questioning tone.

"Shut up!" Tucker said to Gibson. Then to Luke, "We done nothin' wrong. I shot that deer fair and square with my bow. You seen the arrow marks and the blood on the arrow."

"I did," Luke said. "But it sure looks like the arrow was stuck into the animal after it was dead."

Neither of the men responded to that.

"Let's keep moving," Luke said and started walking.

The men moved along the trail, slowly, keeping an eye on Jack as the yellow Lab loped in front of them, sniffing bushes and tree trunks. Luke knew the dog was probably smelling for grouse or squirrels, but Tucker and Gibson didn't know that.

At one point, Jack paused and lifted his nose into the gentle westerly breeze that was blowing and stood taking in the smells.

Luke gave a quick look at the men, who again had stopped to watch Jack. He could see Gibson smiling ever so slightly. Jack wasn't smelling a rifle.

"Let's go, boy," Luke said to Jack. The dog, hearing his name, broke from his scent-sniffing trance and started loping ahead of the trio of men again.

Luke was surprised when they finally reached the spot where the buck had died and Jack hadn't smelled anything worth investigating.

"Here's the gut pile," Tucker said. "You won't find no bullets in it."

"Hand me that bow," Luke said to Tucker. "And you two go stand over there."

Tucker gave Luke his bow and then moved over to where Gibson was standing. Again, the two men looked at each other like they were trying to communicate something without saying anything.

Luke looked around the area. There was plenty of blood, which would be common if the buck had been mortally wounded by an arrow or a bullet.

"Where were you standing when you shot the buck?" Luke asked.

"Up over by that little hogback over there," Tucker said with a point in that direction.

"And it ran down here and died?" Luke asked.

"Yessir," Tucker said. "Just like we told you. Right, Rafe?"

"That's right," Gibson said.

"And where were you when you shot it with the rifle?" Luke said to Gibson.

Gibson started to point in a direction and say something, but Tucker elbowed him in the ribs.

"We didn't shoot it with no rifle," Tucker said.

"You fellas come over here," Luke said. "We're going to backtrack the blood trail to where you shot from."

The two men walked over to where the deer had died, and Luke said, "Go ahead, let's follow the blood."

Tucker looked down, pointed at a blood spot in the dirt a few feet from the pile of entrails, which were now attracting a swarm of flies, along with a few hungry yellow jackets, and started walking in the direction of the hogback.

Luke had considered looking through the pile of innards but knew the soft tissues of the intestines, lungs, and other organs would not stop a bullet. There had been an exit wound on the other side of the deer, but from what Luke had been able to see, the men had stuck the arrow in that hole as well to give it the impression the arrow had flown through the buck.

They slowly moved toward the top of the hogback ridge, with Tucker pointing out blood splotches as they went. Jack again moved out ahead of the trio, searching for any kind of game.

Luke kept one eye on the men and another on the brush and rocks on either side of the path they were taking up the slight incline. The blood trail was easy to follow, and Luke occasionally would see one or both of the men's boot prints walking downhill where there was dried dirt in the path.

"That's where I shot from," Tucker said, pointing at a tree by a large gray rock.

"You go sit over there on that stump," Luke said to Gibson, pointing him in another direction, away from the rock Tucker had just identified.

Gibson obeyed, and Luke said to Tucker, "You come with me."

The two men walked over by the rock, but Luke took him on past it another thirty yards. He could still see Gibson but wanted to be far enough away from him that the man couldn't hear the conversation he was about to have with Tucker.

"Okay, Mr. Tucker," Luke said. "Explain to me exactly where you were standing and where the deer was when you shot."

Tucker started talking loudly, and Luke stopped him.

"Explain it to me," Luke said. "Every critter in the forest doesn't need to hear you."

"I was standing by that big gray rock," Tucker said, much quieter this time. "And Rafe spotted the buck eating on that green bush down there by that little stand of tamaracks."

Luke looked at the spot and did some calculations. From the gray rock to the stand of trees Tucker identified looked to be pushing fifty yards. Doable with a recurve bow, but the shooter would have to be very good.

"Then what happened?" Luke asked.

"I hit him right behind the shoulder," Tucker said, "and the buck whirled and ran down to where we showed you where it died."

"Was the buck standing facing uphill or down?" Luke asked.

"Uphill," Tucker said.

"Did the arrow go through the deer?"

"No, I could see it sticking out of its side when it run off."

"Sticking out about how far?"

"I don't know, maybe four inches. I could see some of the shaft and the feathers."

"Which side of the deer was it sticking out of?"

Tucker hesitated a few seconds and said, "On the left side."

Luke thought about the wound he had seen on the deer carcass, and it all added up. All except for the fact that the arrow he had looked at didn't have enough blood on it to be sticking that far into the deer's body. And he was pretty sure the arrow had been placed to make it look like the deer had been killed by the projectile.

"You sit down right here, Mr. Tucker," Luke said. "I'm going to go talk to your partner."

"He'll tell you the same thing I did," Tucker said.

Gibson pretty much confirmed the story. He told Luke where he and Tucker had been when the shot was made, and where the deer was standing.

"Was the buck standing facing uphill or down?" Luke asked.

"Downhill," Gibson said.

"So, it shot straight downhill when you shot?"

"Yep," Gibson said.

"I thought Tucker shot the deer, not you."

"What?"

"I just asked if the deer ran downhill when you shot, and you said yes."

"I didn't shoot the deer, Max did."

"Okay, so what side of the deer was the arrow sticking out of when it ran down the hill?"

Gibson thought about it. Luke could see the confusion on his face. He hadn't seen an arrow in the deer, and now he was trying to figure out what side Tucker might have said.

"I think it was on the right side. Yeah, it was the right side. 'Cause the deer was facing downhill."

"How much of the arrow was sticking out?" Luke asked.

"I don't know, maybe eight inches."

Luke thought about that for a couple minutes, mostly to make the two men stew for a bit, and then he called Tucker down to the rock where he claimed to have made the shot.

When the three men all arrived at the rock, Luke told Tucker and Gibson to stay there, and he stepped off the distance to where the men said the deer was standing when it had been shot.

"Fifty-four yards," Luke said when he walked back up the hill to where the men were now sitting. "That's a pretty good shot with a recurve, Mr. Tucker. You must practice a lot to be good enough to make that shot."

"I practice some," Tucker said.

Luke then turned and pointed to the stump where Gibson had been sitting.

"How far you think that stump is?" Luke asked.

"I dunno," Tucker said. "Maybe seventy yards."

"Let's just see," Luke said and started stepping it off.

Luke couldn't hear them, but he knew that both men were counting every one of his steps.

"I count forty-nine," Luke said as he turned and walked back to the men. "Is that what you got?"

Both men nodded their heads.

Luke handed the bow to Tucker and said, "Go ahead and take a shot at that stump."

"I might break an arrow," Tucker said with some hesitancy in his voice.

"You might at that," Luke said. "I'll tell you what, if you hit the stump and break an arrow, I'll pay for it. But if you miss the stump and you break an arrow, that's on you."

Tucker was looking down at his feet, shuffling a small pine cone around in a circle with the toe of his boot.

"As good a shot as you are, hitting that buck at fifty-four yards and all, you surely can hit that stump. It's half again the size of your deer."

Tucker started to pull the arrow with the blood on it out of the quiver, and Luke stopped him.

"Hand that one to me. Use another one," Luke said.

The skinny man pulled another arrow out of the quiver, put his finger tabs on the first three fingers of his right hand, nocked the arrow, and started to pull the bowstring back. Luke could see Tucker was using every ounce of strength he had to pull the string back to full draw but never made it. Tucker let the arrow go, and it hit ten yards short of the stump, rattling around in some rocks.

"That's what I thought," Luke said. "The good news is your arrow didn't break. The bad news is that you boys are in a bit of a pickle here. Your stories don't match, and I'm not sure you could hit a deer at fifteen yards, let alone fifty."

Luke took the bow from Tucker and then walked over, picked up the arrow, and placed it—along with the one with the blood on it—back in the quiver. Then he pointed up the trail back to the trucks and said, "Let's go."

Luke whistled for Jack, who came running out of the stand of tamaracks, and the three men and the yellow dog walked back to the trucks.

As they walked, Luke heard Gibson whisper to Tucker, "I can't afford no ticket."

"And you think I can?" Tucker whispered back.

When they got back to the vehicles, Luke said, "Okay, time for a confession. Let's get to the truth right now, and I'll try to help you get the fines reduced."

Finally, Tucker said, "I shot that deer with an arrow, and you can't prove I didn't."

Luke had wondered if he was going to stick to his story. Tucker was right: all the evidence Luke had was circumstantial. He strongly believed one of the men, probably Gibson, shot the deer with a rifle, but if he did write them up for illegally killing the buck, and they hired a good attorney, he or she would most likely get the fines eliminated.

"Okay," Luke said. "If that is your story. Go ahead and get your deer, and I'll let you be on your way."

The two men smiled at each other, went over to the back of Luke's truck, pulled the buck out of the bed, and dragged it to the old Explorer.

After they loaded the deer into the back of the SUV, Tucker turned to Luke and said, "Don't know why you made us go through all that when you knew we was right."

"Just doing my job," Luke said. "I'll be seeing you boys."

He watched as the two men climbed into the SUV, started the engine, backed out, and drove past him. Neither man looked at him. They were too busy laughing.

CHAPTER 5

Trey Creech saw the birds first. As he and the ranch hands drove the two-track road that followed Clear Creek up the mountain, a bald eagle flew up and landed in the top of a tall, old-growth fir tree. Then about twenty magpies scattered in every direction, squawking as they flew off.

"There's the steer right there," Artie Miller said, pointing out the right side of the windshield of the Ford F-350 pickup he was riding in with Creech and Deke Price. "Damn wolves got it, I bet."

Two ravens were still on the ground next to the steer's carcass. They were reluctant to leave the giant meal that sat before them.

"We don't know that yet," Price said. "Coulda just died from infection or something."

"Too soon for infection to take it," Creech said. "It wasn't that sick when we doctored it the other day."

Creech pulled the truck to a stop, and the men climbed out. The tallest of the three men, Creech stood almost six foot one. He was built like his grandfather, only about sixty pounds lighter. His clean-shaven face made him look younger than he was. At twenty-three, Creech had spent some time on the regional rodeo circuit bulldogging and calf roping. He struggled to make a living at it, and when he tore a meniscus in his right knee while trying to throw an exceptionally heavy and overzealous calf in Lewiston, Idaho, he called it quits.

Miller was a short, stocky twenty-three-year-old with thinning, sandy brown hair. Everyone knew the young man would be bald in a few short years, but he was trying his best to hold on to the hair he had. Most of the time, he wore a tan-colored Stetson that, like his male-pattern baldness, was inherited from his father. The cowboy hat worked as an effective cover at hiding his rapidly receding hairline.

Price was best described as average. He wasn't tall or short. He wasn't fat or thin. He wasn't handsome or ugly. He had neatly cropped, jet-black hair with eyes that matched, and he wore a scraggly, patchy black beard. Where he wasn't average was in the brains department. Price had tested as a genius in middle school. He was the valedictorian at his high school in La Grande, Oregon, and if he hadn't gotten into some serious trouble with the law the summer after high school, he might have gone on to some Ivy League school and become the next Bill Gates.

He had never told anyone what he had done, or why he had come to the wilds of northcentral Washington, but when Price met Creech and Miller at a tavern in Omak, he hit it off immediately with the two. In short order, he was hired as a hand at the Creech Family Ranch.

It was only later that Creech learned of Price's intellect and his ability with programming and other geeky computer stuff. He was the one who had developed the dark website for the group now called the Renegades.

The ravens flew up into the same fir tree as the eagle had and sat on a branch like Heckle and Jeckle, watching the men. The overgrown crows were smart enough to know that the men would leave sooner or later. Then they would have another opportunity to be back at the giant black smorgasbord.

"I was right," Miller said as the men walked up to the dead steer. "You can see where they tore its back end out. Standard operating procedure for a pack of wolves."

Creech and Price looked at the animal and knew their friend was right. If the steer had been killed by a cougar, it would have had claw marks raked down its side and puncture wounds in its throat. No other predator, except for maybe a grizzly bear, could take down a three-hundred-pound steer. And while there were rumors of grizzlies in the high mountains, no one had ever laid eyes on one.

"The thing couldn't run, being injured and lame," Price said. "Easy pickin's for even a couple of wolves."

"They'll be back," Creech said.

"If we didn't just run them off," Miller said.

"So, what do you want to do?" Price asked.

"We got work to do," Creech said. "We need to check on the rest of this bunch of steers, and there's that fence on the back twenty that needs to be fixed."

"One of us could stay here and wait for them," Miller said. "I've got an itchy trigger finger that only a wolf can scratch."

"Who knows when those things will be back," Creech said. "Or if they'll be back. Let's go do what we came up here to do, and then we'll figure out how to deal with los lobos."

The men climbed back into the big white Ford pickup, and as soon as the truck was bouncing up the road, Heckle and Jeckle were back at the dead steer, picking morsels of meat off the carcass.

* * *

The broken fence took longer to fix than Creech had estimated. A big windstorm the week before had blown two old dead pine trees over onto the fence, about three hundred yards apart, breaking two of the four barbed wire strands, pulling three cedar posts out of the ground, and breaking two others in half.

Knowing they were going to be fixing fence, Creech had brought along four 100-foot rolls of barbed wire and three six-foot long metal t-posts, the kind you drive into the ground with a weighted post driver.

"We're going to have to reuse two of those cedar posts," Creech said after assessing the situation. "You guys get started on putting them back into the ground, and I'll get these metal posts in."

Two hours later, the three metal posts were solidly in the ground, and the cedar posts were, if not solid, at least functional after Price and Miller had dug new holes as deep as the rocky soil would allow. They got the posts somewhat straight up and down with the help of some large rocks stacked around the base. New barbed wire was strung, and the fence, if not as good as new, was certainly capable of keeping the cattle in.

"Let's hope that big fir tree doesn't decide to blow over," Price said with a head nod down the fence line as they were loading the tools back into Creech's truck.

"It will one of these days," Creech said. "Let's just hope the wind is blowing the other direction when it does. Now, let's go check on the cattle."

They drove a rough circle around the area known to the Creeches as the "far twenty," the parcel of land that sat in the northwest corner of their ranch. In that time, they counted thirty-seven Black Angus steers. Each animal was branded with the Creech Family Ranch brand—a three-letter CFR inside a circle—and there was a tag in each steer's right ear with a number large enough to be read with the naked eye up close, and with binoculars at a distance.

As Miller looked at the steers, he called out a tag number, and Price would make a check mark next to the corresponding number on the list of the small herd of cattle that had been moved up into the far twenty in late spring.

"We're missing three," Price said.

"They were all here last week, so they gotta be around somewhere," Creech said.

They decided they would park the truck and take a walk to see if they could find the missing steers. Creech went west, Miller went east, and Price went south. The road they had driven in on was on the far north boundary of the property, so they figured they could cover the rest of the area fairly quickly on foot. Each man had binoculars around their neck and a rifle slung over their shoulder.

"If you find something, try to text," Creech said.

Cell phone service could be sketchy in this part of the state, but there were small areas of the ranch where you could get a bar or two.

"Meet back here in forty-five minutes," Creech instructed and then set off to the west.

The other two men followed suit, and in ten minutes all three were out of sight of the truck.

Miller spotted the three missing steers ten minutes later. The black animals were backed up against a small group of trees, surrounded by five wolves. One shot in the air from his .308-caliber Winchester rifle, or just walking toward them, would have likely sent the wolves on the run, but Miller hated wolves as much as the other Renegades. Here was his chance to finally shoot a wolf. Maybe two if things worked out in his favor.

The wolves and cattle were a hundred and fifty yards slightly downhill. Miller had killed deer at that distance many times, so he was confident he could make the shot without a rest. He picked out the biggest wolf, a dark gray male, raised his rifle, put the crosshairs on its right shoulder, and fired.

The big wolf humped up at the shot and turned and ran with the other four. But within fifteen yards, the big gray canine dropped his head and did a somersault into some sagebrush.

It all happened so quickly, Miller didn't have a chance to get a shot at the other fleeing wolves.

He kept his rifle up and his crosshairs on the portion of the wolf he could see through his scope, lying in the brush. The animal didn't move. So, with rifle at the ready, he slowly worked his way toward the downed animal.

When Miller got to the wolf, he poked it in the side with the barrel of his rifle. The animal didn't move. He looked into the big canine's eyes and saw there was no sign of life. Then, the stocky man with the Stetson hat began to shake.

He had dreamed of shooting a wolf someday, and that day had come. He had done so protecting his employer's cattle, which made it totally justified, if not in the eyes of the law, for sure in the eyes of cattle ranchers around the West.

"Miller!" came a shout from up the hill.

"Down here!" Miller yelled back. "I got one. I shot a wolf!"

CHAPTER 6

It was an hour before dark when Luke returned to the area where the men had shot the deer earlier that day. He drove a half mile past where the old Explorer had been parked, pulled off the road, and parked his truck.

"C'mon, boy," Luke said to Jack as he climbed out of the truck and opened the back driver's side door so the yellow dog could jump out.

His plan was to cut cross-country to the hogback ridge, above where the men's SUV had been parked earlier in the day, and sit and watch. The weather reports were for some light mountain rains arriving overnight, and if the men had hidden a firearm somewhere along the trail, as Luke suspected, there was a good chance they wouldn't want the weapon to sit out in the weather.

Finding the men in possession of a recently fired rifle would be one more piece of evidence that the buck had been killed with a bullet, and Luke believed he could get a confession out of one of them. Luke hoped it would be Rafe Gibson who showed up, because he seemed to be the weakest link in the suspected two-man poaching chain.

As it turned out, Luke didn't have long to wait. He was sitting, back against the trunk, under a fifteen-foot-tall Douglas fir that had branches drooping to the ground, when he heard a vehicle coming up the road. By the engine's growl, Luke knew it wasn't the Ford Explorer. The groan and rattle of the engine told him the truck coming up the road had to be a diesel, and Luke guessed it was a 1990s-model Dodge Ram.

The sun had set, and the forest was growing darker, but there was still enough light to see. When the pickup came around the bend, Luke saw he was right. The truck was a '90s-vintage Dodge, with the original blue paint faded to almost no color on the hood and the top of the cab. Luke tried to see who was driving, but he couldn't make out any features on the driver's face. He checked to see if there was anyone in the passenger seat and saw no one there.

Jack sensed Luke's heightened awareness and started to whine quietly.

"Shsssh," Luke shushed the dog.

Jack did as he was told but sat with his ears forward and alert. He knew something was going to happen soon.

The driver's door on the blue Dodge creaked and then clunked as it opened, and Luke saw a skinny leg stepping out. Tucker or Gibson? His money was on Gibson.

"Bingo," Luke whispered to Jack. The yellow dog stood and started quietly whining again. "Shush," Luke whispered in the dog's ear.

Gibson, still dressed in the blue jeans and old white sneakers from earlier in the day, but now wearing a black nylon windbreaker with a yellow logo that was faded into unreadability on the left breast, started hiking up the trail. Luke looked to see if the man was carrying a weapon, but the only thing in Gibson's hand was a cheap, aluminum flashlight.

Jack moved slightly, rustling the duff under the tree. Luke again whispered in the dog's ear, this time telling him to sit still.

As Gibson got closer, Luke could hear the man whistling. It was a nervous whistle of no recognizable tune. The slender man looked left and right as he hiked up the trail.

From what had transpired that morning, Luke figured the rifle was stashed somewhere over the ridge, so he wasn't surprised when Gibson kept walking up the trail, within twenty yards of where he and Jack sat, and disappeared over the hill, continuing to whistle nervously as he went.

Luke waited thirty seconds and then inched over to the trail, slowly following Gibson. He whispered to Jack to "heel," and the dog obeyed, moving only when Luke did.

At the top of the rise, Luke looked down the path and saw Gibson still moving, but within a few steps, the thin man stopped whistling as he slowed and started looking away from the trail, down the hill to his left. Ducking down quickly so Gibson wouldn't see him if he happened to look back up the trail, Luke put a hand in front of Jack to get him to stop. Luke sank down so just his eyes and the top of his head were visible on the break of the hill, and Jack dropped to his belly.

"Good boy," Luke whispered to Jack. The yellow dog was staring intently at Luke's face.

Gibson cut off the trail through some young pine trees. The trees were spindly and four feet tall, so Luke could track the man's movements. Then Gibson quickly dropped out of sight, like he'd gone down an escalator.

Luke stood and moved as rapidly as he dared down the trail without making too much noise. Jack walked with his head at Luke's right hip, matching his speed. Luke kept his eyes on the spot where Gibson had vanished into the trees.

When he got to where he had seen the man walk into the young pines, Luke stopped. He was almost positive Gibson hadn't seen or heard him, but for safety's sake, he pulled his pistol from the holster on his utility belt. The man was most likely retrieving a rifle, and Luke had to believe the rifle was still loaded. Best to be safe.

Luke was semi-proficient with the Glock .45-caliber pistol the state issued to all Fish and Wildlife enforcement officers, but in tight situations, he preferred to have his trusty Remington Model 870 shotgun in his hands. Unfortunately, the shotgun was locked up in his truck, so the pistol would have to do.

Man and dog stood steady on the trail. Both looked down through the trees to where they could see nothing but a tangle of brush amongst some large, dark gray rocks.

A few seconds later, Gibson almost magically appeared from behind the brush with a rifle in his hands. The rifle had a black synthetic stock and a scope mounted above the bolt action. Gibson was again whistling, and even though he seemed to be looking right at Luke, he didn't see him. Or he didn't see him until he did, a half-second later.

"Freeze!" Luke yelled when he saw Gibson's eyes open wide in recognition of what he was seeing in the dusky light. Luke had his pistol up and was aiming center mass at the man's chest.

"I'm serious, Gibson," Luke said. "Move a muscle, and I'll shoot."

"I ain't gunna shoot," Gibson said in a quivering voice as he started to raise his hands like someone who was being robbed in an old TV western.

"Is that freezing?" Luke asked.

"Oh, sorry," Gibson said, stopping his arms mid-raise. "The gun ain't loaded anyway."

Luke slowly worked his way to Gibson. When he got two feet away from the man, he said, "Lower that rifle down to me." He kept the pistol aimed at the man's chest.

Gibson did as he was told, and as soon as Luke had the rifle in his hand, he asked him if he had any other weapons.

"No, sir," Gibson said.

"Where's your flashlight?"

"Oh, shoot," Gibson said and started to turn around. "I left it over there."

"Don't move," Luke said again. "For right now, we'll leave the light right where it is."

"That's my only flashlight," Gibson said.

"We'll get it later," Luke said. "First, we're going to talk."

Luke stepped aside and told Gibson to walk slowly out to the trail.

"Don't try to run," Luke said. "My dog here loves nothing more than running someone down. He likes to bite them just below the butt cheek and sometimes, if his aim is off, he might even get a hold of other parts that you don't want bit."

Gibson looked at Jack and gulped. Jack looked at Gibson with a goofy, happy Labrador retriever face that could be taken a couple different ways, one being that he was hoping the man would run.

Over the years, Jack had attacked a suspect here and there, but only when they were about to do his human partner some harm. Otherwise, the big yellow dog was pretty much a pussycat and would probably sit and watch with some interest if Gibson actually did start running off down the trail.

"I don't want no dog to bite me," Gibson said. "The sheriff's K-9 dog got after my brother once, and he had to have shots and stitches and said it hurt like hell."

"Well, there you go," Luke said as he holstered his pistol and opened the bolt action on the rifle. Gibson was telling the truth; the rifle, a .270-caliber Weatherby Vanguard, was not loaded. While the action was open, Luke stuck his nose down close to the opening and could smell that the rifle had been fired recently.

Luke told Gibson to take a seat on a large rock just off the trail. Gibson obeyed, all the while looking at Jack.

"So, let's have a little chat," Luke said as he stepped over by Gibson, who looked at Luke and then back at Jack. "The hidden rifle, along with some of the other evidence I have, tells me that you or Mr. Tucker shot the deer with this rifle this morning. I have enough to drop about thirteen citations on you guys, and they're going to be expensive. However, I might see my way clear to be kind to you if you tell me the truth, but I'm only going to give you one chance."

Gibson thought about it for a few seconds and then said, "Max told me not to say a word to no one. He said if I did, he'd kill me."

"So, who shot the deer with the rifle?" Luke asked.

"Max did," Gibson said. "I missed with the first shot, so he grabbed the rifle out of my hands and he shot it, right in the side. I never shot nuthin' before and was nervous, so I guess that's why I missed."

Luke remembered that the bowhunter he'd been talking with on the road said he'd heard a rifle shot just before Luke arrived. That must have been when Gibson shot and missed.

"So, he shot it and then stuck the arrow in the bullet hole?" Luke asked.

"Yup," Gibson said, nodding his head. "Just like you said he did. On the way home, he was pissed that he didn't stick the arrow farther into the buck to get more blood on the shaft. Then you wouldn't have known."

"What else did he say?" Luke asked.

"He said he would remember that for the next time."

"Is he planning on doing this again?" Luke asked.

"I'm not sure," Gibson said. "I really don't know him all that well. We met at work. I told him I wanted to learn how to hunt, and he said he'd take me along. I knew it wasn't right what he done, but I was too afraid to say something."

"Afraid of me?" Luke asked.

"No, afraid of Max. Everyone says he killed a guy already, so I didn't want to get on his bad side."

"Who did he supposedly kill?" Luke asked.

"Some Mexican guy who was shacking up with his old lady," Gibson said. "Or that's what they said."

"Who are they?"

"Guys at work. They all believe it."

"Did you hear the name of the man Tucker supposedly killed?"

"Gonzalez or Gomez. Something like that."

Luke thought about that for a few seconds and decided to shift gears. "So, is this your rifle or is it Tucker's?"

"It's Max's."

"So, why are you the one up here picking it up?"

"Max told me to hide the rifle while he was taking the innards out of the deer. I took the gun and hid it over there. He didn't know where I put it."

"You think Tucker might have used this rifle on the man he supposedly killed?"

Gibson thought about it for a minute and then said, "Dunno. Never heard, I guess."

"Can you remember, did Tucker keep the shell casing after he shot the deer?"

Gibson looked confused and then said, "What?"

"After you shot at the deer, did you work the bolt action to put another shell in the chamber?"

"No," Gibson said. "Max grabbed the rifle right outta my hands when I missed. He was pissed I couldn't hit the deer."

"Take me to exactly where you were when you shot," Luke said.

The light had continued to fade as the two men talked, and now it was getting difficult to see.

"But first, go grab your flashlight," Luke instructed. "And remember what I said about my dog here just hoping that you'll run."

Gibson gulped again, looked at Jack, and slowly walked to where he had set his flashlight.

Jack watched, ears forward, grinning that familiar Lab grin as Gibson retrieved the light.

Luke wanted to have the shell casing, or casings, if he could find them. If what Gibson was saying was true, there was a chance that Tucker had used the same rifle to kill a man, and any evidence he could find might help the sheriff's department or whoever was investigating the murder.

Gibson led the way back to the spot where they had told Luke they'd shot the buck with the bow and arrow. Luke pulled his flashlight off his utility belt and turned it on.

"Start looking for the shell casing," Luke said to Gibson. "Unless Tucker picked them up, they should be around here somewhere."

"I never seen him pick up nuthin'," Gibson said. "He just shot, and when the buck run up over the hill, we took off after it."

After just a minute of looking, Gibson said, "There's something shiny right there." He was pointing his flashlight into some tall grass.

Luke looked and saw the telltale gold color of what shooters call "spent brass." It was the casing from a high-powered rifle shell.

"Don't touch it," Luke said.

"There's the other one," Gibson said a few seconds later, pointing his light into the same tall grass, only two feet from the first shell casing.

Using a small twig and sticking it into the hole where the bullet had been seated into the brass casing, Luke gathered the two empty casings like marshmallows on a stick and slid them off into his pocket without touching them. Then he grabbed the rifle and pointed Gibson up the trail, back toward Gibson's pickup.

CHAPTER 7

On the short walk back to where the blue Dodge diesel was parked, Luke told Gibson that since he hadn't shot the deer, he wasn't going to cite him for any game infractions.

"But," Luke said, "there is a chance I might need you to come to court and testify that it was Tucker who shot the buck with a rifle out of season, with the wrong tag, and lied about it to a state police officer."

"I dunno about that," Gibson said. "I mean, there's that whole thing about him telling me he was gunna kill me if I ratted on him."

"I don't think he'd kill you over a few hundred dollars in fines," Luke said.

"He ain't got a few hundred dollars," Gibson said. "He's gunna blame someone, and that person is me."

"If he can't pay his fines, then he'll likely spend some time in jail," Luke said. "Maybe that would be a good time to move on, find a job somewhere else."

"Yeah, maybe," Gibson said. "I'll think about it."

When they reached Gibson's truck, Luke told him he was going to hold on to Tucker's rifle as evidence and that he would be contacting Tucker when he got back to town to confiscate the deer carcass and issue the appropriate citations.

"Do not call him and tell him I am coming," Luke said.

"Okay," Gibson said. "What if he calls me?"

"Don't answer."

Gibson said, "Okay," but Luke knew it was likely the two men would talk, maybe before Luke could get to Tucker's place.

* * *

After leaving Gibson at the Dodge, Luke and Jack hoofed it back to Luke's truck. They jumped into the truck and started back down the mountain. When Luke had phone service, a text buzzed on his phone.

It was from his wife, Sara. The text had been sent forty-five minutes earlier and read: *Meeting Magic for dinner. Call if you get to town in time to join us.*

Magic was a young lady that Luke had encountered at a homeless camp in the area. She was being pursued by a man who had killed her fiancé in Seattle. After her testimony at the man's trial, combined with an investigation by Sara and other law enforcement officials, it was found that the man, who was a medical doctor, had killed dozens of homeless people in several cities along the West Coast. Sara, an FBI special agent working out of the Yakima office, befriended Magic, and their friendship grew after the conviction of the killer.

Magic's given name was Madison Harris, a twenty-four-year-old from northern California who'd been raised by a single mother.

After her mother went to prison for killing a man who was trying to molest her daughter, young Madison started taking drugs, landed in a homeless camp in Portland, and ultimately ended up in a camp in Seattle with her fiancé. Somewhere along the line, she'd picked up the nickname of Magic.

Sara pretty much adopted Magic, helping her through the depression of losing the man she'd loved, and got her back into school. That was just one of the many things Luke loved about his wife. She had a heart of gold. Not that you would want to get on her bad side. Sara could top Luke any day at the shooting range, and she was an excellent investigator, helping solve several cases of missing and murdered native women on the Yakama Nation reservation.

Luke had fallen in love with Sara the first time he met her. She was tall, fit, and beautiful, with black hair and eyes to match. She was the smartest person Luke had ever met, and every day he was thankful she had come into his life. He truly believed he was the luckiest man in the world to have somehow gotten her to fall in love with him.

While Sara's work kept her busy trying to find killers and drug dealers, Luke was often dealing with people like Gibson and Tucker. Not really bad guys, but moronic and making bad decisions. While he had worked at running down some big-time poachers and was once asked by the governor to track down a serial killer in northcentral Washington, Luke's days were mostly filled with contacting hunters and anglers and making sure they were adhering to the laws. It was a job he loved.

Luke called up Sara's number on his phone and pushed the send button. After two rings over the Bluetooth speaker in his truck, Sara answered.

"Where are you?" she asked.

"Coming down out of the mountains," Luke said. "I'm still a half hour from town."

"Well, we're hungry, so we won't wait for you."

"That's okay," Luke said. "I have one more stop to make anyway. I'll grab something and see you at home."

"Sounds good," Sara said. "Magic says 'hi.'"

"Tell her hi back," Luke said. "See you later."

He thought about Magic for a minute. The young lady, who was a recovering drug addict and had been living in a homeless camp near T-Mobile Park in Seattle only a year ago, was now getting A's in her first quarter of classes at Washington State University's College of Nursing in Yakima.

Sara had been instrumental in helping Magic pass her GED tests, get financial aid, and enough scholarships to pay for some of her college. Now, the young lady was thriving.

As Luke got closer to Yakima, he pulled his notepad out of his breast pocket and looked at the notes he had written from his contact with Tucker and Gibson that morning. He recognized Tucker's address. It was a mobile home park on the west side of town.

Pulling into the entrance of the park, Luke slowed his vehicle to a crawl. He was looking for number seventeen. When he got to number fifteen, he pulled to the side of the road and parked. He could see the aged gold Explorer that had been up in the woods that morning sitting in the driveway two houses ahead.

Luke fired up the computer and plugged Tucker's name into the Yakima County Sheriff's database and waited for a response. Two minutes later, the screen on the laptop changed and up popped a photo of Tucker's driver's license and a short history on the man. Besides three speeding tickets over the last five years, Tucker was clean. The tickets had been paid. Luke wondered what they did to Tucker's auto insurance.

Rafe Gibson had not said what kind of work he or Tucker did, but neither man seemed to be working now during the week.

Luke rolled the back window of the truck down and told Jack to stay. With the window down, Jack could come right away if Luke needed him. Then he shut the truck off, climbed out, and walked to the front door of number seventeen. The house was a prefab double-wide mobile home from the 1980s, Luke guessed. There was no grass, just rounded gray river rock, with a couple of unidentifiable shrubs popping in the middle of what was the front yard.

Luke glanced into the back of the Explorer as he walked by and saw that the deer from this morning was gone. The bow that Tucker had been carrying, along with the quiver of arrows, sat in the front passenger seat.

The three steps up to the front door were covered in a brown indoor-outdoor carpet that was unraveling on the edges. The aluminum screen door in front of the main door was now just an aluminum door because the screen was missing.

Luke reached through the unscreened door and knocked on the wooden door. From somewhere inside, Luke heard a man's voice call out, "Yeah, come on in."

Luke opened the useless screen door and then reached for the knob on the main door. It turned easily, and he pushed open the door.

"Mr. Tucker," Luke said loudly. "Officer McCain. We met earlier today."

Tucker came around the corner and said, "Oh, hey, I didn't expect to see you."

Luke looked at the man's face. He seemed genuinely surprised. Gibson had followed directions and hadn't warned Tucker about the visit.

"What's this about?" Tucker asked. "I thought we were all good this morning."

"Well," Luke said, "there have been some developments since this morning."

"Oh?" Tucker said in a questioning tone.

Luke could see the man thinking, starting to put two and two together.

"Didja talk to Rafe again?" Tucker asked.

"Yep. After I watched him walk back up to where you claim you shot that buck with your bow and pick up your rifle."

Tucker's face went from a smile to a frown in an instant.

"He told me the whole story," Luke said. "So, I've come to pick up the buck, and unfortunately, I have to cite you for several game violations."

"I didn't shoot that deer with the rifle," Tucker said. "Rafe did. Yeah, I stuck my arrow in it to make it look like I shot it with my bow, but he's the one who shot it with the rifle."

"That's not the story he told," Luke said. "He said he tried to shoot it but missed. You took the rifle from him and killed the deer."

Luke was watching Tucker's face when he was telling him this and saw the man glance to the left and look down.

"He said he's never even shot at anything before and was so nervous he missed," Luke continued. "I'm of a mind to believe him."

"He's a liar," Tucker said. "He shot the buck."

"Whose rifle is it?" Luke asked.

"It's mine," Tucker said.

"And why did Mr. Gibson have it with you this morning?"

"'Cause he's scared of cougars. He wanted something to protect himself if a cat came after us."

"I ran a check on Mr. Gibson. The records show he has never had a hunting license in Washington State, so he wasn't lying to me about never hunting before. Why would he lie to me about who shot the buck?"

"I guess he doesn't want no fines."

"Unfortunately, you tagged the buck and tried to make it look like it was shot with archery equipment, so I'm going to cite you for those infractions. And I have to take the deer. I didn't see it in your rig, so where is it?"

"It's at my brother's place," Tucker said. "He's a butcher, so he's cutting it up."

"Can you give me his address, please?" Luke asked.

"You know what?" Tucker said. "No, I can't. This is a bunch of bullshit. I didn't shoot that deer with the rifle. You need to be getting after Rafe. He's the one who done it."

"Either way, the deer is going to be confiscated because it was taken illegally. So, get me your brother's address, or I'll add another citation for impeding an investigation."

"This is a whole bunch of bullshit," Tucker said again, getting more agitated. "I'm going to kill that little bastard for lying to you. You know he's lying, right?"

"I know someone is lying," Luke said. "Now, are you going to give me your brother's address or not?"

"Sure," Tucker said finally. "Go get the deer. Rafe's the one who shot it, so you're taking it from him, not me."

Luke didn't say anything and just looked at Tucker until he gave him the address.

"Hope whoever eats it chokes on it," he said as Luke was walking out the front door.

Luke had written over six hundred dollars in citations, including one violation for shooting a game animal out of season with a rifle.

Chapter 8

Trey Creech, Deke Price, and Artie Miller were standing in a half circle, looking down at the dead wolf. There had been plenty of congratulations and back-slapping when Creech and Price arrived at the kill. Miller described the shot and told how the big wolf did a death roll, "ass over tea kettle" into the sagebrush.

"So, what should we do now?" Price asked.

"I see it we have two options," Creech said. "We can call the local game warden and tell him that Artie shot the wolf as the pack was about to attack the steers."

"Or?" Price asked.

"The three S's," Creech said. "Shoot, shovel and shut up. We grab a couple of shovels and bury the thing on the neighbor's property."

"No way," Miller said. "I'm not going to just throw away this beautiful pelt. I mean, look at it. I'm going to skin it and make it into a rug."

They all stood and looked at the dead wolf and thought about that for a minute.

"I believe we would have a legitimate argument that the wolf was about to do harm to the cattle," Price said. "And shooting it to protect the steers is justified."

"Maybe," said Creech. "But even if they did say it was a legal kill, they'd take the wolf, and Artie would have nothing but a photo on his phone."

"So, you want to just take it and skin it?" Price asked.

"I do," Miller said. "To hell with them wolf lovers. I can always say I shot the thing in Idaho or Montana, all legal-like."

"I know a taxidermist down by Boise that will do the rug for you, no questions asked," Creech said.

"Then it's a done deal," Miller said. "Let's pack this thing back to the truck, and I'll skin it in the tool shed."

After loading the wolf's body in the back of Creech's pickup, the three men drove back down toward the ranch. As they went by the dead steer, the bald eagle was standing on the carcass, pulling meat from the now-exposed ribs. The two ravens were working on the back end of the animal, where the wolves had fed, and several magpies were flitting about, trying to steal a bite wherever they could.

"My old man's going to be pissed about this one," Creech said after stopping the truck and taking a few photos with his phone of the carcass and the scavengers. "But he'll justify it as just doing business in today's wolf-loving world."

"The state will reimburse you for the steer, right?" Price said.

"Yeah, but it'll take forever," Creech said. "They'll send some folks out to investigate to see that it was actually a wolf kill, and then they'll have to send it through about six other agencies and departments before someone cuts a check. We won't see the money until after Christmas."

"Well, I know one wolf that won't be eating beef steak for dinner tonight," Miller said. Creech and Price laughed.

"That's for damn sure," Creech said. "Just remember, don't say a word to no one."

"Time to sound the bell out to the group," Price said.

"Let freedom ring," Creech said, and again the three men laughed.

* * *

The wolf bell rang three times that night. In addition to the big gray male wolf Miller had killed earlier in the day, two other wolves in Washington State died at the hands of Renegade gang members. It was the most successful day since the group had formed shortly after Eli Creech Sr. died of a massive heart attack in his driveway.

As the third gong sounded, the message board on the dark web lit up.

One message read: *The boys have been busy today! Congratulations to the shooters!*

Another one read: *It was a bad day to be a livestock-killing wolf. Kudos to the good guys.*

And yet another one read: *I'm jealous. Heading out tomorrow to see if I can do my part. Congrats to the successful ones.*

No one, not even Deke Price, knew the identity or location of the people writing the messages. And unless the dead wolves were just left out where they were killed and someone came across them, the public might never know either.

Depending on the situation, most of the members of the Renegades adhered to the shoot, shovel, and shut-up rule. Sometimes, though, worried they might not have time to bury the evidence, or were in the wrong place to do so, they would leave the dead wolf where it lay. And there were other times when a wolf might just be wounded by the shooter and would run off to die later. Those wolves might eventually be discovered and reported.

One of the wolves killed that day happened to be a collared juvenile male member of the Skookum Pack, located in the Colville

National Forest north of Spokane, just east of the Pend Oreille River near the Washington-Idaho border. The person who shot the wolf hadn't realized the young animal was collared when he shot it, got scared when he saw the identifying sleeve around its neck, and basically turned and ran.

A grouse hunter found the dead wolf two days later and reported it to the Pend Oreille County Sheriff's Department. The sheriff's deputy who took the call immediately called the Region One office of the Department of Fish and Wildlife in Spokane, where Officer Cody Stephens took the pertinent information, including GPS coordinates, for the wolf's location.

Two hours later, Stephens, an eleven-year veteran of the WDFW enforcement division, was standing at the kill site. Without even bending over to look, he could see by the dime-sized hole in its side that the wolf had been shot by a high-powered rifle. Stephens took photos of the wolf and the area where it had died, then put the dead canine in a plastic bag and threw it over his shoulder for the short, quarter-mile pack out. He estimated the young wolf may have weighed sixty pounds when it was alive.

Standing five-foot ten-inches tall and weighing one hundred and eighty pounds, Stephens was boot-leather tough, and he kept himself in good shape. During the hike out with the dead wolf, Stephens thought about the last time he was involved in a wolf-poaching case.

It had been four years earlier, when he was working with an undercover WDFW officer who had infiltrated a gang of poachers that, among other things, were targeting wolves near Colville. The investigation led to a surprise sting on the poachers. Unfortunately, one of the wolf killers was in a position to start shooting at the officers, and Stephens caught a bullet high in the chest. As all WDFW officers do when they are on the job, he was wearing his protective Kevlar vest, and it saved him from serious injury, if not death.

Luke McCain was the WDFW officer who was working

undercover on that operation. After the shooting and the arrest of two of the poachers, McCain had tracked down the man who had shot Stephens.

Since the wolf that Stephens had just recovered was abandoned in the field, he assumed the animal was not the victim of a similar poaching ring. The poachers he and McCain were dealing with a few years back were selling the hides on the black market for five hundred dollars apiece or more, so it was unlikely this collared wolf had been killed for its hide, or it wouldn't have been left out where someone might find it.

When he got back to his office, Stephens called Joe Ames, the head of wolf recovery for the Department of Fish and Wildlife.

"Yeah, this is Ames."

"Hey, Joe, this is Cody Stephens. I got a call today about a dead wolf up north of here. I went and picked it up. It has a collar on it. Number 2311."

"Hit by a car?" Ames asked.

"No, hit by a bullet."

"Crap," Ames said. "Hate to hear that. I know that wolf. Member of the Skookum Pack."

"I assume you want to see it, do some tests and what have you?"

"Yessir. I'll come and get it. I'm over by Wenatchee right now, but I'll pick it up tomorrow morning. You got someplace to keep it cool?"

Stephens told him he did, and they set a time to meet the following day.

It had been a while since Stephens had talked to Luke McCain. Since the fellow officer was on his mind, he called him just to check in.

"Hey, Cody," Luke said as he answered his phone. "Haven't talked to you in a while. How's the shoulder?"

"It's as good as new, so no complaints," Stephens said. "Although I'll still have nightmares now and again about getting shot."

"Yeah, I hear ya," Luke said. "I have them too."

"That's right," Stephens said. "You caught a bullet from that guy who was pretending to be Bigfoot."

"None the worse for wear," Luke said with a laugh. "So, what's going on up in Region One?"

"I took a call on a poached wolf, and that brought back memories of our little dust-up with those guys up in Colville. You haven't heard any rumblings about them, or someone else starting up again, have you?"

"No, but there do seem to be higher numbers of poached wolves being reported, not just up your way but all over Eastern Washington. They even found a wolf that had been shot down in Klickitat County a couple weeks ago."

"I saw that," Stephens said. "I don't think there is a confirmed pack down that way."

"Whether it's a pack or not, they're there," Luke said. "We're getting more and more wolf sighting calls coming from around that area."

"Seems weird the number of poached wolves is ticking up all of a sudden," Stephens said.

"More wolves mean more potential interactions with humans," Luke said. "Hunters mistake them for a coyote or hate that the wolves are competing for the deer and elk, so they shoot them."

"That has always been the case," Stephens said. "But I just looked at the numbers, and there's more poached wolves in the last two months than all last year. And those are just the ones we know about."

"You think there is a concerted effort by someone who is purposely out to kill the wolves?" Luke asked.

"I hate to think so," Stephens said. "I'm going to talk to Joe Ames in the morning and get his take on all of this. He might have some thoughts."

"I'm sure he will," Luke said. "The man lives and breathes wolves. Let me know what he says. And I'll talk to the captain here to see if he's heard anything."

"Sounds good," Stephens said. "I'll stay in touch."

After he hung up from the call, Luke started thinking back to the day when Stephens was shot. Luke hadn't really been involved in the shoot-out. He'd had his hands full arresting the two other members of the poaching ring. Luke was glad he was able to track down Ricky Carter, the man who shot Stephens, and help put him away for fifteen years.

Then he started thinking about what Stephens had said, that poaching numbers were way up. Could there be a concerted effort by some radical wolf-haters to reduce the number of wolves competing for the big game in Washington?

CHAPTER 9

Peter Covington hated hunting. He hated the idea of hunting. And he hated hunters. Just the thought of someone killing an innocent animal or bird made him physically ill.

When the state of Washington banned the use of dogs to track cougars for the purpose of running them down and shooting them out of a tree, he cheered. And when the game commissioners, two of whom he knew well, decided to cancel the spring bear hunt in the state, Covington was ecstatic. Who in their right mind wanted to shoot a bear anyway? Certainly, in today's world, no one wants to shoot bears for the meat.

The day his father died in 1989 and left Covington an inheritance of just north of twenty-six million dollars, he decided he would dedicate his life, and his money, to stopping all sport hunting in his beloved Washington State. Never having to work again, Covington became involved in every anti-hunting organization he could find. With his time and passion, and with his money, he helped them all.

His greatest joy was assisting a covert operation to reintroduce wolves into Washington State back in the early 2000s. He had financed the unauthorized release of twenty-four wolves from Montana, Idaho, and British Columbia into the northeast corner of the state.

With the help of local and state politicians, including a governor whose personal feelings about hunting more closely aligned with Covington than those who spent millions of dollars each year buying hunting licenses and tags, he believed he was making some headway. Even, some twenty years later, when the WDFW biologists made recommendations to take the wolves off the state's endangered species list, the governor and the wildlife commission persisted in keeping the canines listed.

Covington had tracked the growth of the wolf populations carefully. And every year when a new population census showed the wolf numbers had grown, and new packs were popping up here and there on the east side of the Cascade Mountains, he jumped for joy. And he cringed every time wolves were exterminated by the Department of Fish and Wildlife's hired wolf killers after the canines had been identified as predating on some rancher's livestock. Two different times, a whole pack had to be totally wiped out because they had killed so many domestic animals.

It was out-and-out legalized poaching, Covington believed, when gunmen from the state wildlife department eliminated problem wolves. He believed not enough had been done by the ranchers to protect their livestock.

In the hopes of stopping the culling of the cattle-killing wolves by the state shooters, Covington stepped up and anonymously sent even more money into the fund that helped pay ranchers for the livestock that were confirmed to be wolf kills. If the ranchers were paid above market price for their cattle and sheep, he thought maybe they wouldn't want to go on the war path against his beautiful, cherished wolves.

Covington seethed when he heard of the occasional wolf that died at the hands of poachers. He figured the killings were done by hunters who, based on who they were and what they enjoyed doing, shot the wolves just for the joy of killing.

When a wolf kill was confirmed as a poaching, Covington would immediately contact one of the animal rights organizations he supported and offer a sizable reward for the identification and the conviction of the weak, miserable snivelings who did the killing.

Over the years, only once did he have to pay a reward. The half dozen other times he had offered up the money, it had gone unspent. Mostly, it was because there never seemed to be enough evidence to catch the murdering criminals.

Fifty-four years old, with graying around the temples of his black hair, Covington was what might be best described as distinguished-looking. He sported a mid-summer tan all year long and wore perfectly pressed, high thread count, white cotton dress shirts tucked into neatly pressed Levi's jeans. The white shirts, he believed, showed off his tanned face. If Covington wasn't wearing penny loafers, he was wearing Birkenstock sandals.

During late fall and winter, Covington lived with his thirty-seven-year-old, former model girlfriend in a large house on Mercer Island. The rest of the year, he lived in an 11,000-square-foot "summer cabin" along the shores of Cle Elum Lake. The girlfriend didn't accompany him to the east side of the Cascades because to her it was "dirty and cold with too many uncouth people running around."

Covington suspected that she had a boyfriend on the side to keep her company during the months he was gone, but he didn't press it. She looked good on his arm at the different money-raising galas he attended that supported the different animal-saving organizations. As long as she didn't spend over her ten-thousand-dollar-a-month allowance, he was happy.

When he heard about the young wolf that had been killed by poachers over by Spokane, Covington became enraged. Why the hell couldn't the authorities find out who was doing these killings?

He had talked to the governor, who was on the receiving end of tens of thousands of dollars from Covington for his re-election campaign every four years. But the man was pretty useless in Covington's opinion. He believed the governor to be a typical politician. He talked a good game, but with the homeless problems around the state, and being billions of dollars over budget, the least of his worries was a few wolves being killed.

So, after thinking about it one evening while sipping on a glass of Mackinlay's Highland Scotch Whiskey, Covington decided it was time to take the problem into his own hands. He picked up his phone, scrolled through the contacts listed within, tapped on a name, and pressed the call button.

"Mr. Covington, how may I help you?" the man on the other end of the line said after two rings.

Covington didn't know the man's name. He was just listed in the phone as "the fixer." He had used the man once before to track down a former friend who had stolen $200,000 of Covington's much beloved inheritance.

At the time, Covington told the fixer, "Don't kill him, but let him know that I am very disappointed in his behavior. And try to get my damn money back."

"It will be done," the voice on the other end said.

Two weeks later, a small box arrived via courier to Covington at his Mercer Island mansion with $120,000 inside. A note accompanying the money said: *Your friend is very sorry for what he did. I have taken my fee of 50k out of the funds. Not sure where the other 30k went, but I suspect up his nose along with payment to prostitutes.*

Covington told the fixer about his new problem and asked the man if he had the ability to find out who might be poaching wolves around the state.

"I think I can do that," the fixer said. "Might take me a while, and I would need some funds for procuring the information that is needed."

"Certainly," Covington said. "Whatever you need."

He then told the fixer that he only needed the information, and none of his other services would be desired at this time.

"Depending on what you find out," Covington told the man on the phone. "Then we'll see how we want to handle it."

"Yes, sir, Mr. Covington," the fixer said.

"Wire the money to the same place?" Covington asked.

The fixer again said, "Yes, sir." Then he was gone.

Covington poured himself another tumbler of Mackinlay's and sat in his favorite overstuffed leather chair. As he sipped the smooth Scotch and looked out the giant window at the stars and half-moon reflecting off Cle Elum Lake, he smiled.

"To hell with the governor," he said to himself. "There's more than one way to deal with these miscreants."

* * *

The fixer went to work immediately. He called a computer hacker who was the best money could buy and told him what he wanted.

"Scour the internet and see what you can find," he told the hacker. "Look for anything about the illegal killing of wolves in Washington State. I need to find out who, where, and when. I'm sure you know where to look."

The hacker confirmed the fixer's order and told him his rate of $500 per hour had, unfortunately, gone up to $600 per hour, what with inflation and all. The fixer told him to do whatever it took but to find him something, anything, that he might use to identify the person, or persons, who had poached a wolf.

"I'm on it," the hacker said.

It took him less than an hour to discover the group that identified themselves as "the Renegades." Of course, he would bill the fixer for a full hour, plus an extra hour as a bonus for being so good.

CHAPTER 10

It had been almost two months since Luke had cited Max Tucker for the multiple game violations. Tucker's brother, while not cordial, was at least cooperative and had handed over three cardboard apple boxes with cut and wrapped venison from the ill-gotten buck. Luke had taken the deer meat to the mission, where it was received with gratitude.

The big game hunting seasons were now in full swing, and Luke was working every day, checking on hunters. He had contacted dozens and dozens of hunters, and nearly everyone was legal and doing their part to make the season safe and enjoyable for all.

Luke had just finished a quick lunch when a call came through on his radio. He had met fellow WDFW officer Stan Hargraves at the little restaurant in the small unincorporated area known as the Nile. They were walking out to their trucks when both their personal radios crackled.

"Wildlife 148 or 136, you have a copy?"

"This is Wildlife 136," Hargraves said. "Go ahead."

"We have a call about a dead hunter in the Gold Creek area—can you respond?"

"Roger that," Hargraves said. "I'm with 148. We'll head that way now."

"Another heart attack?" Luke said to Hargraves as he was climbing into his truck.

"Oh, probably," Hargraves said, climbing into his own pickup.

During the different general hunting seasons, it was not uncommon to have a hunter, sometimes two, suffer a heart attack while out hunting. It was usually older men, out of shape, who had tried to do too much.

Luke had been called in on one death where the hunter, who looked to be in good physical condition, had died after he walked up to a bull elk he had just killed. Evidently, the excitement had been too much for the man, and his heart gave out on the spot.

Luke was thinking about that call from a few years before while driving up the Forest Service road into the mountains north of State Route 410 when his radio again crackled. The emergency response operator said a Yakima County Sheriff's deputy and an ambulance were on the way, but they were both about fifteen minutes behind Luke and Hargraves.

When they arrived at the spot on the Forest Service road that dispatch had given them, there were two hunters standing next to a side-by-side ATV. The hunters, a man and a teenage boy, were outfitted in the standard hunting attire of the modern-day rifle hunter. Each wore pants, a coat, and a hat in some version of camouflage, with a bright orange vest over the coat.

Luke always thought it was somewhat ironic to be outfitted from head to toe in camo when the law then required a bright-colored vest to be worn over the top. Ironic, yes, but when he hunted, he did the same thing. Most of today's best hunting clothing was built to be dry and warm, and it all came in an array of different camouflages to match all kinds of different habitats.

He parked his truck in a turnout just past the ATV and got out. He almost said something to Jack but remembered the yellow dog had chosen to stay home on this day. Still, Luke opened the back door to get his coat out of the back seat. As he put the coat on, he walked over to the hunters who were already talking to Hargraves.

Luke heard Hargraves say, "So you found the body?"

The teenage kid said, "Yessir. I just thought he was sleeping, but then I looked closer and saw he wasn't breathing. I radioed my dad, and he came over and told me I was right, the man was dead."

"Did you touch the body?" Hargraves asked the man and his son. Both shook their heads.

"No, sir," the man said. "We hiked out to the ATV, and I rode up to where I could get cell service and called 911."

Luke took identification information from the man and the boy and then said, "Can one of you take us to where the body is? And someone else bring the deputy in when he gets here?"

The man, whose name was Chris Bass, said to his son, "Why don't you take them in, Jaydon, and I'll bring in the other officer."

"Okay," Jaydon Bass said and started walking up an overgrown two-track road that followed a small creek. Luke and Hargraves followed.

"How old are you, Jaydon?" Hargraves asked.

"I'm fifteen."

"Have you seen any elk?" Luke asked as they hiked along.

"Yeah, I saw a huge bull this morning. Close, too. He ran right by me. But I don't have a big bull tag."

"Still was exciting though, huh?" Luke said.

"Yes, it was. I've never shot an elk, but I did get my buck earlier this year."

"Good for you," Hargraves said. "So, this dead guy, is he older, maybe a little overweight?"

"No, sir. He's really skinny. I can't tell how old he is. He's face down in the grass."

Hargraves looked at Luke with raised eyebrows. They'd both been on several dead hunter calls, and almost to a one, they were older. And many were overweight to some extent.

"Did you see his rifle anywhere near the body?" Hargraves asked.

"No, sir. But I don't think he was a hunter."

"How's that?" Hargraves asked.

"Because he wasn't dressed like one. He was wearing blue jeans and old white tennis shoes. And he didn't have any orange on at all."

They walked another half mile up the rough two-track, and then the young man cut up the hill.

"He's right over there, by those rocks," Jaydon said.

"Okay," Luke said. "Maybe wait here for a bit while we go check it out."

The young man found a stump to sit on and watched as Luke and Hargraves walked up the hill to the rocks. When they got there, they found the man lying face down in the grass.

"The kid's right," Hargraves said. "Doesn't look like a hunter."

"And doesn't fit the description of a typical heart attack victim either," Luke said as he bent down to look closer at the body.

"Roll him over," Hargraves said.

Luke grabbed the right shoulder of the deceased man, pulled him downhill to roll him over, and stared right into the dead, cold eyes of Rafe Gibson.

"Well, I'll be danged," Luke said after looking at Gibson for a few seconds, running the dead man's face through his memory banks.

"You know this guy?"

"I do," Luke said. "Name is Gibson. I caught him and another guy with a buck they shot with a rifle during early archery season."

Hargraves still hadn't gotten a good look at the ashen-colored face of the deceased man and said, "Heart attack?"

"Don't think he had time for one," Luke said. "What with the bullet hole in his forehead."

"No, probably not," Hargraves said as he moved in for a closer look. "Looks like a small caliber, maybe a twenty-two?"

The small hole in Gibson's forehead was almost perfectly centered above the bridge of his nose.

Both men stepped back from the body and started looking around for any clues as to what might have happened.

After a couple minutes, Luke said, "All I see is a bunch of trampled grass where people have been walking. No blood, no gun, no shell casings, nothing."

"Most likely the trampling was done by us and the man and his son who found him," Hargraves said. "You think he was shot right here?"

"No idea," Luke said. "But whoever did it had to have been pretty close to hit him perfectly between the eyes."

"Wouldn't you be ducking and running if someone was pointing a gun at your face?" Hargraves asked.

"Maybe he didn't have time for any of that," Luke said. "But the more I think about it, I don't think he was killed here. I think he was shot somewhere else and dumped out here."

"Long way to bring a body just to dump it," Hargraves said. "It would have been much easier to just throw him into the river."

Luke didn't say anything. He was thinking about Rafe Gibson and Max Tucker—and what Tucker had said he was going to do to Gibson because he had ratted him out.

"Luke?" Hargraves said.

"Yeah, no," Luke said. "I have no clue why."

"Must have been someone strong enough to pack the body up this way," Hargraves said.

Luke thought about Max Tucker. He was as skinny as Gibson. And after Luke had witnessed him trying to draw his recurve bow that day back in September, he believed Tucker wasn't terribly strong either. No way the man could have packed a dead body, even as light as Gibson's was, up here from the road.

"Someone could have shot Gibson a short way away and then dragged the body here," Luke said.

"Still doesn't make sense," Hargraves said. "He looks pretty light. Probably anyone with any strength at all could have carried his body a good distance with a fireman's carry."

A fireman's carry allows one person to carry another person without assistance by placing the carried person across the shoulders of the carrier.

"Heck, a person with average strength could have carried him under their arm," Luke said. "I don't think he weighed a hundred and twenty pounds."

"Well," Hargraves said, "he didn't just fall out of the sky."

A minute later, they heard voices coming up the trail. Then they heard Jaydon Bass say, "Hi, Dad. The two game wardens are up at the body."

Then Luke heard the familiar voice of Bill Williams, a longtime Yakima County sheriff's deputy who periodically kidded him about his name being the same as the lead character on the old TV Western show *The Rifleman*.

"Whatcha got cooking?" Williams asked Luke when he saw him.

"Dead guy," Luke said. "Shot in the head."

"Guess it wasn't a heart attack then?" Williams asked.

"Probably should let the coroner make that determination," Luke said. "But if I was a betting man, I'd say the bullet between the eyes did the deed."

Williams looked at the dead man's body and asked, "Any ID yet?"

"I just happen to know who he is," Luke said. "I investigated him and another guy on a poaching case back in September. His name is Rafe Gibson."

"Was he this skinny in September?" Williams asked.

"Yep," Luke said.

"Meth head?" Williams asked.

"No sign of it back in September," Luke said. "Might have been a smoker, though. You know how some of them are. Every time they feel hungry, they light up a Marlboro and forget to eat."

Williams patted his round belly and said, "Maybe I should take up smoking." Then he said, "See anything else around here that might tell what happened?"

Luke and Hargraves told them what their thoughts were on Gibson's body being dumped there. And Luke told him about Max Tucker and what the man had said about killing Gibson if he snitched on him.

"Did he snitch?" Williams asked.

"Yep," Luke said.

"That's kind of a crappy thing to do to a hunting buddy," Williams said.

"Sounded like they weren't really buddies," Luke said. "And Mr. Gibson here wasn't really much of a hunter, at least according to what he told me. I looked up his history, and he's never had a hunting license."

"That doesn't stop some guys," Williams said. "I guess we better have a chat with Tucker."

"And here's one other thing," Luke said. "Gibson told me that there was a rumor that Tucker had killed another man. Slept with his wife or something. Don't know how long ago. Hispanic, by the name of Gomez or Gonzales."

"Cold case?" Williams asked.

"I guess so," Luke said. "Although Gibson didn't seem the type to be reading the newspaper. So he may not have known if a person was arrested for that one or not."

"I'll look into it," Williams said. "If this Tucker killed one guy, he certainly could have killed another."

After talking for a few more minutes, Luke and Hargraves told Williams good luck with the investigation and headed back down the hill to where Chris and Jaydon Bass were waiting.

"Yeah, thanks," Williams said to the men as they walked down the hill. "If you think of anything else, let me know."

Chapter 11

Eli Creech Jr. was upset at hearing the wolves had killed the steer with the bum leg.

"Did you see the wolves?" Creech Jr. asked his son.

"We did," Trey said. "And we shot at them to scare them off."

"Good, but it most likely won't do much good."

"There are other alternatives," Trey said, trying again to get his father to agree to the more permanent measures that he and his buddies had ultimately used.

"No. It's illegal, and we're not going there. Understand?"

"Yessir," Trey said, knowing that Price and Miller were at this very moment skinning the wolf Miller had shot earlier that day.

"We'll contact the game warden tomorrow to get someone out here to investigate."

"No investigation needed," Trey said. "We know it was the wolves. We saw them."

"Still," his father said, "we need to go through the appropriate channels."

"Yessir," Trey said again and headed for the door.

When he reached the tool shed, the other two men had the hide off the wolf carcass and were scraping the bits and pieces of remaining flesh off the skin.

"What should we do with the carcass?" Miller asked when Trey came in.

"We'll throw it in the back of the truck and run it over to the river. It'll be nothing but bones in no time."

"I'm gunna take the hide and drop it into my old man's freezer," Miller said. "He never uses it anymore. Then I can run it down to Boise when we get a day off."

"Sounds good," Trey said. "Let's get rid of the carcass and go grab a beer."

"You guys go," Price said. "I'm going to go check out what's happening out there on the internet."

When they were up on the mountain, Price had taken a picture of Trey and Miller with the dead wolf. A hero shot, the hunters called it. Two smiling nimrods holding up the head of a lifeless wolf, tongue hanging out, eyes glazed over.

He knew it was a risk to post the photo on the Renegades' site, but a couple of others had done so, with the face or faces of the shooters blanked out. Some put a yellow happy face over the human faces, and Price decided that would work just fine for the photo he had of his friends with the dark gray wolf.

He worked the picture over in Photoshop and covered Trey and Miller's faces, scrubbed the rifle out of Miller's hand, and looked for any other identifying things in the photo. Seeing nothing else, he saved the photo and then posted it to the site with the caption "Queen for a day."

The caption was in reference to the Queen song, "Another One Bites the Dust."

Within seconds, the photo was getting likes and comments such as *Lucky bastards* and *It's a bad day to be a wolf.*

*   *   *

The hacker saw the photo too. He had been in the Renegades' site on the dark web for only a few minutes when the photo popped up. He immediately went to work trying to trace the source of the photo, but whoever had posted it was good. They were using coding and algorithms that made it almost impossible to track. Almost. It would take him a while, but the hacker was determined to find out who was running the Renegades' site.

In the meantime, he looked at the photo that had just been posted. Seeing the dead wolf didn't bother him. He had no problem with people shooting wolves, or any other animal for that matter, but he did always wonder why hunters took photos of themselves with the animals they'd killed. Did it make them feel superior? Or was it just another memento of the hunt?

Then, as he studied the photo, he noticed some kind of tower way back behind the hunters who were now wearing happy face masks. He enlarged the background as much as he could before it became blurry. The tower was an old fire lookout where forest service employees sat and watched for smoke in the surrounding mountains. And there was a barbed wire fence in the closer distance.

The hacker had read about the fire lookouts but had never seen one in person. From what he remembered, the lookouts were built in the mid-1900s, but most had been dismantled in the last decade or two because satellites and other modern technology had made them obsolete. Some western states rented a few of the remaining old lookouts to hikers who would spend a night or two in the small cabins on stilts.

As the hacker continued researching the old lookouts, he realized he might be able to pinpoint this exact one. And if he could, he would be closer to figuring out who the two men were with the dead wolf in the photo that had been uploaded that night.

* * *

"You sure no one will find the wolf carcass?" Miller asked Trey as they drove to the Okanogan River.

"Pretty sure," Trey said. "And even if they do, what can they do? It'll look like a skinned coyote or some other animal."

"I guess," Miller said. "I'm just starting to get a little scared about what would happen to me if someone found out that I shot it."

"No worries," Trey said. "We'll be fine."

They dumped the carcass into a deep hole in the river and watched it sink into the dark depths.

"That should do it," Trey said. "Problem solved. I'll call the taxidermist in Boise tomorrow and get it set for you to take the hide to him. Next year at this time, you'll have a beautiful wolf rug."

"You think they can get DNA from a tanned hide?" Miller asked.

"I don't know," Trey said. "Maybe from some fur, but so what if they do—that won't matter. A wolf is a wolf, whether it is from Montana or Washington. No one will know where you shot this one."

"I guess," Miller said again.

"I'd do the same thing if it were me," Trey said. "In fact, we're going back up to where you shot yours in a few days to see if the pack is back in the area. I want to shoot one too."

"You'll get your chance sooner or later," Miller said. "They'll be back on that herd of cattle at some point."

"I hope so," Trey said as the pickup bounced down the road, headed to their favorite tavern.

* * *

The hacker spent thirteen minutes getting into the U.S. Forest Service mainframe computer. The files for the information on the still-standing fire lookouts were not as heavily protected as was the personal information of the tens of thousands of USFS employees.

He found photos of all the still-existing lookouts, but the issue was that they all pretty much looked the same. And the one in the photo with the men and the dead wolf was so far away, there were no distinguishing marks that might have made a match easier.

There were twenty-one lookouts still standing and in use as a rented camping spot in the western United States. And only eight of those were located in Washington. The hacker copied photos of the eight and moved them onto a separate screen. Then he put the enlarged version of the dead wolf photo next to each of the eight Washington photos.

He still couldn't determine if the wolf photo lookout was one of the eight. It could be any of them, or none of them.

To help him whittle it down even more, he brought up a map of the known wolf packs in Washington State. He didn't have to hack into anything to get it, as the map was available to the general public through a simple Google search.

Then, one by one, he placed the location of the eight lookouts onto the wolf pack map. Three of the lookouts were in counties where there were no known wolves.

Finally, the hacker brought up Google Earth images of the five remaining lookouts based on the latitude and longitude numbers accompanying the photos and started meticulously looking at the surrounding geography and vegetation of each. This helped him to narrow the choice down to one of two lookouts. One was in Chelan County, in country that looked to be remote wilderness. The other was in Okanogan County, where there were patches of private land.

The barbed wire fence in the background didn't guarantee the photo was taken on private land, but it made it much more likely.

Now, all he had to do was look up who owned land around the fire lookout, maybe within five miles or so based on the photo, and he would have an excellent starting point for narrowing down the identity of the men in the photo.

The fixer had asked him for a name. The hacker might be able to provide the man with two. That would be worth another bonus, for sure.

*   *   *

There were currently nineteen members of the Renegades. Through a program Price had written specifically for the purpose of keeping track of who was visiting the Renegades' site and how often, he would know if someone had hacked their page. When he saw that someone new had been into the site, he started to panic a little.

Of course, it could have been some computer geek, like himself, who was nosing around in the backgrounds of different sites on the dark web and landed on theirs. Or, and he didn't want to think about this, it might be someone who was specifically searching for wolf killings.

"Damn it!" Price said to himself and immediately took the photo of his friends with the dead wolf down. Of course, it was too late, but he didn't know that.

Then he started tracking whoever it was who had broken through the highly intricate firewall into their page. When he couldn't track the person, he really started to panic.

He picked up his phone and dialed Trey.

"What's up?" Trey said, with a bit of a slur in his speech.

"We have a potential problem," Price said. "You guys need to get to my place as soon as possible."

"Tonight?" Trey slurred. "We're celebrating the life and death of el lobo."

"Shut up about that," Price said. "And yes, you need to get here, like right away. Drink some coffee, sober up, and get over here."

"Aw, man, okay. We'll get there as fast as we can."

In the background, he heard Miller order two more Budweisers. It was going to be a long night.

CHAPTER 12

Rafe Gibson's corpse had been found by Jaydon Bass on a Friday afternoon. The following Monday, as Luke McCain drove into the Region Three office of the Department of Fish and Wildlife, he started thinking about the thin man.

It was hard for him to believe that Max Tucker would actually kill Gibson just for telling Luke about who really shot the buck with a rifle. Then again, Tucker had sounded pretty believable when Luke went to his house that night to confiscate the deer.

He decided to call Bill Williams to see if he had talked to Tucker.

"Hey, Rifleman," Williams's voice crackled over the Bluetooth in Luke's truck. "What's up?"

"Did you go talk to Max Tucker about Rafe Gibson?"

"As a matter of fact, I did," Williams said without elaboration.

"Let me guess, he didn't confess."

"No, he didn't. He seemed truly surprised. He wasn't broken-hearted or anything, but he did seem a bit perplexed."

"Did you tell him why you were asking?"

"Yes, and he laughed it off. He said he says he's going to kill someone about once a week. Said he never means it."

"Hmmm," Luke hummed. "You mind if I go over and have a little chat with him?"

"Be my guest," Williams said. "Other than Tucker, we have no solid leads at all. Gibson lived by himself, and we can't even find anyone who might have seen him in the last week."

"Did you check where he worked?"

"We would, if we knew where that was."

"Tucker didn't know?"

"No, he said that Gibson quit the job over at Thompson's Trucking, where Tucker works now, right after you cited him for those hunting violations and hasn't talked to him since."

"Okay," Luke said. "What did you find out about the other man that Gibson said might have been killed by Tucker?"

"The guy's name was Gomez. Took a knife to the chest. Tucker said he knew the guy, but he seemed to have a solid alibi for the night Gomez was killed. If it had been a twenty-two-caliber bullet to the forehead, I might be looking into it a little more closely."

"They still have no suspects on that one?" Luke asked.

"Nope. Our detectives are working it, but nothing solid has popped up."

"I'll let you know if I learn anything else after I talk to Tucker," Luke said.

Williams thanked him and disconnected the call.

At the office, Luke ran through a bunch of emails and three voicemails, then went and checked in with his boss.

"Morning, Cap," Luke said after knocking on the frame of the door to Captain Bob Davis's office.

"Hey, Luke," Davis said.

Luke thought Davis looked like a combination of Wilfred Brimley and Andy Reid, the coach of the Kansas City Chiefs. Davis was a large man, overweight to some degree, with a big bushy gray mustache hiding his upper lip. Gold rim glasses were perched on his nose, and short gray hair ringed a shiny bald head.

"I hear you were able to ID the body that was found up off of 410 on Friday," Davis said.

"Yessir," Luke said. "He was the guy who ratted on his friend about shooting that buck with a rifle during archery season. Name is Rafe Gibson."

"You think his partner did it?" Davis asked.

"I don't know. Seems to be the likely suspect. But Williams over at the sheriff's department questioned him and says the guy doesn't seem good for it."

"They'll figure it out," Davis said. "They're pretty good at their job."

"I might follow up with the guy I wrote up, just to get my take on it. On another subject, have you heard anything about the increase in poached wolves in the region?"

"Only through the reports that are coming out of Olympia," Davis said. "I guess because we really don't have many wolves around here, we haven't seen the problem first-hand."

"I got a call from Stephens up in Region One the other day," Luke said. "He's concerned that someone, or maybe even a group, is targeting wolves."

"Like back in the 1890s?" Davis asked. "Ranchers wanting to exterminate them?"

"I don't know exactly what he is thinking. It's likely hunters who are pissed that the wolves are competing with them for the deer and elk. But it could be ranchers, I guess."

"There are definitely some outspoken ranchers who hate that the wolves are now back amongst their cattle. But they're getting well-paid for the occasional animal they lose to wolves."

"I told him we'd keep our ears open down this way," Luke said.

"I'm guessing you're not willing to go undercover again," Davis said.

"I'd just as soon not. Besides, I think everyone up in that neck of the woods has seen my picture since then. Undercover is no longer an option for me."

They talked for a few more minutes, and Luke started to head out the door when Davis said, "Oh, I almost forgot. I got a call from a guy my wife works with. He lives down around Sunnyside and says his neighbor is putting out cracked corn to get the ducks and geese to come into an old wheat field near his place. He claims the birds are coming in, and whoever is hunting them is shooting after hours."

Luke said he would check into it and took the neighbor's phone number from Davis.

On his way to Max Tucker's house, Luke called the number that Davis had given him. A man by the name of Delmar Berry answered.

Luke identified himself, and Berry said, "Yes, Officer McCain, thanks for calling. My neighbor is shooting well past hunting hours, and when I looked out into the field this morning, I could see corn spread all over the place. They haven't grown corn in that field in a coon's age."

"Okay, Mr. Berry. Give me your address, and I will come down and check it out."

"Come just before shooting time ends, and you will see what I'm talking about," Berry said.

"Alright. I'll see you then," Luke said and pushed the Bluetooth button on his steering wheel to disconnect the call.

He pulled into Max Tucker's driveway seven minutes later. When he had visited Tucker at his home two months earlier, the few flowers in the garden were still vibrant. Now, in early November, the flowers were wilted and dead.

Luke parked his truck, got out, and walked up to the front

door of the mobile home. The brown indoor-outdoor carpet on the steps looked even more tattered, and the screen door was still screenless and serving no purpose. He often could tell when a house was empty, and Luke was getting that feeling now. Still, he knocked on the front door and listened for footsteps or any other noise that might tell him that someone was home.

After a minute and hearing nothing, Luke knocked again, this time a little harder. Still no response, so he decided to walk around the side of the house and take a look in the backyard. He was surprised to see a small mule deer buck hanging from the branch of a maple tree. The buck had been gutted but otherwise was intact.

Luke walked over to the deer to see if a tag had been affixed to its antlers or was tied to a leg. Finding none, he backed up a few steps and pulled his phone out to take a picture.

He inspected the buck and found a bullet hole just behind the shoulder. A similar hole in size and placement to the buck Tucker had killed back in September. Luke moved around to the back side of the tree so that he could also get a photo of the deer and the back of the house for proof that the buck was in Tucker's yard. He was taking his photo when a man called out from the next house over.

"Hey, what are you doing over there?" the man hollered.

"Game warden," Luke said as he walked toward the neighbor's house. "Have you seen Mr. Tucker lately?"

The man ignored Luke's question.

"You supposed to be snooping around people's houses without some kind of warrant?" the man asked. He was a withered-up old man, Luke guessed to be in his late eighties or early nineties, wearing a gray cardigan sweater over a checkered flannel shirt. His tan chino trousers were cinched up with a belt about midway between his shoulders and his hips. What little hair that was left on the old-timer's head was white and shot up in a bunch of different directions.

"I need to talk to Mr. Tucker, and I was just looking to see if he was back here," Luke said. "So, you haven't seen him lately?"

"Don't know," the old man said. "I'm not one of those kind of neighbors, always looking at what everyone else is doing."

"You sure spotted me pretty quickly," Luke said.

"I saw your truck, so I wondered what you was up to."

"Well, now you know," Luke said. "When did Tucker hang this buck here?"

"Last night, not that I was paying any attention."

"Did you know that Tucker shot a deer earlier this year?"

"Yep, he had one hanging in that tree two weeks ago, not that I was paying attention."

Luke paused and thought about it. The deer hanging in the tree now was most likely shot the day before, and only special permit hunters were allowed to take a deer during this time in November. He knew from looking at Tucker's information that the man had no special permit, let alone the fact that his one and only tag was used illegally during early archery season.

The deer he was looking at now, and the one that the neighbor had seen in the tree two weeks earlier, could have been taken by a family member or friend who used Tucker's tree, but this deer had no tag on it. That was a violation.

"Any other deer in the last couple months?" Luke asked.

"Just one other. 'Bout a month ago," the old man said.

"Do you remember, were they bucks or does?"

"All young bucks like that one there. I thought it was illegal to shoot forked-horns in Washington?"

"It is in most of the east side of the state," Luke said. "I really need to talk to Mr. Tucker. Any idea when he gets home from work?"

"No idea," the old man said. "Like I said, I don't pay much attention to what goes on over here."

Luke chuckled. The old timer probably knew exactly what went on over here and when.

"Okay," Luke said and walked over to the man. "My name is Luke McCain. Here's my card. If you see anything out of the ordinary, or any more game animals appearing in this tree, give me a call."

"Charlie Zimmerman," the old timer said, reaching out his right hand for Luke to shake. "Lived in this here park for forty-one years. Seen a lot of changes over the years. And a lot of animals hanging in that tree right there."

"But you really don't pay much attention?" Luke asked with a smile.

Zimmerman huffed and waved a hand like he was shooing a fly.

"Oh, you know, stuff is going on around here all the time. It's hard to miss."

"Well, it is nice to meet you, Mr. Zimmerman. If you happen to see Mr. Tucker before I do, let him know I'm looking to speak to him. He can call me on the number on that card."

Zimmerman held up Luke's card, winked his right eye at Luke, and bobbed his head as he made a clicking noise with his tongue. Then he turned and went back into the house.

Luke took a few more photos of the dead deer hanging in the tree and headed back to his truck. Tucker seemed to be one of those guys who had no problem breaking the law. How many laws that might be was the question, including possibly the murder of Rafe Gibson.

CHAPTER 13

"We may have a problem," Deke Price said to Trey Creech and Artie Miller when they finally arrived at his house. It was nearly three o'clock in the morning, and both men were showing signs of lingering inebriation.

"What's so important that we couldn't go home and get some sleep first?" Creech asked with a slight slur in his speech.

"Someone's been into our website," Price said.

"That's what we want, isn't it?" Creech said.

"Someone who isn't supposed to be was in there snooping around tonight. They saw the photo I posted of you guys with the wolf, and the other two photos of members with wolves they killed."

"WHAT?!" Miller yelled. "You posted my photo with the wolf?"

"Your face was covered. No one will ever know it was you. And they can't find out where we are or who we are. But still."

"You also said no one without permission would be able to get into the site," Miller said. "And here we are."

"I'm worried it might be the law," Price said. "They have some pretty good I.T. people. They wouldn't know who we are, but they might be able to figure out there is a group who is purposely killing wolves."

"So, what then?" Creech asked. "If they can't figure out who we are, what good does that do?"

"I don't know," Price said. "I just wanted you guys to know someone hacked our site. I think we should shut it down."

"You're the computer geek," Miller said. "Can you track the person who hacked us?"

"I tried," Price said. "Whoever it is, is good. I'll keep working on it, but so far they've covered their tracks."

After a moment of silence, Creech said, "You better shut it down, at least until we know who it is. Now, I'm going home to go to bed."

*　*　*

The hacker was very good. He saw Price trying to track him to learn his identity, but he was having no luck. No one had ever discovered who he was.

Just after midnight, he had texted the fixer and told him he was making some headway.

Found a website with some photos of poached wolves. Working on location and IDs now. Should have something for you in the next 12 hours.

The fixer immediately texted back: *Great news. Standing by for the information.*

Then the fixer picked up his phone to call Peter Covington. He worried that he might wake the man, but Covington sounded awake and alert when he answered the phone after the first ring.

"Tell me you found someone," Covington said without so much as a hello.

"Getting very close," the fixer said. "I should have a name and location, maybe more, by this evening."

"Excellent," Covington said and ended the call.

The man set the phone down and thought about the call. He was right. Someone was purposely killing the wolves he worked so hard to get back into his treasured home state.

When he was a child, he did a report for school on the gray wolf and what had happened to them. He learned the wolves had been native to the Northwest, but they had been systematically exterminated by ranchers and hunters. By the early 1900s, the wolves were basically gone. He remembered crying at the thought of such regal animals being murdered just because they lived on land where ranchers wanted to graze their cattle and sheep free from predators.

Covington's father was a man of means. The family lived in a huge house in Seattle, and they had servants who did the cooking, cleaning, and kept up the grounds. One day after doing his report on wolves, young Peter went to his father and asked if there was not something they could do to help bring the wolves back.

"It would take a great deal of money and patience," his father told him. "I don't have enough of either."

And that was that.

Still, young Covington told himself, if he ever had the means, he would do something to help the wolves.

Years later, his money and contacts were instrumental in getting the wolves started again in Washington, and as he watched the number of packs grow and expand, he couldn't be happier.

Over time, he even started thinking of himself as the brother of the wolf. His hair was black and gray, and his green eyes sometimes glowed in the right light. He was a kindred spirit. He was their savior.

"I'm coming, my brothers," he whispered to himself. "Help will soon be on the way."

*　　*　　*

The hacker narrowed his list of landowners down to three names. All three families owned large tracks of land within sight of the fire tower in Okanogan County. As he did his research on each, he found some interesting information on a family by the name of Creech. Newspaper clippings showed that the family raised cattle and grazed them on their expansive ranch, and had been doing so since the late 1800s.

A recent obituary told the story of Eli Creech dying of a heart attack as he ran to save some calves from being attacked by wolves. Could that be enough to push the other family members into some kind of war against the big canines?

The obituary noted that the elder Creech was survived by a son, Eli Creech Jr., and a grandson, Eli Creech III, among others. Could they be the men in the photo wearing Photoshopped happy faces?

More checking showed that since 2012, the state of Washington had made payments of nearly $32,000 to the Creech Family Ranch in reparation for confirmed losses of livestock due to wolf predation.

"Interesting," the hacker said to himself.

Then, after making some notes on the Creech men, the hacker went back into the dark web to look at the other photos on the Renegades' site. He was somewhat surprised to find that the site had been taken down.

No worries. He had been smart enough to copy the other two photos on the site, including one of a man and a dead gray-colored wolf, and another of three men with a wolf that was almost black in color. The photo of the single man also had a happy face covering his head. The faces of the three men in the other photo had been removed as if a pencil eraser had been used to scrub them off the image.

Again, by close inspection, he found clues as to where the wolves had died. Those sent him down more paths to try to discover the identity of the people in the photos.

With the single man and the gray wolf, he didn't have to look too hard. The proud hunter, if you could call him that, had some mirrored sunglasses in his shirt pocket. By enlarging the one visible lens and doing some tinkering to get added focus, the hacker could make out the first three digits of a license plate on a silver vehicle reflecting from the lens. The digits were backwards in the reflection, but still, easy to figure out.

The hacker then worked his way into the Department of Motor Vehicles' mainframe, put the digits into a search engine, and found four potential licenses. Only one license was shown to be affixed to a silver vehicle. It was a Nissan Frontier pickup registered to a man by the name of James Henricks.

Next, he brought up the driver's license for Henricks and copied it.

With the name and photo of the man in hand, the hacker went back into the site that showed property ownership. The site showed Henricks owned some 300 acres that butted up against the Wenatchee National Forest near a town called Thorp in Kittitas County. It didn't look like Henricks was a commercial beef rancher, but with that amount of land, it was logical to think he might graze some cattle on his property.

"Bingo," the hacker said to himself. Yes, he had some information on the Creech family, and they might be the men in the photo with the happy faces. But he knew for sure that Henricks was the man in the photo with the gray wolf.

He attached the photo of Henricks' driver's license to an email and sent it to the fixer. Then he typed two words into a text message and pressed send.

Check email.

It took seven minutes for a response.

Fixer: *Wonderful news. Send invoice.*

The hacker sent a second text.

I am working on more. Do you want them?
Fixer: *Yes.*

The fixer called Covington for the second time that morning.

"You are good. It's not even nine o'clock," Covington said, sounding sleepy.

"I'm sorry if I woke you," the fixer said. "But I have a name and address for you, and I thought you would like to know."

"No apologies needed. Yes, please. Give me the name."

"Not over this phone," the fixer said. "Go purchase a cheap throw-away phone from Walmart or someplace and then text me the number when you have it. I will text the pertinent information to the new phone, and once you have it, destroy the phone."

"It'll take me a bit. I'm not close to any big stores at the moment."

"That's okay," the fixer said. "Unless you want me to just handle the problem."

He was hoping Covington would give him the order because it meant another $50,000 on top of the money he had earned to find the wolf poacher.

"No," Covington said. "I'll handle this one myself."

"I'll await your text," the fixer said and clicked off.

* * *

Covington had been thinking about the people who were killing his beloved wolves. He could hire the fixer to take a couple of the poachers out, which would hopefully put the scare of Jesus in the rest of the group and get them to quit. Or he could do it himself.

He wanted to do it himself, but up until three days before, he wasn't sure he could take another person's life. Sure, he had paid for the fixer to rough up the friend who had embezzled his money. And he believed he could have given the order to have the man taken out. Killing someone with his own hands was something totally different.

His opportunity came late one afternoon as he was driving from his cabin on Cle Elum Lake. As he drove toward the town of Roslyn, he spotted a man walking alongside the road. The man was very thin and looked to be in ill health. When he heard Covington's SUV coming down the road, the man turned and stuck out his thumb.

Covington slowed and pulled up alongside him. He buzzed his window down and asked, "Where you headed?"

"To Yakima, but if I can get to Cle Elum, I can probably hitch a ride from there," the skinny man said.

"Hop in," Covington said. "I'm headed that way."

"Thanks a lot," the thin man said as he climbed into the passenger seat. "My truck broke down up by the lake. Damn thing is always costing me money."

Covington laughed and said, "Isn't that always the way. I haven't been to Yakima in a while, but I'd be happy to drive you there."

"That'd be great," the skinny man said. "My name is Rafe, by the way. I don't have much money, but I'd be glad to help pay for some gas."

"No worries," Covington said. "Just call me Pete."

Covington shot Rafe right between the eyes with his Ruger Wrangler .22-caliber revolver as they drove down the freeway into the Yakima Valley. He'd waited until it was nearly dark and there was no traffic coming from behind or ahead of him. The skinny man had been watching out the windshield, talking about something, and with one quick movement, Covington pulled the pistol out from behind his back. The instant the man looked over at him, Covington squeezed the trigger.

The man named Rafe slumped over in the seat and never moved another muscle.

The blast of the revolver was deafening inside the cab of the SUV. Covington's ears were ringing, and his heart was beating so fast. With adrenaline pumping through his body, he had to pull over to get settled down. He had done it. He had killed another human being. He was another step closer to his ultimate goal. He now knew he could and would kill the people who were hunting down his wolves.

The rest of the night was a blur. Covington needed to get rid of the body, so he just kept driving. He drove around Yakima and up into the Cascades on one of the smaller highways leading out of town. Then he took a Forest Service road farther up into the hills. When he found a wide spot in the road, he pulled over, got out, grabbed the skinny man's body, threw it over his shoulder, and walked up a small creek.

When he felt he was far enough off the road, Covington dropped the body in some rocks. He figured it would take weeks for someone to find the man's remains. He didn't realize elk hunting season opened the next day.

Chapter 14

Luke had written dozens and dozens of citations for shooting after legal hunting hours. And virtually all of them had been given to duck hunters. It was the nature of the beast. Unless it is incredibly cold, ducks mostly feed at night. The birds rested on the water or next to water throughout the day, and then in late afternoon, they would get up and head out to feed.

Ducks will eat most types of grain, but one of their favorites is corn. And if they find a spot, such as a recently tilled corn field where there are plenty of kernels of corn scattered about, they will feed in that field until the corn is all gone or the need to migrate overtakes them and they head farther south.

Using bait to attract game animals and birds is illegal in Washington State. But that doesn't stop some hunters. If they can gain even the slightest advantage by spreading corn or wheat to attract waterfowl, they will do it.

Evidently, that is what was going on down by Sunnyside, according to Delmar Berry, whom Luke had called earlier that morning.

He followed his phone map system to the address Berry had given him and soon was pulling into a long gravel driveway. An older white farmhouse sat at the end of the lane, with several pieces of equipment sitting in front of a shop. A man in bib overalls was walking from the shop toward the house. When he saw Luke's truck coming down the driveway, he stopped and waited.

"You must be Officer McCain," Berry said when Luke climbed out of the parked truck.

"Yessir," Luke said, reaching out his right hand to shake Berry's. "So, you think your neighbor is baiting one of his fields?"

"It's pretty obvious when you see it," Berry said. "Piles of corn here and there, with kernels scattered around. What else would he be doing that for?"

"They're hunting over it every evening?" Luke asked.

"The last few nights," Berry said. "Ticks me off because they have to be shooting after hours. It's dark, and they're still blasting away. I got nothing against hunting, but folks should stay within the rules."

"Okay," Luke said. "So where is this field?"

Berry started walking back toward the shop, and Luke followed.

"You got binoculars?" Berry asked as they walked.

"I have a spotting scope in the truck," Luke said.

"All the better," Berry said.

A few minutes later, he and Berry were standing along a fence looking across an asparagus field into an old wheat field that had been burned off at some point in the past couple of months. With his spotting scope, Luke could see the piles of yellow corn kernels standing out like gold nuggets against the fire-darkened soil. Tiny kernels of yellow twinkled like glitter strewn about the field.

"Sure enough," Luke said.

"Just wait," Berry said. "They have a blind built on the far end of the field along that fence. See those tumbleweeds? They'll be showing up shortly."

Luke checked the pile of tumbleweeds in the scope and could see it was a makeshift blind.

The two men knelt along Berry's fence, shielded by the rows of four-foot-high asparagus that had gone to seed. The thick fronds of the mature asparagus grew so close together, it made for a perfect screen to hide behind.

They waited only ten minutes before they saw movement on the far end of the burned field. Three men dressed in camouflage and carrying shotguns walked single-file along the far fence out to the tumbleweed blind. The men had come from a small barn next to a farmhouse that sat near one corner of the field.

Luke looked at his phone. There were twenty-seven minutes left of legal shooting time. The ducks had better arrive soon, or these men were going to be in deeper hot water than they already were.

They heard the ducks before they saw them. The familiar feeding chuckles ducks make when they are getting close to the dinner table got louder and louder. The chuckles were mixed in with the occasional loud quack, quack, quack of different hen mallards, along with the growling quacks of a drake here and there.

Luke looked up and spotted the birds as they started to circle from high in the darkening sky.

The ducks must have been out of shotgun range because the men didn't shoot as the birds cupped their wings and dropped, feet extended, into the field.

The next small flock wasn't as lucky. Luke saw the birds flare an instant before he heard the shots from the men. Five ducks fell in the barrage. He checked his phone again. Twelve minutes until the end of shooting time.

He could have gone then and talked to the men about the

baiting situation, but since the hunters, according to Berry, seemed to be habitually ignoring the legal shooting times, he decided to stand by and see what happened.

When the time came to legally stop shooting, Luke told Berry to stay there, and he started working along the asparagus field toward the blind. It was getting darker by the minute, and when the next small flock of mallards dropped into the field, he could see fire coming out the ends of the shotgun barrels when the men stood to shoot.

The hunters shot at one more flock before Luke arrived. The men didn't see him coming because of the fading light, but there was evidently enough light in the sky to see the ducks, because after the last salvo, one of the men hustled out to pick up three more downed ducks.

When he was ten yards from the blind, coming in from the side, Luke yelled out to the men. "Game warden! Empty your guns and step out of the blind!"

He heard one of the men say, "Oh shit!" and then saw the smallest of the three exit the other side of the blind and start running for the end of the field.

"Stop!" Luke yelled. But it was to no avail. The man was not going to stop.

Luke heard shotguns being pumped and shells being ejected. A minute later, the two remaining men came out of the blind.

He pulled his flashlight off his belt and shined the light into the two men's faces.

"I guess your buddy didn't want to talk to me tonight," Luke said. "Looks like you fellas were having some luck."

Neither man spoke. They just stood, looking guilty.

After asking the men to lay their shotguns against the blind, Luke said, "Can I see your hunting licenses, please? And, let me see your shells."

The men put their shotguns down, dug wallets out, and took shells out of their coat pockets. Luke grabbed the licenses and put them in his pocket without even looking at them, then pulled a magnet out of one of the pouches on his utility belt. In virtually every state in the union, waterfowl hunters are required to use non-toxic shotgun shells. Ammunition with lead shot in them is illegal to use when hunting ducks and geese, and a magnet is the quickest way to tell if the shells are loaded with lead because shells loaded with non-toxic shot stick to the magnet while lead-filled shells do not.

The oldest of the two men, maybe fifty and wearing a camouflage Cabela's hat, handed over his shells. Luke scanned them with the magnet. They all stuck to the magnet, so they were legal.

The other man, younger by maybe ten years and wearing a brown hat with a Duck's Unlimited logo on it, handed over his shells. They, too, were lead-free.

Luke noticed more shell-sized items bulging in the man's other pocket and said, "Please empty that pocket for me."

The man dropped his head. He put his hand into his other pocket and pulled out a half dozen more shotshells. None of the shells stuck to the magnet. They were filled with lead.

As they stood there, a flock of about thirty mallards circled just overhead, wings whistling, and dropped into the field.

"You gentlemen found a pretty good field to hunt, huh?" Luke said.

Again, the men didn't say anything.

"Do you know what legal shooting hours are?"

"Yes," the man in the Cabela's hat said.

"What are they?"

"Like, five-twenty," the man said.

"Shooting hours were over at five straight up. You shot at five-o-seven and again at five-thirteen, and you didn't show any signs of quitting."

"I guess we didn't look," the older man said.

Luke pulled the men's hunting licenses out of his pocket and, with the flashlight in his mouth, looked them over. They were legal with the appropriate state and federal migratory bird endorsements and stamps.

"Do one of you gentlemen own this property?" Luke asked.

"My father does," the man in the DU hat said.

"Did you or your father dump the corn in the field?" Luke asked.

"He did," the man said. "But it wasn't to get the ducks to come in. He just needed a place to dump the stuff."

"Unfortunately, it doesn't matter what his reason was. Shooting ducks coming into the dumped grain is illegal."

"You gunna fine my dad?"

"Yes, unless you tell me that you put the corn out, then I'll be citing you instead. That is in addition to tickets for shooting after hours and using shotgun shells that are illegal."

The man didn't say anything.

Luke spent ten minutes writing out citations for the different violations. The man in the DU hat admitted that he, and not his father, had dumped corn in the field. So, he was given an additional fine. Luke told the man that the corn needed to be cleaned up and disposed of properly.

When he was all done, Luke handed the citations and licenses back to the men.

"I'm going to be checking on this place to make sure you get the corn cleaned up. No more hunting over bait or after hours."

Both men nodded their heads slowly.

"And let your friend know I got a good look at him through my spotting scope. I'll be keeping an eye out for him."

The two men glanced at each other but didn't say anything.

Luke told the men good night and headed back the way he had come to where his pickup was parked at Berry's place. But instead of going to Berry's, he circled back around and watched the men walk back to their truck.

They arrived in the big yard of Berry's neighbor's house, where an older white Chevy Suburban was parked under a bright halogen light attached to a twenty-foot pole. Luke watched as the men put their shotguns and dead ducks in the back of the rig, and then, like magic, the third man who had run from the blind appeared out of the dark. The two men turned and talked to the guy, gesturing with their hands.

Luke smiled to himself and hurried over to where the men were talking. He was in the cover of darkness, and because the men were so involved in their conversation, they didn't see or hear him walk up behind them.

"One more thing," Luke said loudly, and all three men jumped and turned to see who it was. "I have a couple more tickets to hand out."

The third guy, the shortest and youngest of the three, dropped his head.

"Hunting license, and hand over all the shells in your pocket," Luke said to the man who was wearing a black hat with a drawing of a yellow Labrador retriever's head on the front panel. The dog looked a lot like Jack.

The man handed Luke his license and started digging in his pockets for the shells. Luke ran the magnet over the shells and found none that were loaded with lead.

"Why'd you run?" Luke asked.

"There may be a warrant out on me because I have three outstanding speeding tickets. I thought if you found out about it, you would take me to jail. My wife would kill me if I went to jail. She's been nagging me about those tickets for a couple of months now."

"Not smart," Luke said.

"I know," the man said. "If I went to jail, I might as well just stay there, because it would be better than at home."

"I have your information," Luke said. "If you promise me to take care of the traffic fines this week, I'll let it slide. But I'm going to check, and if you don't pay them, I will help the county sheriff run you down. He can figure out what to do with you from there."

"Thanks," the guy said. "I'll take care of it on Monday."

Just then, a flock of ducks, wings whistling, swooped over the house and dropped into the field.

They all looked up and then at each other.

"Don't even think about it," Luke said.

And they all started laughing.

As he walked away, Luke looked at the man with the yellow Lab on his hat and said, "By the way, nice hat."

CHAPTER 15

The state and federal wolf experts arrived at the Creech's dead steer two days after Eli Creech Jr. reported the wolf kill. Following their standard investigation, they determined that yes, the year-old Angus had been killed by wolves.

In the process of their investigation, they interviewed Trey Creech, Deke Price, and Artie Miller, who told them they had seen five wolves feeding on the carcass. Unfortunately, eye-witness testimony wasn't enough evidence to prove the canines had been the killers. Tracks in the dirt, and what physical evidence was left on the steer's dead body after the coyotes and birds had worked on it, were enough to determine the outcome.

With a promise to receive payment for the steer in the mail within four to six weeks, which meant more like eight, the wolf experts loaded their gear up into their respective government vehicles and headed down the road.

Four days after the investigation, Renegade members Creech, Miller, and Price were on the mountain again. This time, they weren't there to mend broken fences. They were there to try to take out as many of the remaining wolves in the local cattle-killing pack as they could.

"What's the chances of seeing them?" Price asked.

"Pretty good, I would think," Creech said as they drove up the bumpy two-track road. "No one's been up here bothering them in a while. And we still have a bunch of steers in this upper pasture. They get a taste of prime, grass-fed beef, and they'll be done eating wild turkeys, jackrabbits, and whatever else they can catch."

"You mean like one of those steers?" Miller said.

He was looking back down the hill into a small ravine. Creech slowed the truck, and they all turned to look. A Black Angus steer was down, and four wolves were feeding ravenously on its hind end, pulling and tearing meat off the hindquarters.

"Damn it!" Creech said, but he didn't stop. He kept the truck rolling up the road, out of sight of the ravine and the wolves.

"Grab your rifles," Creech said. "Get out and quietly close your doors."

Miller and Price followed directions, and in less than a minute, the three men were walking slowly down the backside of the ridge above the ravine where the steer's carcass was.

"Slowly," Creech hissed as they angled up the ridge to look into the ravine.

As is the case with virtually every critter that spends every second of its life in the wilds, wolves have an uncanny sixth sense when trouble is approaching. Whether they heard something, smelled something, or just "felt" something, they were running down the ravine when the men peeked up over the hill.

Creech and Miller, the two most experienced hunters in the group, dropped to a knee and aimed at the running wolves. Creech put the crosshairs of his nine-power scope just in front of the big, light, gray-colored wolf leading the pack and touched the trigger. The wolf stumbled once and then rolled.

Miller blazed away at the other three, but he never really aimed, and the two shots he was able to get off before the fleeing wolves disappeared around a bend in the small canyon missed badly.

"I got one," Creech said. "Did you see that? I got one!"

"I missed," Miller said.

"I didn't even shoot," Price said.

"Let's go check it out," Creech said.

When they got down to where they had last seen the wolf, the big male was not dead. He was facing the men, head down, teeth bared, snarling at them.

"You broke its back," Miller said.

Creech just stared.

"Well, do something," Price said. "It's creeping me out."

About that time, the wolf, which only had the use of its front legs, started lurching at them, growling and snarling.

Miller and Creech fired at the same time. One of them, they were never sure who, hit the wolf in the head and put it out of its misery instantly.

"Holy hell," Miller said. "That scared the shit outta me."

"Me too," Price said.

"Can you imagine one of those things coming at you with all four legs working?" Miller said.

"I hate 'em," Creech said, his hands shaking after the shot. "And now there is one less wolf killing our cattle."

This time, there was no discussion about what to do with the wolf. They could have left the big male at the site near the dead steer where Creech shot it so that the government officials could come do their investigation and take the animal. But after looking at the wolf for a couple of minutes, Creech and Miller grabbed the dead wolf by the back legs and dragged it up the ravine, back to the truck.

"This one's bigger than mine," Miller said. "I'm guessing a hundred and fifty pounds."

"Or more," Creech said. "It's as bad as dragging a big buck."

At the truck, it took all three men to hoist the dead wolf into the bed.

"Here," Creech said, handing his phone to Price after the wolf was loaded. "Take my picture."

Creech sat on the open tailgate with the deceased wolf's head in his lap. He held his rifle with one hand, butt of the gun on his thigh, rifle pointed at the sky. Creech didn't smile. He tried to look tough.

"Looks like some of the photos from back in the day when your grandfather was getting rid of these things," Miller said after looking at the photo Price snapped on Creech's phone. "Badass!"

"Except for the almost new pickup in the background," Price said.

"Well, there is that," Miller said.

"DO NOT post this photo on the site," Creech said. "Got it?"

"Don't worry," Price said. "Whoever that was rooting around in there the other day scared me. The guy was really good."

The men loaded up and started back down the mountain.

"You gunna tell your old man about the dead steer?" Miller asked Creech as the pickup slowly bumped down the two-track.

"I pretty much have to," Creech said. "Why?"

"I got to thinking," Miller said. "There's quite a bit of evidence around there that we shot that wolf. Blood in the dirt, drag marks, probably some fur here and there."

"I hadn't thought of that," Creech said and stopped the truck. "Let's go back and see if we can get rid of some of it."

After hiking back down into the ravine, they did find drops of blood, lots of their boot tracks, and drag marks from where the wolf died. They kicked dirt over the blood drops, and Miller cut branches out of a tall sagebrush bush, which they used as brooms to sweep out all the drag marks and boot tracks. When they were done, they stopped and looked.

"Looks pretty good to me," Price said.

"If we get some wind and snow, that would help too," Miller said.

"We'll get some wind, but not sure about the snow," Creech said. "My old man will be up here pretty quick after we tell him about the dead steer."

"He won't notice anything out of the ordinary, will he?" Price asked.

"Not if he's not looking for it," Creech said.

Confident they had covered up the evidence of the wolf shooting, the men headed back to the truck.

*   *   *

"Another one?" Eli Creech Jr. said after his son told him about the dead steer in the ravine.

"Those wolves got a taste for beef," Trey said.

"The state might have to come in and take the pack out," Creech Jr. said. "There was four wolves at the kill site?"

"Yessir," Trey said. "Working on the back end of the steer when we seen 'em."

"Okay," Creech Jr. said. "I'll make the call."

Then he asked, looking his son right in the eye, "And you shot at them but didn't kill any?"

"Yessir," Trey lied, looking away.

"I almost wish you had," his father said quietly under his breath.

Trey Creech smiled. He might yet persuade his father to join his group of Renegades.

*   *   *

Back at his computer after the big male wolf had been skinned in the tool shed, Deke Price downloaded the photo of Creech and the wolf to a file he had that was encrypted and protected. The file included all the photos that had appeared on the Renegades' website prior to it being taken down. Maybe it wasn't smart to keep the photos, but Price believed they might be wanted or needed by the group at some point.

He also believed that if the members of the group were ever to get caught, the photos would be valuable bargaining chips in keeping him out of hot water. He was fine with helping Creech and Miller, but he, personally, hadn't shot any wolves, and he wasn't going to. He knew nothing about any of the other members of the Renegades except that they hated wolves and liked killing them. There was no personal connection to any of the others, and he would have no problem sending them, like the wolf carcasses, down the river. The photos he had of the other members of the group, all with dead wolves, would certainly be valuable evidence any federal prosecutor would like to have.

Next, as requested by Trey, Price texted out one gong of the Liberty Bell to all the Renegade members, letting them know a member had been successful in killing another wolf. Immediately, responses began rolling in, including thumbs-up emojis and assorted comments of congratulations. Counting the wolf Trey had killed today, the Renegades were now claiming seventeen wolf kills.

Finally, Price went back out onto the dark web and did some looking. He found where someone, probably the same person, had tried to find the Renegades' website. A cold shiver ran down his spine. How much did the person know?

* * *

The hacker knew enough and was learning more and more. He found out more about the Creech Family Ranch, and specifically more about Eli Creech III. The young man's Facebook page and Twitter account were easily accessed, and by reading the posts and comments over the past months and years, the hacker was convinced Creech hated wolves.

Evidently, the young man and his father had been regular attendees at the Department of Fish and Wildlife public meetings. They lobbied to get the wolves delisted in Eastern Washington and met with their state representatives, testifying about the damage the wolves were doing to their livestock.

Just by the tone and content of the younger Creech's social media posts, the hacker was convinced the man could be one of the people who was killing wolves. He decided it was time to send that information to the fixer and let him do with it what he may.

He hacked into the DMV once again and found the driver's license for Eli Creech III. He copied the photo of the license, attached it to an email, and sent it to the fixer.

CHAPTER 16

Luke was on the freeway heading back to Yakima after dealing with the duck hunters when his phone rang. He didn't recognize the number that popped up on his phone, but he often didn't, so he pressed the answer button on his truck's steering wheel, activating the Bluetooth connected to his phone and said, "This is Luke McCain."

"Mr. McCain, this is Charlie Zimmerman, Max Tucker's neighbor."

"Sure, Mr. Zimmerman, how can I help you?"

"You can't help me, but I might be able to help you."

"Okay," Luke said. "Go ahead."

"Not that I was snooping or anything, but Tucker is in his backyard right now skinning that young buck you were looking at earlier. If you get here quick, you might nab him with the evidence."

"I'm not sure there's been any laws broken, but I would like to talk to him."

"I'm sure," Zimmerman said defiantly. "How many deer can one man shoot in a year?"

"We don't know it is his," Luke said. "But I'm headed that way."

"You want me to try to keep him here?" the old man asked. "I could park my car behind his rig."

"No, no," Luke said. "No need to do that. I just appreciate you calling."

"I took a couple of photos with this piece of crap phone of mine," Zimmerman said. "Long way away, kinda blurry, but they might help."

"Did Tucker see you?" Luke asked.

"Naw, I was shooting out the side window. This piece of crap phone has a piece of crap camera. I keep telling my daughter I need a new phone, but she says I wouldn't know how to operate one of the new ones, so she just ignores me."

Luke said, "Listen, Mr. Zimmerman, I think Mr. Tucker might have a bit of a temper, and I don't want him coming after you, so just sit tight, watch some TV or something. I'll be there in ten minutes."

"That's the other thing," Zimmerman said. "I used to have cable, but my daughter said I couldn't afford it anymore, so she canceled it. Can't even watch the Mariners. The local stations suck."

Luke said, "I'll be there in a few. See you then." And he clicked off.

If Tucker had murdered Rafe Gibson, he might be capable of hurting an old man who was snooping into a poached deer. Maybe even worse. Luke hoped Zimmerman stayed in his house and out of sight.

When he pulled into the mobile home court and got around to Tucker's house, the familiar faded-out gold Ford Explorer was sitting in the driveway. Luke pulled in behind the rig, and as he did, he glanced over at Zimmerman's house and saw the old man sitting on the porch in a rocking chair. Luke made eye contact with the old timer and gave a little wave. Zimmerman just gave a slight head nod.

Luke chuckled to himself. The old boy most likely hadn't had this much fun in years. And if Tucker was a jerk of a neighbor as Luke suspected, Zimmerman was probably more than happy to see the man get into trouble with the law.

He jumped out of the truck and walked around the house to find Tucker and another guy, probably another brother by the looks of the man, taking the skinned deer carcass out of the tree.

Tucker saw Luke and said, "What are you doing here?"

"I needed to ask you a few more questions about your friend, Rafe Gibson," Luke said.

"I told ya, he weren't my friend."

"Nice deer," Luke said, changing subjects. "I assume you have it tagged legally?"

Tucker looked at the other man, who looked at Luke.

"I got the tag at home," the man said. "It's notched properly."

"You know the law says it has to remain with the carcass until it is processed, right?" Luke said.

"I've been hunting this state for thirty years or more," the man said.

"Then you should know. You have your hunting license with you?"

"No, it's with the tag."

"Driver's license then?" Luke asked.

"Why you bothering us about all this?" Tucker said.

"Because I know you've already poached one deer this year, so

I figured two isn't that big of a leap," Luke said to Tucker, and then back to the man, "Driver's license, please."

As the man dug for his wallet, Luke took a glance at Zimmerman's house. In the side window, he saw two eyes under the white, scraggly-haired top of the old man's head peering out at them.

The man handed Luke his driver's license. It confirmed what Luke already knew. Timothy Tucker, age forty-two, weight a hundred and thirty-two pounds, address in Harrah, was most definitely Max Tucker's brother. He wondered how many brothers Tucker had. The three he had met all looked the same. Skinny, same height, same color hair and eyes. As Luke had heard his grandfather say more than once, the Tucker brothers "were kicked by the same mule."

"When did you shoot this deer, Mr. Tucker?" Luke asked.

"Day before yesterday."

"Special permit?" Luke asked.

"Yep."

"Where did you shoot it?"

"Out on the Training Center."

Luke knew there was a late hunt out on the huge area northeast of Yakima known as the Yakima Training Center. Operated by the United States Army, troops from all around the country, and some from around the world, used the Training Center to practice maneuvers with helicopters, tanks, and armory. The sagebrush-covered hills and draws, especially the portion near the Columbia River, were prime habitat for mule deer and elk. You would think all the noise from the weapons and having vehicles driving all over the place would move the wildlife out, but they seemed to coexist just fine with the soldiers and their training exercises.

"Wait here for a moment," Luke said, holding onto the driver's license.

"What you want us to do, just keep holding this deer here?" Max Tucker said with a bit of an attitude.

"I'll only be a minute," Luke said as he walked back around the house to his truck.

It took more than a minute, but Luke was able to pull Timothy Tucker up on the computer that sat on the console between the front seats of his pickup. The information showed that Tucker did have a valid hunting license, and he had been drawn for a special permit for the Training Center. The special season was open for three more days, and if the man hadn't notched the tag like he said he had, there was nothing to stop him from using it again to shoot another deer.

Luke walked back around the house. The Tucker brothers were sitting in lawn chairs, and the deer carcass was lying in the grass. He glanced at Zimmerman's window. The old boy was still peering at them.

"So, I have a bit of a dilemma here," Luke said. "I see you have the special permit, but since you didn't tag it properly, I'm going to have to issue a citation."

"You hand those things out like candy," Max Tucker said.

"Only when guys like you don't follow the rules," Luke said. Then to his brother, he said, "But here's the deal. You bring your hunting license, special permit and the tag, notched on the day before yesterday, to me on Monday, and I will change this to a written warning."

"Why didn't you cut me a break like that?" Max Tucker said.

"Because you lied to me, more than once. If I find your brother is lying to me, he'll get the full ticket, and I'll see about any other charges I can come up with."

"You'd do it too, wouldn't ya?" Max Tucker said.

Luke wrote out the citation and handed it, with his driver's license, to Timothy Tucker.

"Now," Luke said to Max Tucker, "to the real reason I am here. Let's talk about Rafe Gibson."

"I already told the deputy who come by here that I ain't seen Rafe since he quit work down at the truck place."

"When was that?" Luke asked, although he already knew Tucker had told Williams that it was right after he'd shot the deer with a rifle during archery season.

"Right after you give me those tickets," Tucker said. "Which I didn't deserve 'cause he was the one that shot that buck with the rifle."

"That really made you mad, didn't it, Max?" Luke said, using the man's first name for the first time.

"Hell, yeah, it made me mad. I can't afford tickets like that. Luckily, Tim here loaned me the money to pay 'em off."

"Mad enough to shoot Rafe between the eyes?"

Luke watched and saw that there was just a hesitation from Tucker, like he'd been hit in the gut. Tucker didn't know that was how Gibson had been killed.

"I would never do that," Tucker said. "He wasn't a friend, but I could never do that to anyone."

Luke watched the man's eyes and listened, and he believed him.

"Do you know where Rafe went to work after quitting Thompson's?"

"I heard he took a job doing some construction work up around Ellensburg. But I don't know that for a fact. I never saw or talked to him after he quit."

"Do you know who his friends were at work?"

"Oh, a coupla guys hung with him, but I wouldn't call 'em friends."

"Can you give me their names?" Luke asked.

After Tucker gave him the names, Luke asked if they still worked at the truck place.

"Yeah, they do. But if you go in there, don't tell them I gave you their names. I gotta work with 'em, and I don't want 'em pissed at me."

"I won't," Luke said. "Thanks for the information."

He handed Timothy Tucker his card, told him he would see him on Monday, and went back around the house to leave. After he climbed into the truck, Luke looked over at Charlie Zimmerman's porch, and the old man was standing there with his phone in his hand. He held it up to his ear and mouthed the words "Call me."

Luke chuckled again, this time out loud, and then started the truck and backed into the street. He wasn't a block down the road when his phone rang. It was the same number that had popped up before. Luke pushed the answer button on the steering wheel.

"Mr. Zimmerman, everything okay?"

"You let Tucker keep that deer?" he asked.

"For the time being," Luke said. "Besides, it's his brother's deer."

"It was his brother that brought the deer in a couple weeks ago," Zimmerman said.

"The same brother?" Luke asked. "There are at least two of them, and they all look very similar."

"Well, I think it was the same guy," Zimmerman said. "But if you say there's more, I can't be certain."

"I'll ask him about the other deer," Luke said. "I'm meeting with him on Monday to get this all straightened out."

"You want me to keep a watch on them?"

"If you see anything out of the ordinary, let me know, but don't spy on them. I wouldn't want any of the Tucker brothers getting mad at you."

"If they're all that skinny, I'm not too worried," Zimmerman said. "I'll call if I see anything."

Luke thanked him and was about to hang up when the old boy said, "And would you mind calling me when you get this all sorted out. Shows on the TV are crap. I can't understand what half of them are talking about. This is the best entertainment I've had in a long time."

Luke chuckled one more time and promised to call Zimmerman when he had some answers.

Just as he was hanging up, he heard Zimmerman say, "Hello? Hello? This damn phone is a piece of crap."

CHAPTER 17

Peter Covington drove into Ellensburg and stopped at the Fred Meyer store. He was doing as instructed by the fixer. He needed to get a cheap phone he could use and then destroy to get the information he needed.

He found a row of phones packaged in a plastic bubble glued to a card and hung on pegs. He decided to buy two, just in case.

"Will these allow me to text?" Covington asked a kid in the electronics department named Prince, according to his little blue name tag.

"Yep," was all the kid said, not even looking at the phone.

Covington wanted to reach across and slap the pompous little brat but figured it would do no good.

"Thanks," he said to the kid. "By the way, tell your parents they did a great job raising you."

Prince just smiled and still never looked up.

Covington was still pissed when he walked out of the store. Didn't businesses even care one little bit about the type of people they hired? And did they not train them in customer service? Obviously not. And what the hell were those people thinking, naming their kid Prince? They must have been big fans of "Purple Rain." Whatever. He had the phone, and he was anxious to get it back to the cabin and get the information from the fixer.

The phone number for the cheap cell phone was included inside the package. He looked up the fixer's number from his regular cell phone, turned on the new phone, and texted the number with a short message: *Send info. PC.*

Within a minute, a text came through. It was a photo of a Washington State driver's license for a James Henricks, 22034 County Rd. #7, in Thorp.

Twenty seconds later, a second text came through: *Destroy this phone immediately.*

Covington studied the photo of Henricks. He wanted the image burned into his mind so that he would know the wolf killer when he saw him. He wrote the name and address down on the back of one of his business cards, slipped it into his billfold, walked out to the garage where he stored some tools in a small tool chest, placed the phone on the cold concrete floor, and used a sixteen-ounce claw hammer to smash it into a hundred pieces. Then he swept the assorted pieces into a dustpan, walked down to the dock, and tossed the pieces into Cle Elum Lake.

When he got back into the cabin, Covington poured three fingers of his high-dollar Scotch into a crystal tumbler and sat down in his overstuffed chair. After a couple sips to soothe his nerves, he pulled the card out of his wallet and looked at it.

He couldn't believe how fortuitous it was that the address the fixer had sent him was so close. The man he now hunted was not up in the wilds of the northeast corner of the state, or in some wilderness area near the Canadian border. No, this man, this wolf killer, this James Henricks, was a half hour's drive from the very place where he was now sitting.

As he sat and sipped his drink, Covington thought about all the scenarios. He wondered where he would kill the man. He thought about when he would do it and how he would dispose of the body. Or would he? Maybe he should leave the body with some kind of message that let the world know Henricks was a wolf murderer, and this is what would become of the other wolf poachers.

He took another sip, let the smooth alcohol rest on his taste buds before slowly swallowing and grinned. This was going to take some planning. But Covington was going to enjoy every minute of it. Right up to the moment he shot one Mr. James Henricks right between the eyes.

*　*　*

Officer Cody Stephens was starting to believe there was some kind of concerted effort to kill wolves in Eastern Washington. They now had evidence of three wolves killed by high-power rifle fire, besides the collared wolf he had recovered earlier.

The three dead wolves, not surprisingly, were found by late-season whitetail deer hunters in two different counties in northeast Washington. Each of the wolves had been shot and left for dead where they were found in various states of decay. Each body was intact enough to find the bullet holes. Two were shot in the side, and one was shot in the head.

Interestingly, two more skinned wolf bodies were discovered floating in the Okanogan River. Both had bullet holes in their sides. One was spotted by a lady walking her dog, who thought it was a dead person floating in the river.

Joe Ames, the state wolf recovery biologist, was called in on all the dead wolf discoveries, including the skinned carcasses. They were able to identify the carcasses as wolves by the size of the skinned feet.

"This is interesting," Ames said to Stephens when he arrived at the first carcass pulled out of the river. "Someone has kept the hide for whatever reason."

"Probably for a rug, or maybe a full body mount," Stephens said.

The forty-two-year-old Ames, who was short and stocky and wore his long blond hair in a ponytail that fell just below his shoulders, stood with his hand on his chin, looking at the carcass.

"The thing is," Ames said after a minute. "These idiots don't realize that I can easily get DNA from this animal and match it to the hide, even if it is turned into something tanned or mounted."

"If we can find it," Stephens said.

"If we can find it," Ames repeated.

Ames went to work collecting some tissue samples before putting the body in a plastic bag to be transferred to a freezer at the WDFW office in Spokane.

The second floating wolf body, considerably larger than the first, was found two weeks later, not far from where the first body was found. This time, a man riding his bike along the river spotted it. He had heard about the first wolf body, and when he saw the second one floating near the bank, he called the Okanogan County Sheriff's Department to report it.

"Like déjà vu all over again," Stephens said when Ames pulled into where the wolf carcass was lying in the brown grass next to the river.

"This is starting to tick me off a little," Ames said.

"Me too," Stephens said.

Ames did the same postmortem work on the second carcass and then slid it into a plastic bag for transport back to Spokane.

"I've been doing some aerial surveys in the last couple weeks," Ames said. "Some with drones and some flying in helicopters."

"Seeing anything interesting?" Stephens asked.

"Our preliminary findings are that for the first time, the wolf populations are down."

"That is unusual," Stephens said.

"We understand that some of the oldest wolves may be just dying of old age, but some of the packs are down in numbers by half of what they were a year ago."

Ames went on to say that they needed to do more surveying of all the known packs, which was going to take some time, but if the trend held true, there might be something other than natural aging and dying taking the numbers down.

Stephens knew some about wolves and their habits, but he had no idea if there was some disease that might be the culprit.

"Could it be something like rabies or parvo that is killing them?" he asked.

"Wolves can and do contract those diseases," Ames said. "Distemper, too. There have been cases in other continents where wolf populations were severely reduced in number due to an outbreak of parvovirus. But these diseases have rarely been seen in wolves in North America."

"So, something else is getting them," Stephens said.

"We certainly know more are being killed by poaching," Ames said. "Just by the dead animals we've found in the last three months, our numbers are up like four hundred percent."

"Plus, whatever ones are killed by motor vehicles," Stephens said.

"There were only two that we know of in the last year," Ames said. "There's always going to be a few, but there's not much we can do about that."

"Any response to the rewards?" Stephens asked.

He knew the answer to that question. As far as he knew, there had been no calls at all with information regarding collared wolf 2311 that had been killed weeks before. And there were rewards for two other poached wolves from the previous year that remained unsolved.

"No, unfortunately," Ames said. "It would really help. Someone knows something about some of the shootings. But if it was some lone hunter who shot a wolf on purpose, or by accident, thinking it was a coyote, the chances of them telling someone about it are just about zero."

"It's so strange that the numbers would go up so quickly all of a sudden," Stephens said, almost thinking out loud.

"I've been thinking on that too," Ames said. "Think too hard, and it might lead you to the idea that there is a concerted effort by some hunting group taking matters into their own hands."

"Or," Stephens said, "it could be a group of ranchers."

"I just don't see that," Ames said. "We're paying top dollar for every animal they lose. A couple I have talked with have no problem accepting the money."

"The rewards keep going up," Stephens said. "Where's that money coming from?"

"Some rich Seattle dude," Ames said. "I've met him a couple of times at fundraisers. Name is Covington. He would love to see wolves in every county in the state, including over around Seattle."

"That ain't gunna happen," Stephens said.

"I don't know," Ames said. "I think some of our wildlife commissioners are of the same mind."

"I'll be long-retired if it does," Stephens said. "Then I won't have to worry about it. In the meantime, we'll keep investigating the ones poached around here. Someone knows something, and sooner or later they'll go for the reward, especially if the amounts keep going up."

"You might check with all the taxidermists in the region," Ames said. "Maybe someone brought in a hide from this big guy, or from the one the other day."

"Good idea. If I find something, I'll let you know."

Ames loaded up the wolf carcass and headed for Spokane.

Stephens stuck around for a few more minutes to talk to the man on the bike who'd found the dead wolf's body. Evidently, the biker, who rides every day, rain or shine, hadn't noticed the body until that morning.

"I saw it and immediately thought of the one Doris Hartshorn found the other day," the man, whose name was Rupert Markum, said. "It's pretty creepy, really. Why would someone do that?"

"They most likely want the hide for a rug or a mount," Stephens said. "So, you didn't see anyone dropping anything into the river, say, a week or two ago?"

"I see people doing all kinds of stupid things around here," Markum said. "There's no accounting for stupidity these days. They dump grass clippings, rocks, tires, and who knows what all. I call the sheriff, but not much gets done."

Stephens handed him his card and said, "Well, if you see anything else strange in the realm of wildlife, please give me a call, anytime. I can't help much with old tires unless it's stuck around a bear's neck."

"Will do," Markum said, then he got on his bike and pedaled off down the river.

CHAPTER 18

When the pack of wolves killed the two best Bluetick Coonhounds James Henricks had ever known, he went berserk. He couldn't help imagining how the wolves had attacked the two dogs, tearing into them from all angles. His big male, Duke, could probably have held his own against one wolf, but there was no chance against five or six of the bloodthirsty beasts.

And Annabelle, his female hound, wouldn't hurt a flea. She was a hell of a tracker. When Henricks turned both dogs loose on a bobcat, little did he know he was sending his poor dogs to their deaths.

The wolves had already been around his place, stirring things up, when they came into his pasture and started after the little blue roan-colored foal. Luckily, the mare put up a fuss, and when Henricks heard the commotion, he ran out with his rifle and found the wolves surrounding the baby horse.

One shot in the air sent the wolves running. He immediately called the Department of Fish and Wildlife, and they sent a game warden to check it out.

The game warden, named Stan Hargraves, said there wasn't much they could do, but told him to stay vigilant.

"What if I'm gone?" Henricks said. "Then what?"

Henricks was a thirty-eight-year-old bachelor by choice who'd given up a six-figure job as an architect in Tacoma to have some elbow room and fresh air. He was a poor cook, which, along with the hiking he did in the nearby mountains, kept him in excellent shape, carrying just a hundred and sixty-two pounds on his five-foot-nine-inch frame. His thick, dark brown hair matched his full beard and dark brown eyes.

Henricks had saved his nickels and dimes, and when his mother died, leaving him with a house in Portland and a half-million-dollar life insurance payout, Henricks sold the house, took the money, and bought some acreage in the Kittitas Valley.

A pregnant horse came along with the deal, which was fine with him. The two Blueticks became his only family when he bought them from a local hound hunter as pups two years later.

"I don't know," Hargraves said. "If it were me, and it happens again, I'd shoot to kill. You'd be justified in protecting your livestock."

"You say that now," Henricks said. "But there are a bunch of powerful wolf lovers over there in Olympia that would probably send me to jail, or fine me some ungodly amount of money."

"I'll file a report," Hargraves said. "That'll be a record of a continuing problem. I believe you'd be justified."

It took Henricks most of the day to find his two dead hounds and pack their bodies back to the truck. Both had GPS tracking collars, so he was able to go right to them, but each was in some rough country. Locating them was much easier than packing them out.

He considered just burying the dogs where he found them, but he hated the thought of the wolves or some other scavengers digging them up and eating them. No, they deserved a decent, undisturbed, resting place.

He cried when he found Duke. The big hound was torn up something awful. Thankfully, the wolves hadn't eaten him. And he cried again when he found Annabelle. She wasn't as badly injured. Still, she was dead, and it hurt a lot.

It was hard work packing the dogs out, one at a time. The whole time he was doing so, his anger toward the wolves rose. What good were they anyway? They were good for nothing. Stone cold killers taking out elk, deer, and livestock. And, evidently, they were good at killing people's dogs. By the time he had Annabelle back to his truck, he was ready to take matters into his own hands. The game warden had kind of given him the go-ahead, hadn't he?

That night after burying his two hounds, Henricks sent emails to a couple of rancher friends up north he knew had been dealing with wolves in their area for several years. He asked what they did with the wolves harassing or killing their livestock.

One rancher friend wrote: *You didn't hear this from me, but there is a group who is on the warpath with the wolves. Call themselves the Renegades. They have a website. I have no idea how many members, but they post photos of the wolves they've killed.*

Henricks: *Are you a member?*

Rancher: *Not saying a word. Reach out to this address. They'll give you the passwords etc. to join in.*

That night Henricks became the newest Renegade. The wolves in his area had blood on their breath. Blood from two of the best Bluetick Coonhounds in the world. Coonhounds that were his only family. It was time for them to pay.

*   *   *

It took him a while to find the pack. The things roamed for miles, and he hadn't seen any sign that they had been around his place in days. Then one early morning, after it had rained a cold rain all night, he heard the wolves howling. He'd heard them before, and every time he did, it raised the hair on the back of his neck. It was eerie, and this morning, with low clouds hanging down to just above his place, they sounded even spookier.

Henricks, who had been dropping some flakes of hay for his mare and colt, ran and grabbed his rifle. A veteran big game hunter, he knew how to maneuver through the woods. The low clouds and wet forest floor made for perfect stalking conditions.

He was about halfway to where he figured the wolves were based on their continual howling when all of a sudden they stopped and made no sounds at all. Henricks froze right where he was and looked and listened. Then he heard the elk. They sounded like a herd of buffalo coming through the trees, running hell bent to get out of the county. The wolves were chasing them.

He took a knee and watched as about fifteen head of elk, all cows and calves, came thundering by. A couple were almost close enough to reach out and touch.

After the elk dashed by, Henricks switched his attention to whatever had put the fear of death in them. A second later, he saw them. Six wolves—two big ones, and four that must have been the young of the year.

The wolves were running hard along the same path as the elk when all of a sudden the lead wolf veered uphill, and although it didn't seem possible, it ran even faster.

Henricks quickly raised his rifle to try to get one of the wolves in his sights. The lead wolf was almost behind a tree, but the second in line was still in the open just enough. Henricks swung the rifle, with the crosshairs in his scope just ahead of the animal, and touched the trigger.

The wolf he was shooting at disappeared behind the tree, and the four smaller ones followed.

Everything happened so fast, but as Henricks rewound the scene in his mind, he was sure as anything he had hit the wolf he was shooting at.

His confidence faded when he got to the tree and looked all around in the dirt and grass. There was no blood anywhere.

"Damn it," he said as he kicked a pinecone.

Once again, he ran the scenario through his mind. He had to have hit the wolf. So, he started tracking, well, nothing really. He walked the way the wolves had run and looked for anything that might tell him which way they had gone.

Five slow, meticulous steps into the search, he found a track. Then there were more. And finally, he found a spot of blood. Henricks looked ahead on the path and spotted the wolf lying dead under a tree forty-five yards up ahead.

He wanted to jump and shout and hoot and holler. But he kept a calm head. He had no idea what a pack of wolves might do when they lose an older member. He believed he either shot the matriarch or patriarch of the pack, and the remaining adult might come back looking for its mate. So, he proceeded with caution.

The wolf he had killed was the male. Henricks had made the perfect shot, right through the lungs. The big canine had run fifty yards purely on adrenaline before dying.

He didn't dally at the dead wolf. He looked around and grabbed the thing by a back leg and started dragging it down the hill. Henricks was halfway to his place when he heard something. He stopped and listened. Somewhere way up on the hill, in a bank of clouds, the howl of the wolf pack began again. This time, the howls seemed even more mournful and eerie.

At his place, he set up his phone on some bales of hay and set the timer to take a photo of him and the wolf. He now truly felt like he was doing his part as a Renegade and was elated to have some vindication for the death of his two Coonhounds.

After the timer clicked, he went over and looked at the photo. His truck wasn't in the photo, nor was his house. There was nothing in the photo that could identify where he was. He didn't notice the sunglasses in the pocket of his denim shirt, and even if he had, he would probably have thought nothing of it.

That evening, he posted the photo to the Renegades' dark website. Within seconds, he was getting congratulations and attaboys from the other members. Two days later, he was surprised when he went to check the site, and it was gone. Nothing, nada, like it had never existed.

That was weird. Why would they take the site down? He immediately emailed the guy who had given him the contact for the group.

Henricks: *Site is gone. Issues?*

Friend: *No clue. Can't get answers.*

Henricks: *Worried?*

Friend: *No. No way to ID anyone.*

Henricks: *Okay. Thx.*

No way to ID anyone, except by facial recognition. Sure, his face was covered by one of those happy face emojis, but if someone was clever enough to get into the site, they surely would be capable enough to magically make the happy face disappear. If the federal police, or even the state game wardens, secured the photo of him and the wolf, they could run the photo through their computers and somewhere along the line, from a driver's license, or even a high school annual photo, they'd figure out who he was.

Henricks started to worry. The more he thought about it, the more he worried.

He'd been a straight-arrow, law-abiding citizen all his life. Heck, he'd only been stopped by the cops once, and that was for a broken taillight on his truck. And now this. The stuff he'd read in the game laws said that shooting a wolf brought with it big fines and potential prison time. What was he going to do?

The first thing he had to do was get rid of the wolf. He'd left it in the tack room behind the loafing shed next to the corral. The temperatures were cold enough—getting below freezing at night—

that he hadn't worried about the thing starting to decompose and stink, so he had just left it there.

Now it had to go. But where?

He decided he would dump it into the Columbia River. The chances of someone finding it there were slim, and if they did, they would have no way of knowing where it had come from. So, just before sunrise the next morning, he loaded the wolf into the bed of his pickup and headed to the Vantage Bridge on Interstate 90.

He figured that if he timed his arrival on the bridge with the light morning traffic, he could stop, drag the wolf to the edge of the bridge and have it over and into the river in a minute or less.

As he drove down the freeway, he thought about his predicament. How had he been so stupid to post the photo on that website? It was supposed to be protected on the dark web, but now, evidently, there were some problems.

He didn't regret shooting the wolf. In fact, he was still quite happy about that. It meant he had exacted at least some revenge on the pack that had taken out his beloved Duke and Annabelle.

Dropping off Ryegrass Ridge on I-90, driving down to the Columbia River, Henricks maneuvered his placement in the few 18-wheelers and occasional other vehicles traveling east down the hill. When he arrived at the bridge, he put himself well behind regular traffic and the big trucks.

He slowed and pulled as close to the railing of the huge bridge as possible, put the truck in park, jumped out, and ran to the back of the pickup. He dropped the tailgate and, with some effort, hoisted the wolf onto his shoulder. Then he turned, took four steps to the railing, and pushed the dead animal over the edge.

Henricks watched as the wolf fell and splashed an instant later into the black waters of the mighty Columbia. He wanted to watch to see if the wolf sank, but he knew he needed to get going before a vehicle came along.

His hands were shaking as he drove up the freeway, past the

metal wild horses on the sagebrush hill. He wondered if this was what it felt like to dump a human body.

A few moments later, he stopped in George and grabbed a cup of coffee at the mini-mart. With the hot coffee in hand, Henricks went back to his truck and sat and drank and thought about just what kind of trouble he might have gotten himself into.

Chapter 19

It was a busy Monday morning for Luke McCain. At the office at eight sharp, he chatted with Bob Davis and brought him up to speed on the corn-baiting situation down in Sunnyside and the follow-up contact he had with Max Tucker.

"Sounds like that hanging tree is getting plenty of business," Davis said, referring to the tree in Tucker's backyard where the neighbor, Charlie Zimmerman, had seen at least three deer skinned this fall.

"Maybe too much business," Luke said. "Tucker's brother is supposed to bring in his paperwork this morning. If it's all in order, we'll be good. But I'm going to ask him about the other deer Mr. Zimmerman saw in the tree a couple weeks ago."

"You think Tucker is telling the truth about the dead guy with the bullet hole in his forehead?" Davis asked.

"I do," Luke said. "And I told Deputy Williams as much."

After chatting for a few more minutes, Luke headed to his cubicle and, as he went around the corner, he looked out at the lobby and saw Tim Tucker standing there.

"Mr. Tucker," Luke said. "How are you today?"

"Good, but I'll be better if I can get this ticket reduced," Tucker said as he walked toward Luke with his hunting license, special permit card, and notched tag in his hand.

Luke looked it over and said, "Everything checks out. Give me the citation, and I'll trade it for a written warning. Just know, this will be in your file for eternity, and if there are any other violations in the future, it might not go well."

"I understand," Tucker said. "Thank you."

"By the way, I happened to be chatting with your brother's neighbor, and he said he saw another small buck hanging in Max's backyard a little over two weeks ago. You know anything about that?"

"That old coot can't remember what he had for breakfast," Tucker said.

"He seems pretty with it to me," Luke said. "So, do you know anything about another deer your brother would have had hanging in the tree?"

Tucker hesitated before saying he had no clue what the old man was talking about. It was just enough of a pause for Luke to realize that Tucker knew something about it.

"If you think of anything, let me know," Luke said and handed the man the written warning.

"I will," Tucker said as he turned and headed for the door. "I gotta run. I'm already late for work."

Luke let him go. He was watching him walk through the parking lot when the duck hunter from the other evening came walking in.

"Officer McCain," the man said. "I've just left the sheriff's office, and my fines are paid."

"You have a receipt?" Luke asked.

The man handed a piece of paper to Luke, and after looking at it, he sent the man on his way.

"No more baiting or after-hours hunting," Luke said as the man was leaving.

"No worries," the man said with a laugh. "I'm on timeout from hunting anyway, according to my wife. And I might be for quite a while because she was extra pissed when I told her about getting the ticket for hunting after hours."

"You need to know the laws," Luke said.

The man just kept walking and gave a little wave.

Luke took care of a few emails that needed immediate attention and then listened to his voicemails. Done with those, he headed to his truck. His plan was to spend the rest of the day checking on elk hunters up in the Colockum.

As he often did, Luke ran by his house before heading up into the mountains and picked up Jack. The dog had been a constant companion on these patrols over the years, but now, pushing eleven years old, Jack was just as happy to sleep on the couch at home as he was to go with Luke.

"C'mon, lazy dog," Luke said when he opened the back door to his house. "You need some fresh air and exercise."

Jack had heard Luke's truck pull in and was at the back door to greet him. Luke let Jack wander around the backyard for a couple of minutes so he could empty his bladder, and when the dog was done, Luke told him to load up and opened the back door of the truck so Jack could jump in.

The big dog used to fly into the back of the truck. Now it was a lot less jumping and much more climbing. Still, Jack scrambled in on his own and sat in his preferred spot on the back seat.

Luke liked having Jack along. There had been times over the years when the yellow dog had saved him from harm in the form of a bad guy trying to attack. Once, Jack had been instrumental in alerting Luke to the pending attack of a wounded black bear, which saved Luke from injury and possible death.

Plus, Luke just liked the company. He talked to Jack often as they patrolled the mountains, and even though the dog couldn't talk back, Luke believed Jack knew what he was saying. That is, if he wasn't asleep, which was happening more often these days.

"Let's go see what kind of trouble we can find," Luke said to Jack as they hit the highway that would take them north and east.

A yellow tail thumped the backseat, which told Luke that Jack had heard him and was ready to go.

They were between Yakima and Ellensburg, on SR 821, the old highway that ran along the Yakima River, when the radio crackled.

"Wildlife 148?" the voice on the radio said.

"Yeah, this is 148," Luke said. "Go ahead."

"We have a call from a fisherman who says he has found a dead wolf in the Columbia River. He believes the wolf has been shot with a rifle."

"Roger," Luke said. "Give me the contact information, and I'll give him a call."

The dispatcher gave Luke the man's name and phone number. As he was jotting the information down, he wondered if the fisherman knew the difference between a wolf and a coyote. Ever since confirmed wolf packs started popping up in the eastern half of the state, the number of wolf sightings called in to the department had jumped about five hundred percent. In his experience, most of those sightings had actually been coyotes or domesticated wolf-dog hybrids.

Luke pulled over, punched the man's phone number into his phone, and pushed connect. The ringing on the other end immediately came through the Bluetooth speakers in his truck.

"Hello?" a man's voice said after the connection was made.

"Yes, Mr. Jones. This is Officer Luke McCain from the Department of Wildlife."

"Yessir," Jones said. "Thanks for calling."

"So, you say you found a wolf?"

"Yep, big sucker too. Just floating down the Columbia as nice as you please."

"You sure it's a wolf?"

"If it's not, I'll eat your hat," Jones said.

Luke chuckled hearing that. He found out where the man with the dead wolf was located and started that way.

"I'm a half hour away," Luke said. "I'll get there as quickly as I can."

"No hurry," Jones said. "The fishing has been pretty slow, and I was going to head home, but I'll wait for ya."

Jones said he was at the boat launch at the state park downriver from the Vantage Bridge. Luke thought about that and wondered how a dead wolf had ended up there. The closest wolf pack was up in the Naneum, not far from the Columbia River, but a long way from the state park. Someone must have dumped it somewhere upriver.

When Luke pulled into the boat launch at the park, he spotted a small aluminum boat sitting on a trailer behind a red Toyota Tacoma pickup. A man dressed in brown Carhartt coveralls, wearing an Elmer Fudd-style hat, flaps pulled down over his ears, was sitting on the middle boat seat.

Luke pulled up to the boat, buzzed his window down, and said, "Dean Jones?"

"Yessir," Jones said. "By the way, did you know you have the same name as the main character in that old TV western, *The Rifleman*?"

"So I've been told," Luke said. "And you have the same name as the actor who starred in those Disney movies with Suzanne Pleshette."

"So I have been told, but aren't you too young to know that?"

"Saturday afternoon movies on TV when I was a kid," Luke said. "Saw *The Ugly Dachshund* several times."

"I'm sorry," Jones said with a laugh and nodded at Luke's truck. "Speaking of dogs, who you got there with ya?"

Jack was sitting up and looking out the back door window.

"That's Jack. He's a cross between a yellow Lab, a chowhound, and Rip Van Winkle. Anymore, when he's not eating, he's sleeping."

"Kinda sounds like me," Jones said with another laugh. "So, you wanna see this dead wolf I fished outta the river?"

Jones climbed out of the boat as Luke and Jack jumped out of Luke's pickup. They followed the man in the coveralls down to the edge of the river. Sure enough, there lay a very dead, very waterlogged wolf.

Jack spent a few seconds sniffing the dead wolf, then, as if he smelled dead wolves every day, he wandered off to look for squirrels.

"Wolf, right?" Jones said.

"Yessir. That's a wolf," Luke said. "But I can't figure out what it's doing down here. Closest wolf pack is a good twenty-five miles from here."

"Well, it wasn't out for a swim, I can tell you that," Jones said, pulling some of the wet, thick fur apart to reveal a clean, round bullet hole in the skin on the animal's side.

Luke thought about the discussion he'd had with Cody Stephens, the game warden up in Spokane. More and more poached wolves seemed to indeed be popping up, and here was another one.

"What are you gunna do with it?" Jones asked.

"I'll take it back to headquarters for our wolf biologist to look it over. Then he will likely send it to the forensics lab so they can run some tests on it."

"What kinda tests do they do?"

"Cause of death, how long it's been dead, genetics, things like that."

"That seems like a waste of time," Jones said. "I can tell you this animal is a wolf, and it died of lead poisoning. Probably a hundred-and-fifty-grain ballistic tip right through the boiler room. Maybe a day or so ago."

"I wouldn't argue with you, Mr. Jones, but we have to do our due diligence."

The two men talked for a few more minutes. Luke found out that Jones had spotted the wolf floating just off the shoreline while he was fishing for smallmouth bass. He didn't know it was a wolf at first, but saw it was an animal and went over to check it out. When he saw it was a wolf, he made the call to 911. After talking to the dispatcher, Jones had grabbed the wolf by the tail and towed it to the shore next to the boat launch.

"Catch any bass?" Luke asked.

"A couple, but they were too small to mess with," Jones said. "I like the three-pounders. They got a little meat on their bones. Make great fish and chips."

"Yes, they do," Luke said and grabbed the wolf by the back legs to drag it to his pickup.

Jones jumped in and grabbed the front legs, and the two men carried the wolf up the ramp to the truck.

"Thing is heavier than it looks," Luke said.

"Probably has ten pounds of water soaked up in its fur," Jones said.

"Still," Luke said. "Jack over there is a hundred and ten pounds, and this wolf is a fair bit heavier than Jack."

"That's how they can take down an elk," Jones said.

They placed the dead wolf into the bed of Luke's truck, and Luke thanked Jones for calling it in.

"No problem," Jones said. "Kinda made my day. I've never seen a wild wolf before. Even a dead one is a rarity, I'd say."

Luke called Jack to the truck, had him load up, jumped into the driver's seat, and gave a wave to the man in the coveralls. As he drove out of the park and back toward the big bridge that spanned the Columbia, he started thinking about how the wolf had made it into the river. He wondered if someone might have thrown the dead wolf off the bridge.

When he got to the on-ramp to I-90, Luke took the eastbound entrance and drove across the bridge. He knew they had been doing some upgrades to the bridge over the past several months and wondered if part of those improvements might include cameras. He slowed some and looked carefully. Sure enough, he spotted what looked to be cameras on both sides of the bridge, pointing east and west.

Luke called into the office and asked the assistant if he could run down someone at the Department of Transportation.

"If you find someone who can talk to me about the cameras on the Vantage Bridge, can you have them give me a call?"

"Will do," the assistant said and signed off.

Luke drove to the next exit, crossed under the freeway, and made his way back onto I-90 going west. He drove a few miles, thinking about the dead wolf, and was just about to the top of Ryegrass when his phone rang.

"This is Luke McCain."

"Yeah, Officer McCain, this is Martin Vaughn. I work for Transportation and oversee the video equipment on the public roadways."

Luke told Vaughn what he was looking for and asked if there was a way he could check the cameras on the Vantage Bridge for the last forty-eight hours.

"It'll take a little time," Vaughn said. "If you have an estimated time for when this happened, I could get it to you sooner. But that's a lot to look at."

"Can't help you there," Luke said. "I'm just guessing it was some time in the past couple of days by the lack of decomposition of the wolf, but I have no idea."

"Okay," Vaughn said. "We'll take a look and get back to you if we find anything."

Luke thanked him, told him to call at any time if he found something, and clicked off. The chances of finding anything were slim, he knew, but it was worth a shot.

"Okay, boy," Luke said to Jack. "Let's go check on some hunters."

He glanced in the back. The big yellow dog was sound asleep.

CHAPTER 20

Peter Covington found the house of the man the fixer had given him quite easily. He plugged the location into the map app on his phone, and in a second, a female voice came over the speakers, telling him exactly when and where to turn until he spotted James Henricks' ranch house.

It was mid-morning, and the house, which sat a quarter mile from the road, surrounded by fences and some outbuildings, looked to be unoccupied. Two horses, a larger one and a smaller one, fed in a pasture close to the house. A few chickens pecked around the horses and in the gravel driveway.

From the road, Covington could see a tractor and a red ATV sitting near a shed, but he found no other vehicles parked nearby. Henricks, he assumed, was at work. He thought about risking driving up to the house to look around, but decided not to take the chance. He now knew where the house was, and by looking at the surrounding terrain and outbuildings, he could start putting together a plan for taking out the wolf killer.

He punched his own address at Cle Elum Lake into the map program, and the digital voice directed him back around in a different route than he had come in on. He sped off and started thinking about being back here come dark, when he could get close enough to shoot one Mr. James Henricks.

* * *

Henricks came around the corner just in time to see a big black SUV pull away from his mailbox. Was someone trying to steal his mail? Maybe they were just stopped to talk on the phone. Henricks didn't get many visitors out this way, and so it was weird that someone had stopped right there.

The SUV disappeared in a cloud of dust around the corner, and as Henricks drove up his driveway, he watched his rearview mirror to see if the rig came back down the road. When it didn't, he stopped thinking about it, believing he was being a little paranoid about the whole deal with the dead wolf. The chances that anyone would ever find out he had killed the wolf were very small. And then, what could they do about it? The county sheriff or the game wardens might harass him, but without the animal, which was now on the bottom of the Columbia River, possibly even banging up against the Wanapum Dam, there wasn't much they could do.

He'd been thinking about the photo he had posted on the Renegades' website, and there was nothing there that would tell anyone the wolf had been shot in Washington. If someone were to press him on it, he'd say it was shot in Montana, where wolf hunting is not only legal, it's encouraged. He had a couple of buddies in Bozeman who would vouch for him and say they were there when the wolf in the photo was shot.

He spent the rest of the morning doing chores around the

place. It was weird not having Duke and Annabelle there. They had been his constant companions when he was out working around the farm, and now they weren't there. He missed them dearly.

*　*　*

About the same time as Henricks was outside feeding the horses and the chickens, the hacker sent the fixer a text.

Hacker: *Email incoming.*

The fixer didn't even respond. He just went to his computer, opened the secure email site, and waited. A moment later, the email popped up. It read: *Good news. Another wolf poacher identified. Name and address will be sent in a second email. Stand by.*

Another moment later, a second email landed. This email just had a copy of a driver's license for a young man by the name of Eli Creech III. His address was in some place called Okanogan.

The fixer texted the hacker: *Thanks. Send invoice*

The hacker's email notification dinger dinged, telling him he had another email.

A second later, a text from the hacker arrived: *Just sent.*

The hacker knew this information was like gold. Covington expected his sources to provide good information in a timely fashion, but this was above and beyond. Two names in less than a week. The new information was going to be worth a serious bonus.

The fixer immediately texted Covington on his main phone. *I have more information. Same procedure as last time. Text with a new phone number.*

Covington was just arriving home from his reconnoiter of James Henricks' place when the text from the fixer came through. He was glad he had purchased two of the throw-away phones. The last thing he wanted to do was go deal with Prince, the rude clerk at Fred Meyer. He immediately went into his house, grabbed the phone, and punched the number for the fixer to send the text.

Covington: *Send info here*

A moment later, a text from the fixer came in with the photo of the driver's license of Eli Creech III.

Covington was looking at the photo when a second text buzzed in: *Destroy phone immediately*

Just as he had done with the photo of Henricks, Covington studied the photo of the man on the driver's license. He looked at it for several minutes until he was convinced he would recognize the man when he saw him.

Then, he pulled the business card out of his wallet, wrote Creech's address next to the one he had written for Henricks, put it back, and headed for the garage with the phone. Using the same claw hammer as before, Covington placed the cheap phone on the concrete floor and smashed it to smithereens. For the second time in a week, the shattered remains of a cell phone were flung out of a dustpan into the dark, cold waters of Cle Elum Lake.

After returning to his favorite chair, with his favorite tumbler filled with his favorite Scotch, Covington sat down to think about everything.

He knew he could kill a human being. He'd shot the skinny hitchhiker without so much as a second thought. Now he had two new targets. They were confirmed wolf killers. If he killed them, would he be considered a serial killer? That didn't bother him, thinking he might be a serial killer. But after some thought, he came to the conclusion he wouldn't be labeled as a serial killer because he didn't have a type and didn't kill just for the fun of it. He was going to kill the wolf poachers for a very sound and sane reason. He was saving his wolves.

He knew where James Henricks lived. With the new name in hand, he decided to go check out this Eli Creech. From there, he would figure out how to proceed.

Covington took another sip of his drink and smiled. The money he was spending with the fixer was paying off. Tomorrow, he would locate the second wolf killer that had just been added to his list.

*　*　*

Rarely did he drink too much, but Covington awoke the next morning with a dull headache. He looked at the clock and saw it was nearly nine-thirty, a good two hours later than he usually slept. He checked his phone and saw he had a text from his girlfriend. She was informing him that she was going with a couple of friends down to Los Angeles for a few days, and not to be shocked if there were some extra charges on the American Express.

"Bitch," Covington muttered to himself after reading the text. If she weren't so good-looking, he would dump her right now and cancel the charge cards.

He decided he wasn't going to worry about it. He had spent much of the night drinking Scotch and scheming on how he was going to take out the two wolf killers. He envisioned several scenarios where he would walk up to them, tell them he was doing this for the wolves they had killed, and shoot them in the forehead.

He thought about taking out the man on the ranch near Thorp first, but decided he wanted to check out the new man before he made that decision. He wasn't going to take his pistol on the drive north, but changed his mind, because if the perfect situation arose and he could take out this Creech fellow, that would save him another four-hour drive back to Okanogan.

By the time Covington got on the road, it was nearly eleven o'clock. He stopped for some lunch in Wenatchee and then continued up the highway, along the Columbia River to Brewster. He got gas and a cold soft drink at a mini-mart and plugged the address he had for Creech into the map app on his phone.

The app directed him to and through Omak, then through Okanogan, and out into the country. He took increasingly less-traveled asphalt roads and ended up on one that eventually turned into gravel. Finally, the voice on the app said he had reached his destination, so he slowed and saw a large sign hanging from a crossbeam strung from two giant poles that read "CREECH FAMILY RANCH."

Covington stopped his rig and looked up the driveway. Three young men were working in some corrals with maybe twenty head of cattle. They were moving the cattle from one corral to another, where a huge silver trailer attached to a semi-truck was parked. The trailer had about a thousand holes the size of tennis balls punched in it, and a ramp ran from the back of the trailer into the corral. With some effort, the men navigated the black cows into the trailer, and when the last cow disappeared inside, two of the men closed the back doors and swung a metal bar across to keep them closed.

Covington watched with interest as the men worked and then noticed another older man standing on the porch of a nearby house. The man was looking at Covington's SUV. Seeing the man looking at him, Covington put the black Lincoln Navigator into drive and went on down the road.

* * *

Trey Creech, Artie Miller, and Deke Price finished getting the two dozen Black Angus steers loaded into the stock trailer and headed to the house. Creech's father was standing on the porch as the three young men walked his way.

"Good job," Eli Creech Jr. said. "We'll get them down to the stockyard this afternoon, and they'll be ready for the sale in the morning."

"Yessir," Trey said. "Artie and I will drive them down there now."

"You guys see that black SUV at the end of the drive just now?" the older Creech asked.

"No, sir," Trey said and looked at Miller and Price. They both shook their heads.

"Don't see a fancy rig like that out here very often," Creech said. "As soon as the driver saw me looking at him, he took off."

The three young men just shrugged their shoulders and climbed the stairs to the porch. They were thirsty and ready for something to drink.

Price looked unconcerned, but the second he heard that someone in a fancy black rig was watching them, he immediately thought about the person who had been snooping around in the Renegades' website. Someone with the ability to hack into the site might have the ability to identify them. He didn't know how, but nothing was impossible.

When Trey and Miller left to take the steers into the sales yard, Price headed home to do some more work on the computer. He had been trying with very little luck to figure out who had hacked the site, but he needed to keep at it.

The man in the expensive black SUV was a proper motivator. That, and knowing if the police were ever to discover the existence of the Renegades, he might be going to jail, or worse yet, federal prison.

*   *   *

Covington headed back to Okanogan to find a place to stay for the night. He spotted a Quality Inn and Suites with the red vacancy sign lit, so he pulled in. The helpful girl at the front desk took his credit card and gave him a keycard. The room was not up to his usual standards, but it would be fine for one night. Covington could smell the high-powered cleaning solutions typical of small-town motels. And the twenty-eight-inch television was almost laughable. But he wasn't there to watch TV. He was there for one purpose.

As he lay on the too-soft bed in the suite, he thought about what he had seen at the Creech ranch. He was almost positive that one of the three young men he had seen working the cattle was Eli Creech III. It excited him to think about taking out the wolf killer.

He wondered if one of the three young men in the corrals was the other man in the photo with the happy face hiding his identity. Could he shoot both of the men? If the opportunity presented itself, he believed he could.

Covington was tired from the long drive and little rest the night before. He closed his eyes, thinking about the men in the corrals, and fell into a hard sleep.

CHAPTER 21

Luke's phone was ringing on the dresser. It was a little before five o'clock in the morning, and calls that came in at that hour were rarely good. But this one was.

"Yeah, this is McCain," Luke said sleepily, not even looking at the number on his phone's screen.

"Officer McCain, this is Martin Vaughn with D.O.T.," the voice on the other end of the phone said.

"Oh, yeah, Mr. Vaughn, sure, how can I help you?"

"Sorry to call so early, but I think we found the man who dumped that wolf off the Vantage Bridge."

"Really, that's great," Luke said, wide awake now.

Vaughn went on to tell Luke that they had scoured through the video and found where, on the morning before the wolf was found floating in the Columbia River, a pickup truck had parked and dumped something off the bridge.

"The video isn't great," Vaughn said. "And the lighting is bad, but this guy definitely parked on the bridge for a minute, jumped out, retrieved something heavy from the bed of the truck, and hoisted it over the railing of the bridge."

"Were you able to get an ID on the truck's tags?" Luke asked.

"We're still working on that," Vaughn said. "We're looking at the other cameras on both sides of the bridge to see if there is an angle that allows us to read the license plate."

"Okay," Luke said. "If you get anything definite, let me know."

After thanking Vaughn for the call, who again apologized for calling so early, Luke clicked off.

"What was that all about?" Sara said from the bed. She was still lying on her side with her eyes closed.

"That dead wolf thing I was telling you about," Luke said. "The D.O.T. might have video of someone dumping it into the river."

"He had to call and wake us up to tell us he might have something?"

"I told him to call anytime if he found anything."

"You need to stop telling people that," Sara said.

Luke laughed.

"It's not funny. I'm a very special agent with the FBI, and I need my sleep."

That gave Luke an idea. He padded over to the bed and slipped under the covers. He snuggled up to Sara's backside, spooning her, and wrapped his arms around her.

"Don't even think about it," she said sternly.

"No, no," Luke said. "Remember when your guy in D.C. helped to make the video of the Bigfoot more focused and viewable?"

"Yes. You think Bigfoot threw the wolf off the bridge?"

"No, but if we could get clearer images of the man and what he is throwing off the bridge, and maybe his license plate numbers, it would help a lot."

"I'm not going to get to go back to sleep, am I?" Sara asked.

"It's nearly eight o'clock at the Hoover Building. Think your buddy there would help you again?"

Sara groaned and rolled over to look at Luke. He looked like a kid with a brand-new puppy.

"How can I resist that face?" she said and pulled him in to kiss her. "You owe me big time, mister."

While Sara was showering and getting ready for work, Luke called Martin Vaughn back and told him that he might be able to get the brainiacs at the FBI to work their magic on the video from the traffic cameras if he could send over the original files.

"Wow, that's great," Vaughn said. "Who do you know that can make that happen?"

"I'm married to her," Luke said.

He went on to explain about Sara, asked him to send her the files, and gave Vaughn her email address.

"We should have the other angle shortly," Vaughn said. "My guy has spotted the truck coming back across the bridge about fifty minutes after it stopped and dumped the wolf, if it was the wolf."

"I gotta believe it was the wolf," Luke said. "What else would someone be dumping there then?"

"There's always a chance someone was dumping a human body," Vaughn said.

"Let's not think that way," Luke said. "Send the video files as soon as you have them. And thanks for the good work, Mr. Vaughn. I appreciate it greatly."

"We're all part of the same team," Vaughn said. "Happy to help."

When Luke was off the call, he went into the kitchen and got some scrambled eggs and sausage going. Fixing Sara breakfast would ease the earlier-than-normal wake-up call.

As he was cooking, Jack wandered in.

"Hey, boy," Luke said. "Ready to start your day?"

Jack wagged his tail and plodded over to the back door. Luke opened it to let the dog out to do his morning business.

A couple minutes later, he heard Sara talking on the phone. She explained to the person on the other end of the line what she needed, and after listening for a minute, she thanked the person and said goodbye.

"You're lucky that Roger likes me," Sara said. "He said he'd look at the files as soon as I send them."

"He knows you're married, right?" Luke said.

"Sure, but I'm guessing he hopes it doesn't stick."

"What are the odds it doesn't?" Luke asked with a smile.

"About fifty-fifty as of this morning," Sara said.

"Would a hot breakfast help?" Luke asked.

"It might. And dinner out tonight would help too."

"Done," Luke said and went to dish up the sausage and eggs.

* * *

The video files from Vaughn were waiting for Sara when she fired up her computer at her office. She immediately forwarded them to Roger in Washington, D.C., who replied almost immediately that he would get them into the supercomputer to clean up the video and return the files to Sara as quickly as possible.

The files came back less than an hour later. Sara took a quick look at them and then called Luke.

"Hey," she said after Luke answered. "Looks like you were right. The upgraded video definitely shows a man dumping an animal over the railing of the bridge. Can't tell for sure if it's a dog or a coyote or a wolf. It might even be a small bear, but it is an animal."

"That's great," Luke said. "And what about the license plate?"

"Got it," she said and gave Luke the numbers.

"That Roger dude must really like you to get the information that fast."

"Well, he did ask me to dinner the next time I'm at headquarters."

"What did you tell him?"

"I said, 'Sure, it would be fun.'"

"Well, I think you should go," Luke said with a laugh. "If you can get this kind of service every time, it's worth it."

There was a click on the end of the line. Sara was gone. Evidently, she didn't think his suggestion was all that funny.

Luke immediately brought up the state website for running license plates and tapped the keys to enter the number Sara had given him into the system. He pushed enter and waited.

A few minutes later, the information popped up on Luke's computer screen. The license came back to a 2016 silver Nissan Frontier pickup, registered to a man by the name of James Henricks. The address shown for Henricks was in Thorp.

Luke wrote the information down and headed to the captain's office. When he got there, the door was closed, and he remembered that Captain Davis was in Olympia for some meetings. Luke went back to his cubicle and wrote Davis a quick email recapping what he had learned about the dead wolf and the man who they believed had dumped it into the Columbia.

He was just about to head out the door to go talk to Henricks when his office phone started jangling.

"This is McCain," Luke said.

"Hey, Luke, this is Joe Ames calling."

Luke had almost forgotten that the wolf biologist had come and retrieved the body of the wolf that was fished out of the Columbia.

"Oh, hey, Joe," Luke said. "I think we found who dumped the wolf in the river."

"That's great," Ames said. "And I think I know which pack the wolf came from."

Ames went on to tell Luke that over the years, they had trapped at least one wolf from the various wolf packs in Eastern Washington, and through a DNA sampling match, they were able to tell the one found in the river was part of the Teanaway Pack.

He told Luke the wolf was a six-year-old male and looked to be in excellent shape.

"It didn't die of natural causes," Ames said. "It was definitely a bullet through the lungs that killed it."

"That's very helpful, Joe," Luke said. "The guy we think killed the wolf, or at least who we believe dumped it into the Columbia, lives up around Thorp, which is darned close to the Teanaway."

"We've had a few wolf complaints from ranchers up around Thorp," Ames said. "But no one has reported that they shot at any wolves."

"Well, I'm about to head up that way to have a chat with the guy who was on video dropping the wolf into the river."

"Good luck," Ames said. "Let me know what you find out."

"Will do," Luke said and hung up.

Before he left, Luke looked Henricks up in the state's Triple I system, where he searched for any prior arrests or criminal activity. The report came back clean as a whistle. No speeding tickets. No parking tickets. Nothing.

Evidently, Mr. Henricks was a model citizen. Except for possibly killing a federally protected endangered species, that is.

CHAPTER 22

When Covington woke up, it was pitch black in his room. For a few seconds, he had no idea where he was or even what day it was. Then it started to come back to him. He fumbled for a switch on the light next to his bed and turned it on. He found his phone and looked at it. It was a few minutes after eight o'clock. His head was pounding again, and he was hungry.

He sat up and thought about what he should do. He decided a quick shower was in order, and after that, he would find something to eat. He hoped a hot shower and hot food would help his head.

Dinner was chicken-fried steak at a mom-and-pop diner just down the road from the motel. Not the worst he'd ever eaten, but not the best either. He had a Budweiser with dinner, which made his head feel a bit better. He decided he would find a bar to have a nightcap and think about what he should do.

The first bar he came to was a tavern, and it was hippity-hopping. Pickup trucks were parked in front, on the side, and in the back. Covington pulled in and was looking for a parking spot, but decided a tavern might not have any hard alcohol, and he was dying for a Scotch on the rocks.

He was just pulling out of the parking lot when a white Ford pickup pulled in. In the light of his headlights, Covington could see the driver. The face he saw in the white light was the same one he had been studying in the photo sent by the fixer. It was Eli Creech III.

The pickup pulled past him and disappeared around the back of the tavern. Covington reached for the revolver under his seat and thought about what to do next. He could drive back around and ask Creech a question, and when he came up to his window, he could shoot him in the head.

But what if he wasn't alone? Covington had been so intent on looking at Creech's face, he hadn't paid any attention to see if anyone else was in the truck with him.

He decided that doing it now was not a good idea. It was spur-of-the-moment. There were just too many people in the tavern, every one of them a potential witness. Covington pulled out into the road and drove off to find a bar that served hard liquor.

*　*　*

"Did you see that black rig?" Artie Miller said to Trey Creech as they drove to the back of the tavern. "That might have been the same one your old man saw today hanging out down at the bottom of your driveway."

"So what?" Creech said. "Probably some rich guy from California looking for cheap land to buy. We're getting calls from realtors about once a week looking for land."

"The guy driving was looking pretty hard at you," Miller said.

"If he's got a problem with me, he can bring it on," Creech said as he opened the truck door to head into the tavern. "Now, let's go get a beer."

Just then, Miller saw the big black SUV driving down the road.

"The guy's leaving," Miller said and then asked, "Why didn't Deke want to join us?"

"He's still freaking out about our website being hacked," Creech said. "He wants to try to find out who the hacker is."

"Are you worried about that?" Miller asked.

"No, are you?"

"Kind of," Miller said. "What if it's the cops who got in there and saw that photo of you and me with that wolf?"

"Our faces were blocked out, and there is no way to determine where we were. We could have been in Russia for all anyone knows."

"I don't know," Miller said. "The shit they can do with computers nowadays. I wish Deke had never posted that photo."

"You sound like an old lady," Creech said as he sat at the one open stool at the bar. "Stop worrying and have a beer."

✳   ✳   ✳

Covington found a bar in a restaurant only two blocks from the tavern. He walked in and sat down at the bar. After the bartender—an older guy about Covington's age with tattoos on his hands, forearms, and neck—took his order of a double Scotch on the rocks, he thought about how he should proceed. He was positive it was Creech he had seen driving the white pickup into the tavern's parking lot. If the young man was like most tavern patrons, he would be in there for a while. And when he finally came out of the place, Creech might be in some degree of inebriation. It could be the perfect time to take him out.

The tattooed bartender brought a second double, and as Covington sipped on the drink, he worked on his plan.

He would finish his drink, drive back over to the tavern and look for a place to park where he could walk to the parking lot. There, he would hide behind some rigs and wait for Creech to come out. If the man was alone, and there was no one else around, Covington would walk up to him, tell him this was for the wolves, and shoot him in the head.

If Creech was with someone, or there were other people in the parking lot, Covington would slip back to his SUV and wait for the wolf killer to leave. Then he would follow him and somehow get him to pull over, where Covington could get close enough for a shot.

"You want another one?" the bartender asked, startling Covington out of his planning trance.

"Nah, I'm good," Covington said.

"You're obviously not from around here," the tattooed man said. "What brings you to our little piece of the world?"

"I have some business here," Covington said, keeping it vague.

"Well, I hope it goes well for you. It's twenty-four for the drinks."

Covington handed the bartender a twenty and a ten and told him to keep the change. Then he headed for his vehicle, convinced that he would soon be taking out one of the two wolf killers on his list, making the world a better place.

* * *

At closing time, the tavern manager had to chase a dozen locals out the door. It was standard for a Friday night. They drank their beer, played pool, laughed and talked loudly over the jukebox music until they were forced out into the night.

Creech and Miller were part of the group of seven men and five women who exited the building in one big scrum. In singles, pairs, and a group of three, the people dispersed and headed to their vehicles.

"I'm pretty wasted," Creech said to Miller as they approached the white F-350 parked in the back. "You better drive."

Miller had been down this road before, literally and figuratively. Creech almost always made him drive home after a night of drinking. Miller was afraid that one of these times he was going to get caught driving over the limit, so he'd purposely nursed a couple of beers and drank plenty of water so that if he did get pulled over, he wouldn't get a DUI.

"Okay," Miller said, and Creech flipped him the keys to the truck.

They were just out of town, headed toward the Creech ranch, when Miller noticed headlights from a rig that seemed to be following them.

"Damn, I hope that isn't the sheriff," Miller said.

He looked over at Creech and saw that his buddy was passed out with his head against the passenger door window.

Miller kept driving, staying within the speed limit, making sure he also stayed between the center line and the fog line. The headlights stayed behind him. Even with his lawful driving, Miller expected to see blue lights in his rearview mirror. But they never came.

Finally, tired of having to fight the headlights in his mirrors, Miller sped up. The rig behind him sped up too.

"What the hell?" Miller said. Again, he looked at Creech. His buddy was still asleep.

Miller knew Creech kept a pistol in the center console, so he opened it and reached in for the gun. He didn't need to look to see if the weapon was loaded. Creech always kept it ready to shoot. Then he started slowing the truck.

He figured if he slowed the truck enough, the rig would pass if whoever was driving wasn't really following them. But if the rig slowed too, Miller would stop and jump out with the pistol in his hand and go find out what the hell the problem was.

He slowed the truck's speed to twenty miles an hour, and then to ten. The rig behind them slowed too.

"Okay, asshole, I've had enough," Miller said and stopped the pickup.

He exited the truck with the Ruger 9mm in his hand. But he kept the pistol low and behind his right hip as he walked back to the rig that had stopped ten yards behind them.

With the headlights, it made it hard to see just what kind of vehicle it was, but when he got close enough that the lights were off his face, Miller saw the rig was the black SUV that they had seen earlier at the tavern. As he stepped past the front of the vehicle, he saw the driver's window buzz down.

Miller walked right up to the window and said, "What's your problem, mister?"

He saw the revolver, but it was too late. He started to say "Hey" and raise the Ruger in defense, but there was a flash and an explosion.

Artie Miller would never get to see his wolf hide become a rug. He would never meet the woman of his dreams or have the new pickup he had always wanted. And he would never kill another wolf.

*   *   *

Covington panicked after shooting the man. It was so dark, he wasn't even positive it was Creech he had shot. It was the same truck he had seen Creech driving earlier in the evening, so it went to reason that it had been Creech driving it home. But something hadn't quite looked right.

He was going to get out and double-check, but just then he saw a porch light come on at a house he hadn't even noticed sitting twenty-five yards off the road.

A few seconds later, Covington heard a man shouting from the house, "Hey, what's going on over there?"

Covington dropped the revolver into the passenger seat, put the Navigator in gear, and drove around the body lying in the middle of the road. He needed to get off this road, and out of this county, fast.

Once he was far enough away from the body, the white pickup, and the house, he stopped and put his cabin address into the GPS unit of the Lincoln, and it immediately directed him back to the state highway, which would get him headed south.

As he drove through the darkness, he replayed the event through his mind. The person driving the pickup into the tavern's parking lot was definitely Eli Creech III, the man he had come to kill. But now he wasn't sure the man he had shot was Creech. Something was off. What was it?

Then it came to him. Creech had been wearing a white straw cowboy hat when he was driving into the tavern. The man he'd shot was wearing a tan cowboy hat.

"Shit," Covington said.

Unless Creech had somehow changed hats, which seemed unlikely, he had shot the wrong man. Not that killing an innocent man mattered all that much to him. What really mattered was that he wanted to kill the man who was pictured with the dead wolf, and he had not accomplished that goal.

As he drove south on Highway 97, he met three emergency vehicles, one after the other, heading north. First was a white Washington State Patrol vehicle, followed by a brown SUV with a light rack lit up in red and blue, followed by a red and white ambulance.

Covington murmured to himself, "There'll be no need for the ambulance," after replaying the shooting again. He had hit the man in the forehead right above the bridge of the nose, just like he had with the skinny hitchhiker.

When he reached Wenatchee, Covington was so spent, he could hardly keep his eyes open. He needed to sleep. Knowing that there was a slim possibility the law might already be looking for him, he decided to find a low-budget motel and pay cash for a room.

The Pakistani man who was running the front desk happily took $200 cash and didn't ask for any ID or other information.

"I'll be gone by noon," Covington told the man.

The man just nodded, handed Covington the room key, and turned back to the TV show he'd been watching when Covington had walked in.

In the room, which was old but clean, Covington flopped on the bed and tried to go to sleep. The adrenaline rush was fading, but there was still enough there to keep him awake. He replayed the shooting repeatedly in his head until sometime after about the twentieth time, when he finally fell asleep.

CHAPTER 23

"WHAT?" Trey Creech screamed, tears already running down his cheeks. Then he fell to his knees, put his face in his hands, and muttered, "No, no, no."

A man he didn't know had shaken him awake. Still drunk, Creech was having trouble comprehending what was going on.

"There's been a shooting," the man said as he helped Creech out of the passenger side of the pickup.

"Who's been shot?" Creech slurred as he walked around the back of the truck.

"The guy who was driving this pickup," the man said.

Just then, Creech spotted Miller splayed out on the pavement, a pistol by his side, with a bullet hole in his forehead. That's when the screaming started.

It took fourteen minutes for the first Okanogan County sheriff's deputy to arrive. The deputy, Rolly Dunbar, knew Creech and Miller. They had all gone to high school together.

Dunbar, who was over six foot three and a good two hundred and sixty pounds, came over to Creech and asked, "What the hell happened here, Trey?"

Creech, who was now sitting on the road with his arms wrapped around his knees, said in a quiet voice, "I dunno."

Then a minute later, he said, pointing to Miller's dead body, "I was passed out. Artie was driving. The next thing I know, this guy was shaking me. I got outta the truck and I see this."

The man from the nearby house, who was maybe seventy-five years old, was wearing an old-fashioned checkered robe, tied with a matching sash around his waist. Rubber irrigation boots and a Russian style rabbit fur hat with the ear flaps pulled down completed his middle-of-the-night ensemble.

"I got up to pee," the man said to Dunbar. "And I heard these two rigs stop out here in front of the house. I was just going to the front window to see what the hell was going on, and I heard a gunshot. So, I open the front door, and there's a big Suburban parked behind this white truck."

"What color was the Suburban?" Dunbar asked.

"Too dark to know for sure, but it was a dark color, like blue or black."

"What happened next?"

"The driver of the Suburban was just starting to open his door to get out, and I hollered something like 'What's going on out here?' Then he closes his door and skedaddles outta here."

"Is that when you called 911?" Dunbar asked.

"No, I didn't know someone had been shot until I walked over here."

"Did you see any other vehicles or people?"

"No, sir. I put my boots and hat on and came out here to see if I could help. That's when I saw the young man here on the road. I ran back and called you guys, then came back out. When I looked in the truck, I saw this guy and thought he might be shot too, but he was just asleep, so I woke him up."

Dunbar asked Creech a dozen other questions about where they had been, for how long, and others, but he didn't learn much of anything that might tell him why Miller had been shot.

"No scuffles or arguments with anyone at the tavern?" Dunbar asked.

"No, nothing," Creech said, shaking his head. "You know him. Everyone liked Artie. Why would someone shoot him?"

"Is that Miller's pistol laying there next to him?" Dunbar asked.

Creech looked at the gun. He hadn't even noticed it there before.

"No, I think it's mine," Creech said. "I keep it in the center console, more to shoot at coyotes than anything."

Dunbar went and looked in the truck's center console and found no pistol.

He came back and said, "Miller knew you kept the pistol there?"

"Yep. He saw me use it several times."

"Have you shot it recently?" Dunbar asked.

"Not lately, no. I cleaned it a couple weeks ago and haven't shot it since." Then Creech asked, "Why would someone do this?"

"I don't know," Dunbar said. "But we'll figure it out."

A state patrol officer and two more deputies arrived, followed by an ambulance. Yellow tape was strung around the area, and after about a hundred photos were taken, Miller's body was loaded onto a gurney and rolled into the ambulance.

Eli Creech Jr. showed up forty-five minutes after the shooting. One of the deputies had called him to ask him to come get his son.

After talking to Trey for a few minutes, Creech asked his son where Deke Price was.

"Home in bed or on the computer," Trey said. "He didn't come to the tavern with us."

"We better call him and let him know what happened," Creech said and pulled out his phone.

Price, who had only been asleep for an hour, seemed confused.

"What happened?" he asked sleepily.

Creech told him all he knew again.

Then Price asked a question that Creech himself should have thought of. "Was that big black SUV around when it happened?"

"I don't know," Creech said. "Let me find out, and I'll call you back."

As Creech was helping load his son into his own truck, he asked, "Did you see that black SUV tonight?"

Trey thought about it for a minute and started to say they hadn't, then he remembered turning into the tavern and seeing a fancy black SUV pulling out of the parking lot.

"I didn't pay any attention to it, but Artie said the driver was staring at me," Trey said.

"I wonder if it was the same rig we saw watching us from the end of the driveway yesterday," Creech said.

"I think I heard the old guy over there in the fur hat tell Rolly he saw a Suburban leaving after he heard Artie get shot," Trey said.

Creech went over to the man in the robe, who was talking to a different deputy, and asked, "You saw a Suburban leave after the shot?"

"Yessir."

"Was it black?"

"Coulda been. It was a dark color, but being night and all, I couldn't tell for sure."

"And it was definitely a Suburban?"

"Aren't all them big station wagon rigs Suburbans?"

The deputy jumped in. "No, sir. Just about every car maker makes a big SUV, and they have different designs and names."

"Well, hell, they all look the same to me. We just call them Suburbans."

Creech told the deputy about seeing a large black SUV the previous day at the house, and then Miller and Trey had seen one checking them out at the tavern.

"We already have an APB out for a dark-colored Suburban," the deputy said. "But there are probably five thousand of them in this half of the state."

Eli Creech Jr. called Price back and told him what he had learned about the SUV.

"Damn!" Price said more to himself than Creech.

"What?" Creech asked.

"It's nothing," Price said, not wanting to tell Creech about the Renegades' website and the wolves and everything that had happened in recent days. Someone on the dark web had tracked them down from the website, and they had killed Artie Miller because of what they had seen. He was now convinced of it.

"Tell Trey I'm on my way to the house, and I will see him there," Price said and ended the call.

He had spent hours trying to track the person who had hacked their site without success. He was going to have to do better, or they might all have to leave the state. Especially if there was someone out there hunting them down.

*　*　*

Covington was back on the road before eleven that morning. He had tried to find some news of the shooting on the TV in the motel room before he left, but there was nothing. In his rig driving toward Blewett Pass, he scanned the radio stations but heard nothing of the shooting there either.

He was sure the police must be looking for his vehicle. But as dark as it was, and as far away as the man had been on the porch, he was convinced the guy couldn't have made out the make of his vehicle, let alone his license plate numbers.

He hadn't gone to Okanogan County thinking he was going to kill one of the wolf killers, but it had happened. Maybe it wasn't the right man, but the message was clear, or it would be clear once he had the fixer send a message to the media that the man who had been shot on the road outside of Okanogan had been killed because he was part of a group that was out to exterminate Washington's wolves.

As he drove, Covington turned his thoughts to the other man on his list. He would go home, get some rest, and make his plan to take out James Henricks next.

CHAPTER 24

Luke located Henricks' small ranch and drove up the driveway. No dogs came out to bark at him, which in his experience was unusual because ranches like this seemed to always have a dog or two around to bark at intruders, be it the two- or four-legged variety.

A small flock of a dozen or so chickens was out in the pasture, scratching and picking at whatever they could find to eat, and a chestnut-colored mare and blueish-colored colt were munching away on some flakes of hay.

Luke looked for the Nissan pickup he had seen in the video, but it was nowhere around. The only other vehicles parked near a shed off the driveway were a small tractor and a four-by-four ATV.

He again looked at the horses. The hay they were eating had been tossed out to them not that long ago, based on how much had been consumed. Someone was either still here or had been here recently, so Luke parked his truck, jumped out, and went up to the door. Finding no doorbell, he knocked on the door and stood back to listen.

He heard nothing but silence. He knocked again. This time harder. Still no response, so he went back to his truck.

"No one's home," he said to Jack, who was sitting in the back seat, watching the chickens move around in the barnyard. "We'll catch up to Mr. Henricks later."

Luke backed around, drove down the driveway and up the county road. He watched for Henricks' Nissan pickup but never saw it or any other vehicles until he returned to the freeway.

It was mid-morning, so Luke decided that since it was still elk hunting season, he would run up into the Taneum and check on some hunters.

"Let's go earn our paychecks," Luke said to Jack as he got on I-90 going west. He looked back and saw the big yellow dog zonked out on the back seat.

It had snowed once in the high country about a week prior, but it hadn't been enough to push most of the elk into the lower elevations. There were always some local bunches of elk here and there, but once the hunters hit the woods, the animals would find some deep, dark hole to hide in, and there would be some very unhappy hunters.

Luke had been through twenty elk seasons in this region and knew that if the weather cooperated, there would be more success. But on years like this one, it was the hunters who really worked at it who would be filling their freezers with elk. The old adage of ten percent of the hunters killing ninety percent of the elk always held true.

As he drove the Forest Service roads, he would look into the camps. If he saw something hanging from a meat pole, he would pull in and make sure the animal was legally tagged. The third camp Luke came to had a spike bull hanging from a lodgepole pine that had been nailed crossways to two fir trees. As Luke pulled into the camp, a boy of about thirteen stuck his head out of a white canvas wall tent. As soon as the kid saw Luke in his Fish and Wildlife Enforcement truck, his eyes got big, and he ducked back in.

"That was weird," Luke said to Jack. The dog had awakened at the change in speed of the truck and was now again sitting and looking out the window. "Stay here. I'll let you out in a minute."

As Luke climbed out of the truck, a large man, maybe forty years old with a four-day salt and pepper beard, came out of the tent, followed by two boys, the one Luke had seen and a second who was maybe a year or two younger than the first. The man was wearing a red and black flannel shirt and denim pants that were held up by green suspenders. His black hair was unkempt, like he had just gotten out of bed.

"Hi, fellas," Luke said. "I see someone got an elk."

"Yessir," the big man said. "Ryker here got him his first elk."

Luke looked at the older boy, who he guessed was Ryker, and said, "Well, congratulations, young man."

Ryker smiled sheepishly and started looking at his feet.

"So, tell me the story, Ryker," Luke said.

The man, who was about five foot ten or eleven and weighed two hundred and fifty pounds, said, "He made a great shot."

Luke looked at Ryker again and said, "Is that right?"

Ryker said nothing.

"So, can I see everyone's hunting licenses?" Luke asked.

"Show him your license, Ryker," the big man said.

"I want to see everyone's licenses," Luke said with a little more seriousness in his tone.

The youngest boy said, "I ain't got one yet."

Luke looked at the man.

"I ain't got one neither," the man said.

"How about a driver's license then?" Luke asked.

The man reached into his back pocket and pulled out a brown leather bi-fold wallet that was as thick as a sofa cushion. He dug his license out and handed it to Luke, who read that the man's name was Cliff Buckley. The address on the license was in Sumner.

"So, Mr. Buckley, you don't hunt? Or did you just forget to buy a license?"

"I got into some trouble with the law a while back," Buckley said. "Can't get a hunting license for five years."

"What did you do to lose your hunting privileges?" Luke asked.

"The law called it poaching, but me and a buddy was just trying to feed our families."

"And how were you doing that?"

"We got into a herd of elk down there by St. Helens and shot a couple cows."

"That'll do it," Luke said.

"So, since I can't hunt, my boys here are going to be filling the freezer for us, ain't you boys?"

The older of the two boys was still looking at his feet, and the younger one was smiling up at Luke.

"I ain't got no hunting license," the kid said again.

"What's your name?" Luke asked the younger boy.

"Ranger," the kid said.

"And how old are you?"

"I'm ten, goin' on 'leven."

"You like to hunt?" Luke asked.

"Boy, do I. In fact, I—"

"You shut your mouth, Ranger," the boy's father barked.

"That's okay," Luke said, turning to the man. "Let him speak." Then he said to the boy, "Go ahead, Ranger. You can tell me."

Ranger looked at Luke and then at his father. Then he turned back to Luke and said, "Ryker shot that bull. I can't hunt because I ain't got no hunting license."

Luke looked at Buckley, and the man was smiling.

There was more than one way to skin a cat, and Luke was going to get to the bottom of this. He figured either the father or Ranger had shot the elk, and since Ryker had the only license and tag, he was the one who'd tagged the spike.

"Okay then," Luke said, looking at Ryker. "Let's go have a little chat."

"You can talk to him right here," Buckley said with some anger in his voice.

"No, I can't. He shot the elk, and I'm going to talk to him without you interrupting."

Luke looked at Ryker, and the boy was starting to shake. His face was flushed, and tears started to run down his cheeks.

"All I want you to do is tell me the story of how you shot the elk," Luke said quietly to the boy. "It's not that hard."

"Yes, it is," Ryker said. "Because I wasn't there. I hate hunting. Ranger shot the elk. Dad was so happy for him. He just got me the tag so they could shoot an elk."

Then he started sobbing.

Luke turned and looked at the man and said, "Well, Mr. Buckley, evidently you haven't learned your lesson about breaking the game laws, have you?"

"A man's gotta do what a man's gotta do to feed his family," Buckley said. "The price of beef these days, who can afford to put meat on the table?"

"So, you thought it was a good idea to bring your kids along to break the law?" Luke said.

"We all own the game in this state," Buckley said. "It ain't yours, or the governor's. I just wanted to get our share."

"Well, you've gone about it the wrong way," Luke said. "And unfortunately, I have to confiscate the elk, and with the citation you are going to receive, you would have been better off buying the beef."

"This is a bunch of bullshit," Buckley said, starting to walk toward Luke.

"Don't add injury to insult," Luke said, holding up a hand. "Assaulting a police officer will get you some immediate jail time. What will happen to the boys here?"

Buckley kept coming.

Luke was just figuring out how he was going to handle the man, who, even though he was six inches shorter than Luke, had him by a good thirty pounds, when Ryker jumped in front of his father.

"Stop it, Dad. Haven't you gotten us into enough trouble?"

Buckley stopped. He stared at Luke for a good minute, then turned and headed for the tent.

"Stay out here where I can see you!" Luke ordered. There was at least one rifle in the tent, most likely, and a man with that kind of temper didn't need to be close to a lethal weapon right then. "Go sit on the tailgate of my truck."

Buckley turned and headed toward Luke's truck.

"You boys go sit on that log," Luke said, pointing to a log near their rock fire ring.

Luke followed Buckley to the truck and opened the back door. Jack jumped out and started looking around. The dog had always been able to sense trouble, and he'd gotten a full whiff of it, even if he'd been in the vehicle.

"It's okay," Luke said to Jack. "Go say hello to the boys over there."

Jack loved kids, and as soon as he saw where Luke was pointing, he ran over and started sniffing Ryker. It was the first time Luke had seen the kid smile since he'd pulled into the camp.

"What's his name?" Ranger yelled over to Luke.

"Jack," Luke said.

"Can we give him a cookie?" Ryker asked.

"Only if you want him to be your friend for life," Luke said.

He watched as the younger of the two boys dashed into the tent and came out with some kind of cookie. It didn't matter to Jack what kind it was; he gobbled it up. Then Ryker ran in and came out with another cookie and told Jack to sit. The yellow dog quickly obliged, and the kid gave him a treat.

Ranger started for the tent one more time, and Luke called out, "That's enough. He'll be so fat, he won't be able to keep up with me."

The boy frowned but then looked at Jack and took off running down a trail. Jack followed. Ryker did too. It was good to see boys being boys.

Buckley had simmered down some, and when Luke asked him to help cut the elk down from the meat pole, he stood to help.

"Are you really hurting that bad for meat?" Luke asked as they walked toward the elk.

"Yessir," Buckley said. "I'm not proud of what we done, but I lost my job when they shut down the mill, and my wife, bless her heart, works as a waitress, but it's been hard making ends meet. Those two boys and the daughter about eat us down to nothin'. Not to mention them growing outta their clothes every six months."

Luke stopped and thought about it for a minute. Finally, he said, "Listen, here is what I'm going to do. I'll let you keep the elk. But I still have to give you a citation. It's up to the judge to decide what will happen with your license situation. I'm going to keep an eye on you, and if you have any more infractions, I'll come calling. You don't want that because I can make it so you won't be hunting until your kids have kids of their own."

A short time later, with Jack and the boys back at the fire ring, Luke handed Buckley the ticket.

"Thanks for not taking the elk," Buckley said. "I really do appreciate it." Then he said to his sons, "You boys thank Officer McCain here."

Both boys said "Thank you" in unison. Then Ryker said to Luke, "Do you think I could be a game warden someday?"

"Anything is possible," Luke said. "Work hard in school. Be good. You can be anything you want."

"I'd like to have a dog like Jack," Ranger Buckley said, rubbing Jack's ears.

Luke just smiled and said, "C'mon, boy."

Jack ran over to Luke and followed him to the truck.

As he was walking away, Luke heard Buckley say, "Okay, boys, let's get camp torn down and the elk in the back of the truck. We got some butcherin' to do when we get home."

Luke loaded Jack into the back seat, and then he jumped into the truck. He rolled down his window and watched the Buckleys hauling stuff out of the tent. Ryker looked over, and Luke waved as he backed out onto the road. The boy, arms full of sleeping bags, just smiled.

CHAPTER 25

Word of the Renegades' wolf-killing syndicate hit social media early the next morning. Covington had contacted the fixer, who contacted the hacker and told him to put the information out about the dark website with numbers on how many wolves had been killed by the group.

"Throw those two photos you sent to me in with it," Covington said to the fixer. "That'll prove it is all the truth. And say that one of the members, a man up by Okanogan, has already been killed as punishment for poaching all those wolves."

Deke Price saw the post almost immediately after it showed up on Facebook. He looked at the photos for longer than he needed to, then he called Trey Creech.

"What's up?" Creech said.

Price didn't know if his friend had been crying, but he knew he was grieving for Artie Miller. His voice was quiet and sad.

"We got an issue. It's related to Artie's death. Can I come over?"

"Yeah, give me a half hour," Creech said and clicked off.

Price took the next twenty minutes looking around the internet at social media sites. The story and the photos were everywhere. The photos of Creech and Miller with the dead wolf still had the happy faces blocking their identities, as did the one of the man with the wolf that had been posted just before the site was hacked.

"How in the hell did they know that was Trey and Artie?" Price muttered to himself.

The more he searched, the more postings he found of the photos with the story about the Renegades.

*　*　*

Luke McCain found out about the Renegades around the same time. He was just about to head to the office when his phone buzzed. He looked at the caller ID and saw it was Cody Stephens, the wildlife officer from Spokane.

"Hey, Cody, what's going on?"

"Have you seen the story on the internet about the group that's been poaching wolves in Washington?"

"No, what?"

Stephens went on to tell Luke about a group called the Renegades running a dark website that had evidently been recruiting people to purposely poach wolves.

"They posted photos of their kills," Stephens said. "And cheered anyone who successfully killed a wolf."

"Does it say how many people were part of this group?" Luke asked.

"The post said there were at least twenty members of the group, and although they only posted two photos of dead wolves, they claim to have killed over thirty."

"That might account for the drop in the populations up in your area," Luke said.

"It might," Stephens said. "And here's the kicker. The post claims that even though the faces of the hunters in the photos have been blocked out, members of the Renegades have been identified, and they are going to be taken out. They say they have already killed one of the Renegades."

"What?"

"They claim that a man shot up outside of Okanogan the other night was a member of the Renegades."

"Did you check it out?"

"There was a young man, name of Arthur Miller, aged twenty-three, who was killed night before last in what the sheriff there thought might be a road rage incident. But I have no way of knowing if he was a member of the group."

"How was he killed?"

"Close range, small-caliber bullet to the forehead, just above the bridge of the nose."

Luke immediately thought of Rafe Gibson. The skinny man found up in the Gold Creek area had died the exact same way. He didn't think Gibson had been a wolf killer, or any kind of a killer for that matter, but two men killed a week apart in the same way might be more than a coincidence.

"Is someone following up with the dead guy's family to see if he might be part of the group?" Luke asked.

"Not sure," Stephens said. "But I'm guessing they will now that this information has been released. I'll check with the Okanogan County sheriff."

"When you do, ask if you can get the ballistic report on the bullet that killed the man there."

"Will do," Stephens said. "You think you might have a match somewhere?"

Luke told him about Rafe Gibson and how he had died the same way as the man up in Okanogan.

"Probably a coincidence," Luke said. "But it doesn't take much time to double-check it."

When he was through with the call from Stephens, Luke called Bill Williams.

"Hey, Rifleman, find any more dead guys?" Williams said.

"No, but have you seen the deal on the internet this morning about some syndicate that has been out there poaching wolves?"

Williams told Luke he hadn't seen the story yet, so Luke gave him a quick recap.

"The guy that was supposedly killed as retribution for the wolves that were poached took a small-caliber bullet in the forehead, just like the guy we found last week," Luke explained.

"You think that man, what was his name, Gibbons, was a wolf poacher?" Williams asked.

"Gibson," Luke said. "No, I don't. But it's worth checking out. Did you get the ballistics from the bullet that killed Gibson?"

"Yes," Williams said. "It was a twenty-two long rifle, probably fired from a pistol."

"I'm trying to run down the ballistics from the bullet that killed the guy up north," Luke said. "You might have better luck. Okanogan County is investigating."

"I know the sheriff up there," Williams said. "I'll give him a call and see what I can get. If it's a match, I'll give you a shout."

Luke told him thanks and was about to hang up when Williams said, "Hey, Luke, thanks for the tip. We were getting nowhere on that shooting."

"No problem," Luke said. "Let me know what you find out."

* * *

Trey Creech was sitting in a rocking chair on the porch of his father's house when Deke Price pulled in.

"How you doing, buddy?" Price asked as he climbed the stairs to the porch.

"I've been better," Creech said. "I still can't believe Artie is gone."

There was a long silence as Creech stared off into the gray autumn sky. Then he said, "Do you think whoever shot Artie was trying to kill me?"

"I think he was trying to kill both of you," Price said.

Creech turned his head quickly and looked at Price. "What? Are you serious?"

Price told Creech about the stuff that had hit the internet about the Renegades, along with the photo of him and Miller.

"They said they were going to kill all the members of the group," Price said.

"How could they know it was us in the photo? Our faces were covered."

"I don't know," Price said. "I still have no idea how they hacked the site. Even I don't know the identities of the other members. So, I don't think they have that information."

"Well, they figured something out," Creech said. "Artie killed a wolf, and that was him and me in the photo with the wolf, and now Artie is dead."

"I know, I know," Price said, shaking his head.

Creech didn't say anything.

"You think we should tell the sheriff about all of this?" Price asked.

"No, I don't," Creech said. "I'll just lay low until they find this lunatic, and we'll be fine."

"What if they don't find him?" Price said. "I don't want to be looking over my shoulder for the rest of my life."

"What do you have to worry about?" Creech said. "You didn't shoot a wolf. That's not you in any of those photos."

"But it was my site on my computer," Price said. "I tell you, whoever hacked us is good. I'm thinking I might just head back home to Oregon."

"Just wait for a little while," Creech said. "I'll try to figure something out."

*　*　*

Covington spent the morning on the internet. He was loving it. His post about the Renegades and the photos of the wolf-killers were everywhere. The comments were running about seventy-five, twenty-five, in his favor. People were appalled that there was a group of hunters or whoever out there purposely poaching the wolves. Some were even happy that one of the poachers had been killed.

"Now you know what the wolves felt like," one commenter wrote. Which made no sense to another commenter, who wrote below the first commenter's comment: *If the dude is dead, he can't feel anything, dumbshit.*

A faction of other commenters was glad the wolves had been killed. They felt bad for the ranchers who were losing their livestock to the wolves. Others were happy to see the wolves gone because they wouldn't be killing all the deer and elk in the woods.

Every post Covington found on the Renegades, or the shooting in Okanogan County, had people commenting.

One of the stories he read in Spokane's *Spokesman-Review* newspaper was a report on the shooting death of one Arthur Miller, age twenty-three, of Okanogan. The report had a few facts about the shooting, but in the end, it sounded like the police weren't close to finding the killer. Okanogan sheriff Walt Cooper was quoted in the story as saying, "We know the person who shot Mr. Miller was driving a dark-colored Suburban or similar SUV."

Covington was happy to see the police really had no clue it was him who had killed the man, but when he first read Miller's name, he was a little disappointed. He had hoped to kill Eli Creech III. He had not succeeded, but the death of the other man had served a purpose. The members of the Renegades were put on notice. Any one of them could be next.

Chapter 26

The only person in the world who should have been worried that he might be the next member of the Renegades to be targeted was James Henricks. But he wasn't. He hadn't looked at the internet since he'd discovered the Renegades' website had vanished.

He had taken the wolf to the Columbia River and disposed of the carcass. He was just going to forget about the whole thing and go about his normal daily business.

Henricks did think about Duke and Annabelle, though, especially in the morning when he went out to do chores. The happy hounds were his constant companions as he fed and watered the horses, scattered grain for the chickens, brought in firewood, and tinkered around the place. In the winter, they would lie by the fireplace and occasionally come over to have their ears scratched or bellies rubbed.

He had gotten some semblance of revenge by taking out the big male wolf in the pack that had killed his dogs. He felt no remorse over that. But it still didn't bring his dogs back.

Henricks had just taken a second armload of dried, split tamarack into the house and was coming out the door to go grab another load when he saw a big black SUV coming up the county road. He wasn't positive, but he thought it might be the same rig he'd seen at his mailbox a few days before.

Something in his gut said to stay inside, so he backed back into the house and closed the door. He kept binoculars on the windowsill over the kitchen sink to watch birds and check out the deer and elk that wandered through his place occasionally, so he went to grab them. Looking through a crack in the closed curtains in the front room window, Henricks watched the black rig with his field glasses as it approached his driveway and stopped at the mailbox.

The rig was black and shiny and had fancy, narrow, square headlights. He concentrated on the driver's window to see if he could make out anything on the person driving, but the windows were tinted just enough that all he could see was a reflection.

The rig sat at the mailbox idling, and Henricks had the feeling he was being watched, even though he knew from that distance no one could see him looking through the narrow opening in the drapes. Still, it gave him the creeps, so he went to the gun safe in his bedroom, punched a code into the keypad in the center of the safe door, and opened it up. He grabbed a rifle, the same one he had used to kill the wolf, and headed back to the front room.

When he looked out the crack in the drapes again, the black SUV was gone.

∗ ∗ ∗

Covington decided he would drive by James Henricks' house one more time. If the man was home, he was prepared to drive in and kill him. But as he pulled up to the mailbox at the end of the driveway, it again looked like no one was home.

The horses were in the loafing shed, the chickens he had seen pecking around in the yard were nowhere to be seen, and Henricks' pickup truck was gone.

He sat for another minute or two in the idling rig. Seeing nothing more to entice him to drive to the house, Covington decided he would come back later. Sooner or later, the wolf killer would be home, and then he would pay for his crime.

* * *

Luke had spent two hours at the office, dealing with the mundane but necessary parts of his job. Answering emails, returning calls, filing reports—including the one on his contact with Cliff Buckley and his sons.

One of the calls he returned was to Jim Kingsbury, who had left him a message earlier that morning about having information on some elk poachers.

"I got all the stuff you need to bag these guys," Kingsbury's voice said on the voicemail. "Call me back."

Kingsbury, who Luke had known for years, was a gentleman who lived in Naches and was seen most of the time hanging around with another old-timer by the name Frank Dugdale. The two fought like an old married couple, and Luke wondered why they spent so much time together.

As he was dialing Kingsbury's number, Luke wondered what shirt the man had on today. Kingsbury was well-known for wearing t-shirts with funny or poignant sayings on them. In the time Luke had known him, he had never seen the man wear the same t-shirt twice.

"Hello?" Kingsbury's voice crackled and bubbled on the end of the line.

"Yeah, Jim, this is Luke McCain. You called?"

"Yes, I did," Kingsbury said, and then his voice got really wonky.

"Are you in a submarine?" Luke asked.

"No, why would you ask?"

"Because you sound like you're underwater."

"It's the damn cell service out here. Let me call you back."

"Call me on my cell phone," Luke said. "I'm just heading out the door."

Three minutes later, Luke's cell phone started buzzing, and he switched it to the Bluetooth in his truck. Kingsbury's voice was better, but only a little.

"You found some poachers?" Luke asked when he answered the call.

"Yep, I did. And I want my bonus points," Kingsbury said.

Washington State offered extra special hunt bonus points for turning in hunters who had broken the law.

"You're getting a little ahead of yourself," Luke said. "First, let's see what you got, and then if we catch them and charge them, then you'll get your bonus points."

"I better," Kingsbury said. "I'm getting too old to have to wait much longer to get drawn for big bull elk."

"I'm headed your way," Luke said. "You can tell me all about it when you don't sound like you're gargling."

"Meet me at the hardware store in Naches," Kingsbury said. "I gotta pick up a new toilet seat, the one I have now busted and . . ."

As soon as Kingsbury took a breath, Luke said, "You're still underwater. See you there in fifteen." Then he clicked off.

During hunting seasons, especially during elk season, Luke and the other enforcement officers took plenty of calls from hunters in the field who said they'd witnessed one kind of game law infraction or another. Sometimes they turned out to be nothing, but other times they led to catching someone who had really wandered over the line. Luke wondered which one Kingsbury might offer up.

Luke spotted Kingsbury coming out of the ACE Hardware with a white toilet seat under his arm and a fishing pole in his hand.

"I thought you just needed a toilet seat," Luke said through the driver's side window as he pulled up next to Kingsbury.

Kingsbury was wearing a jacket, and so Luke couldn't see the shirt he had on.

"I needed the toilet seat, but I've had my eye on this pole for a while now. It's almost white fishing season, and this will be perfect."

"Let's go somewhere warm, where we can chat," Luke said.

They decided on the café up the road, and they were sitting in a booth in a matter of minutes. Luke kept looking at Kingsbury's shirt but could only see a piece of an old-style photo of someone's face.

The waitress came, and Luke ordered a hot chocolate. Kingsbury ordered coffee and a piece of pumpkin pie.

"It'll be Thanksgiving in a couple weeks," Luke said. "Won't you get plenty of pumpkin pie then?"

"I'd eat pumpkin pie on the fourth of July," Kingsbury said. "In fact, I have eaten it on the fourth of July."

"Where's that partner of yours?" Luke asked.

"You mean Dugdale?" Kingsbury said. "That damn dummy has gone and found himself a lady friend. Cripes. He never wants to go do nothing anymore."

Luke laughed. Kingsbury was definitely jealous of losing his best buddy to a woman.

"Maybe you should find a lady friend of your own," Luke said.

"Never again," Kingsbury said.

Luke waited for him to tell him more about his history with women, but Kingsbury changed the subject.

"So, you wanna hear about these elk poachers or not?"

"Sure, whatcha got?" Luke asked.

Kingsbury told him he was driving a road up on Bald Mountain when he spotted a small herd of elk feeding in a little meadow.

"It was right at daybreak," Kingsbury said. "I pulled over, put my spotting scope on my window mount, and checked 'em out."

He explained that he, like most elk hunters during the general season, had a tag only good for a spike elk but saw that the little group of elk was made up of only cows and calves. He said he took his spotting scope off the window and was about to drive on down the road when another vehicle coming up the road stopped and two guys bailed out and started shooting.

"Both guys started shooting, right from the road, neither of them in hunter orange, by the way," Kingsbury said. "I looked back at the elk and, of course, they were running into the trees."

"Okay," Luke said.

"There were nine elk in the meadow, and only six were running out. Do the math. Even if both of those idiots had cow tags, which I'm guessing they didn't, that's one elk too many."

Luke had investigated situations like this before. One hunter has a cow tag, but others in a group try to help the hunter fill it. When more than one starts shooting into a herd, often times more than one animal gets hit. It's a bad situation. Luke had had to euthanize wounded animals several times over the years, some from situations just like what Kingsbury had described.

"What happened next?" Luke asked.

"They went back to their truck, put on their hunter orange vests, and went out to where the elk had been."

"Did they see you?"

"Not until I started driving off."

"Did you see what they did when they got to the dead elk?"

"Yeah, they grabbed one by the back legs and started dragging it back toward their rig. After they stopped to take a breather, one of the guys went back to where the elk had been and was looking at something, but the grass was too tall, so I couldn't see if there were any other elk there."

"So, you're not positive they killed any others?"

"Hell yes, I'm positive. Do the math."

"When was this?" Luke asked.

"First thing this morning," Kingsbury said. "I tried to call you as soon as I had cell service, but it went to voicemail."

"Okay," Luke said, wondering why the man hadn't called his cell number to begin with. "Did you happen to get their vehicle license?"

"Yep," Kingsbury said and handed him a slip of paper with some letters and numbers written on it. "I'm sure it's right, but I was in a hurry. The two guys were watching me drive down the road and started walking at me when they saw me stop at their rig. So, I got outta there."

"What kind of vehicle was it?" Luke asked.

"An older blue Dodge Ram pickup, with the paint peeling on the hood."

CHAPTER 27

Luke wanted to get back up to Thorp to talk to James Henricks about the dead wolf, but the potential elk poaching that Kingsbury had just described took priority. If Kingsbury was right, and the men had killed more than one cow elk, he thought he might get there before they got the animals out of the field. That is, if they were going to take the other one, or ones, out.

Based on Kingsbury's description, he had a general idea where the shooting had taken place, but the man was willing to lead Luke to the site. So, Luke took him up on the offer.

Before they took off, Luke used the laptop in his truck to run the tag numbers Kingsbury had given him, but the numbers came back to a white Chevy Tahoe owned by a Gretchen Hayes of Ellensburg. He figured Kingsbury, probably in a hurry to get down the road, had read or written the license number incorrectly.

Something about an older blue Dodge Ram with faded paint seemed familiar, but nothing was coming to Luke at the moment. He had probably seen dozens of Dodge Rams with the paint fading. It was an issue the company had for a few years. Still, it was nagging at him. Who had he dealt with recently that had a truck like that?

Luke followed Kingsbury up Bald Mountain, and once they hit a road that ran the ridge, they drove west along it for a few miles. As they drove, Luke looked into the various elk camps they passed but saw no blue Dodge pickups parked at any of them.

Kingsbury turned onto a green dot spur road, and after a half mile, he stopped. Luke got out and walked up to Kingsbury's open driver-side window.

"This is it," Kingsbury said, pointing out the passenger side of the windshield. "The elk were right up there in that little clearing."

"Okay," Luke said. "By the way, that plate number you gave me was invalid."

"Invalid, what's that mean?"

"It means it didn't go to a blue Dodge. It belongs to a white Chevrolet owned by some lady in Ellensburg."

"I swear I wrote it down right," Kingsbury said.

"We'll figure it out," Luke said. "I'm going to go out there and check to see if there is any sign that more than one elk was killed."

"Want me to go with ya?"

"No, hang here, and when I get out there, help direct me to make sure I'm where you saw the elk standing."

"Will do," Kingsbury said. "How long will it take for me to get my bonus points?"

"First things first," Luke said as he walked back to his truck and grabbed his backpack.

He didn't need any help finding the spot because he quickly found marks where a dead animal had been recently pulled out of the field. Luke followed the drag marks to a fresh gut pile. He was standing and looking at it when Kingsbury called out.

"You're not there yet! Gotta go another forty yards."

Luke looked and saw where the elk had been dragged before it had been gutted and followed those drag marks to a second gut pile. Kingsbury was right. Two elk had been killed.

"Find it?" Kingsbury shouted from the road.

Luke just raised his hand with a thumb up above his head.

Then he spotted the third dead elk, thirty feet from the second gut pile. Whether the two men Kingsbury had seen shoot into the herd had cow tags or not, the third elk had been poached.

He pulled out his phone and took photos of the two gut piles, some of the drag marks, and the dead elk.

Since the third elk had only been dead for four hours, there was a chance the meat would still be salvageable, so Luke rolled up his sleeves and went to work field dressing it. He was just starting to work on the animal when Kingsbury walked out to him.

"Found out I was right, didn't ya?"

"Yep," Luke said. "Two gut piles and this dead cow. Here, give me a hand."

Kingsbury jumped in and grabbed a leg and held it while Luke worked on removing the entrails. When they finished, Luke saw that Kingsbury had taken off his coat. He was wearing an olive-colored shirt with an old-style photo of the face of a bearded Army general from back around the Civil War days. Luke recognized the man in the photo. It was General George Custer. Under Custer's face, there was a caption in dark brown letters that read, "I Like Our Odds"—General George Custer, June 24, 1876

Luke chuckled.

"I'm going to get my bonus points, aren't I?" Kingsbury asked.

"It's looking better all the time," Luke said.

"I knew it. That damn Dugdale could be getting some points too. I'da split 'em with him if he'da been with me. But nooo, he had to go do something with that lady friend of his."

Luke chuckled again and then said, "Come on, help me drag this thing to the road. I need to get it to the butcher."

It took some doing, but they got the dead elk to the road.

Luckily, some hunters came along and jumped out of their Jeep to help drag the elk and load it into the bed of Luke's truck.

"What happened?" one of the hunters asked as they were getting it to the truck.

"Got a report some guys shot into a group of elk," Luke said. "They left this cow to rot."

"Why would anyone do that?" another man in the group asked.

"Who knows," Luke said. "But I think the meat is still good. We'll get it butchered and donated to the mission."

He asked the hunters if they had seen a blue Dodge Ram around the area, and one of the guys said, "Yeah, about thirty of them. You know elk season, there's rigs driving these roads constantly, and every fifth truck is a Dodge."

"Any this morning with elk legs sticking up over the sides?"

They all thought about it for a few seconds and then shook their heads.

Luke gave one of the men his card and said, "If you happen to see an older blue Dodge, faded paint on the hood, with an elk or two in the back, take the license plate numbers and give me a call."

"Don't want to get anyone in trouble that doesn't deserve it," the man holding the card said.

"Neither do I, and it won't," Luke said. "But it might help us catch the guys who poached at least one elk here today."

The hunters climbed into their Jeep, and Kingsbury got into his pickup.

"Thanks for your help, Jim," Luke said, tapping the open window frame. "I'll let you know when I catch these guys."

"And you'll get me my bonus points?"

"Yes, I'll make sure you get your bonus points."

"Good," Kingsbury said and giggled. "Then I'll rub old Dugdale's nose in it."

Kingsbury was still laughing when he put his truck into gear and pulled away from Luke.

On his way to the butcher shop, Luke thought about the elk

shooting. It was an unfortunate situation, but it happened. Guys—and it was always men, never women in his experience—got too excited and let the moment get the better of them. Frustration, greed, or who knows what else took over, and they shot when they shouldn't.

Luke wanted to drive around the area to see if he could locate the blue Dodge, but it was more important to get the elk to the butcher. There, they would skin the animal and let it hang for a few days before cutting it into roasts, steaks, and processing the rest into hamburger. An animal the size of an elk would provide a couple hundred pounds of lean, healthy meat for the kitchens that fed the needy.

After he dropped off the elk, Luke again looked up the license number Kingsbury had given him. The plates belonged to a rig owned by Gretchen Hayes in Ellensburg. He ran the name and address and came up with a telephone number. He punched the phone number into his cell and listened for the ring on the truck's Bluetooth.

After two rings, a woman's voice said, "Hello?"

"Ms. Hayes?"

"Yes, who is this?"

"My name is Luke McCain. I'm an enforcement officer with the Department of Fish and Wildlife."

"Okay," Hayes said. "What did he do now?"

"Who is 'he,' ma'am?"

"My deadbeat husband," Hayes said. "Or I should say my deadbeat ex-husband."

"Well, I'm not sure he has done anything," Luke said. "But a license plate that is supposed to be on your Chevy Tahoe was spotted on a blue Dodge Ram."

"That son-of-a-bitch," Hayes said. "I noticed my plates were missing a couple of days ago. I don't drive that car often, so I didn't say anything to anyone."

"Does he own a blue Dodge pickup?"

"No, but one of his deadbeat buddies has one. Name of Rafe Gibson."

That's where he knew the blue Dodge with the faded hood from. Rafe Gibson had been driving it the evening back in September when Luke had caught him coming back to pick up Max Tucker's rifle.

"Rafe Gibson? About five foot ten, blue eyes with sandy brown hair? Kinda skinny?" Luke asked.

"You mean kinda skinny like he looks like he just got out of a refugee camp?" Hayes said. "That'd be him."

"Did you know Mr. Gibson died a week or so ago?" Luke asked.

There was a long pause, then Hayes said, "No, I didn't. How'd he die?"

"Well, he didn't starve to death," Luke said. "He was murdered."

"Ah, hell," Hayes said. "And you think Zach had something to do with it?"

"Zach? Is that your husband's name?" Luke asked.

"Ex-husband. A real deadbeat," Hayes said. "Yeah, Zachory Taylor, like our twelfth president. Who would name their kid after a president?"

"So, Hayes is your maiden name?"

"Yeah, never took his last name. Never should have married him. I knew it, but still . . . well, you know."

Luke didn't know. He never knew why people married someone they shouldn't have.

"So, any idea how he might have ended up with Rafe Gibson's pickup?" Luke asked.

"No clue. They worked together down at that truck place in Yakima for a while. Maybe he borrowed it from him then?"

"Mr. Gibson left that job two months ago," Luke said. "Does your, um . . . does Mr. Taylor still work there?"

"I don't know, but I would guess that he doesn't. Never could keep a job very long. It's part of the whole deadbeat thing he has going on."

"How about guns, does he own any pistols? Specifically, a twenty-two?"

"He had a whole passel of guns when we were married, but I wouldn't know a twenty-two from a howitzer."

"Has he been to your place recently?"

"Not that I know of, but if my license plates are on Rafe's blue truck, then he had to come by here sometime."

"I'm not positive it is Mr. Gibson's truck," Luke said. "But your license plates were seen on a blue Dodge pickup this morning, and the people in the truck are wanted for poaching at least one elk."

More silence, then Hayes said, "Sounds about right."

"You know how I can reach Mr. Taylor?"

"He ain't a mister. He's a deadbeat."

Then she gave Luke the last phone number she had for Taylor. Luke thanked her for her time and information.

"If you see that son-of-a-bitch, tell him I want my license plates back, or I'm gunna turn him in for stealing them."

"If he's the one who killed those elk, he'll be in a whole lot more trouble than stealing your plates," Luke said.

After he ended the call with Gretchen Hayes, Luke called Bill Williams, the YSO deputy.

"Hey, Luke," Williams said, disregarding his normal habit of calling Luke the Rifleman. "What's going on?"

"I'm following up on a poaching incident and have come across a weird connection to the Gibson fella who was shot and dumped up by Gold Creek."

"You mean different than the possible connection to the man killed up by Okanogan?" Williams asked.

"Yes," Luke said. "The guy who we suspect was involved in the poaching deal was likely driving Rafe Gibson's truck. He stole license plates from his ex-wife's Tahoe and put them on a blue Dodge Ram, just like the truck Gibson was driving at the time of his murder."

"Did you tell the wife about the murder?"

"Yes, I did."

"What did she think?"

"She says her ex is a deadbeat. It sounded like she believed he could be an elk poacher, but I didn't ask her if she thought he could kill someone."

"I guess I should talk to her," Williams said. "By the way, we're still waiting on the ballistics to see if the bullet that killed Gibson matched the bullet that killed the guy up north."

"Probably a long shot," Luke said. "Give the lady a call. Her name is Gretchen Hayes. Lives in Ellensburg. Her ex-husband's name is Zachory Taylor."

"Like the president?"

"Yep," Luke said. "Good luck."

Williams said, "You too," and he was gone.

That business finished, Luke pointed his truck to the freeway. He was going to catch up with James Henricks to have a little chat about dropping the wolf into the Columbia River if it was the last thing he did today.

CHAPTER 28

With the colder November weather already here, and possible snow in the forecast, Henricks had parked his Nissan pickup in the shed the night before. He would never know it, but it may have saved his life.

If he had seen the big black SUV pull up to his mailbox yet again, he might have become worried. But he had been at his desk in the back room, paying bills, so the black rig came and went unnoticed.

Peter Covington was ticked that Henricks hadn't been home and decided he would come back later in the day, after the man returned from work, if that is where he went when he was gone.

Back at his cabin at Cle Elum Lake, Covington turned on his computer and went out to the various social media sites he followed.

The story of the man murdered in Okanogan was everywhere. The wolf-loving anti-hunters were elated to hear someone had had the fortitude and courage to kill a known wolf poacher.

The wolf-haters were just as outraged about the situation. Killing a person who might have been involved in a wolf killing made just about as much sense as killing a doctor who was suspected of doing abortions, they said.

You are insane if you believe wolves are more important than humans, several people wrote in posts on the various sites.

"They're more important to me," Covington said to himself with a smile. "And I'm not insane, or maybe I am." He took a sip of his top-shelf Scotch and kept reading.

The two photos, the one of the two men with the dead wolf, and the other of the man he knew was James Henricks with a second poached wolf, were everywhere as well. The happy face emojis still covered the men's faces in the photos. People speculated on who they might be.

I think the guy on the left was that Miller dude who was killed in Okanogan, one poster said. Others thought Miller was the man on the right, and some believed it was neither of the men.

Covington looked at the photo of the two men with the wolf. The man on the left was the one holding the dead wolf's head up. He could just envision the man smiling, like he was so happy he'd taken the life of such an amazing creature. It about made him ill.

He stared at the photo of the man on the left and said, "I hope that was you!"

Then he started thinking about the man in the second photo. The hatred for him was even greater. He was positive, based on the information he had received from the fixer, that James Henricks was the man in the second photo. He had to die. He was going to die. Covington could feel his face go hot and the muscles in his neck tighten.

After several more sips of the Scotch to settle him down, Covington pulled up Google Earth and tapped Henricks' address into the search bar. A few seconds later, he was looking straight down on the wolf killer's small ranch house, with the shop, shed, and other outbuildings along the long driveway from the county road.

He studied the photo, zooming in and then zooming out. He looked at the terrain and the foliage on the back side of the house. Then he searched down the county road and up the county road. He found an old two-track road that led off the county road about a half mile from Henricks' house.

Covington wasn't in great shape, but he believed he could walk that far, even if he had to hack through the potentially thick brush and trees that covered some of the ground on either side of Henricks' property.

He considered taking a rifle to kill Henricks with a long-range shot. It would be easier with potentially less chance of getting caught by Henricks himself or someone else. But he wanted to let the man know the reason he was being killed. He wanted to look Henricks in the eyes and say, "This is for the beautiful wolf you killed." Then he would pull the trigger and be done with it.

Once Henricks was dead, and his body was discovered, Covington would tell the fixer to put out a second post that another member of the Renegades had been executed as reparations for the wolf he'd killed.

Two killings should do it, he guessed. Seeing another member die would certainly put enough fear in the other members that they would cease and desist.

And if it didn't? Well, there was still Eli Creech III, the man he had originally gone after up in Okanogan. He deserved to die as well, and Covington would have no problem taking him out if he had to.

But back to the task at hand. He would get to the two-track road around four o'clock and be waiting at Henricks' house when he arrived home from work. The surprise alone should create enough time to tell the man what he needed to hear, shoot him, and be gone.

* * *

Luke arrived at Henricks' house at ten after three o'clock. He drove up the driveway, past the horses feeding in the pasture, and the chickens scratching and pecking in the yard. He was looking at the house when he saw someone, presumably Henricks, look out the front window.

The door was opening when Luke stepped up on the porch. Even though he had done this very thing a hundred times or more, it was still always a little scary not knowing if the person was coming out the door with a shotgun or some other lethal weapon they were ready to use.

James Henricks was unarmed. In fact, he looked beaten, and maybe a little relieved.

"Mr. Henricks?" Luke asked.

"Yes, sir. Jim Henricks. Call me Jim."

"My name is Luke McCain. I'm an enforcement officer with the Department of Fish and Wildlife. I'm guessing you know why I'm here?"

"Yessir, I do," Henricks said. "Or I think I do."

"It's about the wolf body you dumped into the Columbia River a few days ago," Luke said.

Henricks smiled.

"Listen, Officer McCain," Henricks said.

Luke interrupted. "Please call me Luke."

"Okay, not that I don't deserve whatever I have coming my way, but I'd like to tell you my story. And I'd like for you to tell me how you found me."

"Fair enough," Luke said. "Let's hear the story."

"Would you like to sit down?" Henricks asked. "This might take a bit. Can I get you a Pepsi or some coffee?"

"You know what, a Pepsi sounds good. I've had a busy day, and a jolt of sugar and caffeine would be welcome right about now."

Henricks came back into the front room two minutes later, carrying a sixteen-ounce bottle of Pepsi for Luke and a mug of coffee for himself. He also had a framed eight-by-ten photo that he handed to Luke.

"Those are, or were, my pride and joy," Henricks said. "Bluetick Coonhounds. Duke and Annabelle. The wolf I killed and dumped into the river was part of the pack that killed my hounds."

Luke was looking at the photo. They looked like great dogs. He looked up at Henricks and could see tears had formed in his eyes. Then he rubbed them away with the heel of his right hand.

"Sorry," Henricks said. "They were my only family."

Luke said, "I'm sorry for your loss, Jim. I have a big old yellow Lab that is just like a child to me and my wife, so I understand."

Henricks went through the whole story. Losing the dogs, tracking their collars, finding their mangled bodies, packing them home, and burying them out back.

"I was so mad, all I could see was red," Henricks said. "Those damned wolves had been around before. They were after my colt out there in the pasture one morning. I shot in the air and scared them off. But I figured they would be back, so I called your department, and Officer Hargraves came out. He told me in not so many words that if the wolves came back, I'd be justified to shoot them to protect my livestock."

Luke knew that's exactly what Hargraves would tell someone. And, truth be told, so would he.

"So, the next time I heard them up on the hill after they killed my hounds, I grabbed my deer rifle and went hunting. I did it for Duke and Annabelle. I knew it wasn't right, but it's also not right for them to hunt down my dogs and kill them when there's deer and elk around."

He told Luke how he'd stalked the wolves and had the elk run right by him, with the wolves in hot pursuit.

"I shot the big male as it ran by," Henricks said. "Then, like an idiot, I posted the photo on a website that was for people who were purposefully hunting wolves."

"The Renegades?" Luke asked.

"Yes, sir, but how did you know?"

"It's been all over the internet, on all the social media sites. You haven't seen it?"

"I'm not much of a social media guy," Henricks said. "Rarely on the computer or watch TV. I might catch a Seahawks game on Sunday, but other than that, I'm either tinkering around here or reading."

"Well, the proverbial shit hit the fan a couple of days ago," Luke said. "As I understand it, someone hacked the Renegades' website and posted some photos in a bunch of places. One man, who supposedly was a member of the Renegades, has already been killed."

"What?" Henricks said and then paused for a minute. "That's why they took the site down. Someone hacked them."

It wasn't a question. It was him figuring out what had happened.

"You should check out the photos," Luke said. "The faces of the hunters were covered, but the wolves weren't. And based on the wolf that we fished out of the river the other day, I'd say one of the photos being shared around is the one you posted."

"I should've never posted that photo," Henricks said. "And I should have never dumped the wolf in the river. But I still have no regrets about shooting it."

"I understand," Luke said again. "Why did you dump it in the river?"

"I got scared after the Renegades' site disappeared. I thought you guys, or the Feds, may have discovered it. I wanted to get rid of the wolf right now, and the river seemed like a safe option. Dump it there, and no one would ever link it to me. But you did. How?"

"Video cameras on the bridge," Luke said. "Cameras are everywhere anymore, and after a fisherman found the wolf floating downstream of the bridge and I saw it had been shot through the lungs, I guessed someone might have dumped it off the bridge."

Henricks was shaking his head.

Luke continued, "The guys at Department of Transportation found the video of you dumping the wolf, although it was a pretty bad video, and we couldn't see you or your truck's license plate. But they looked some more and found your truck coming back over the bridge a while later, and we were able to get the numbers. It was pretty easy to find you from there."

"Big brother, huh?" Henricks said.

"You'd be surprised how many lawbreakers we catch from video camera footage and social media posts," Luke said. "We have one person in Olympia who does nothing but monitor all the hunting and fishing sites."

"So, what do we do from here?" Henricks asked.

"Let's go to your computer and pull up some of the posts," Luke said. "I'm worried that if the one photo is of you and the wolf you killed, and I think it is, you might be in danger."

Henricks looked at Luke like he was kidding.

"You found me because of the bridge video," Henricks said. "How could someone without those connections figure out that was me in the photo when my face is covered?"

"I don't know," Luke said. "I'm a dummy when it comes to all that technical stuff. But they found the guy up in Okanogan, and they killed him. So far, no one has come out to say that the man with the dead wolf in the other photo wasn't a member of the Renegades."

In his back office, Henricks turned on his computer and pulled up one of the Washington hunting sites. Sure enough, there was the photo he'd taken after he'd dragged the dead wolf down into the yard. The numbers below the post said it had been viewed over seven thousand times, and there were well over two thousand comments.

"There's nothing there to tell anyone who I am or where I live," Henricks said, pointing at the photo on the screen.

"I would agree," Luke said. "But these people are good."

"Who are 'these people' anyway?" Henricks asked.

"No one seems to know," Luke said. "Obviously, they are pro-wolf people. Extremists, really, and maybe a little crazy if they believe killing humans who kill a wolf is the answer."

"What do you think I should do?" Henricks asked.

"I think I'd find a place to go where no one could find me," Luke said only half-kiddingly.

He looked at Henricks and could see that the man was thinking about something else. He ignored Luke's comment and said, "You know what, I've seen a big black SUV around here the past couple days. Twice, I saw it stop at my mailbox, and I got the feeling someone was trying to look in here."

Luke said, "Pull up one of the news stories about the man who was shot up in Okanogan. I'm pretty sure the police up there are looking for a black Suburban. Evidently, that is what the person who killed the guy was driving."

Henricks found the story from *The Spokesman-Review* and read it.

"I can't believe it," Henricks said, more to himself than Luke. "How did they find me?"

CHAPTER 29

Covington had struggled through some thick brush and brambles right after he'd parked his rig in the two-track road, but his plan to get to James Henricks' house was on schedule. He would get to the backside of the house and wait until dark. Then he'd move in on the wolf-killer and stop the man from ever murdering another one of his darling wolves.

He made it into a clearing with only some scratches on his face and hands and continued slowly down a game trail, working his way toward the ranch.

When he finally could see the house through the trees, he froze. Instead of seeing Henricks' silver truck parked in the driveway, there was a brown pickup with some kind of insignia on the door.

Covington pulled a small pair of binoculars out of his coat

pocket to take a closer look at the truck. The insignia said it was a Department of Fish and Wildlife police vehicle.

"Damn," Covington whispered to himself.

How had the game wardens found Henricks? Or maybe they hadn't found him. Henricks might have called them to discuss something else, possibly wolf problems? Whatever it was, having a cop at Henricks' house was not part of the plan.

As he worked through the problem, he saw three options on how to proceed. The first was not to proceed at all. He could just backtrack to his rig, through the scratchy brambles, and go home. He could come back tomorrow when the game warden wasn't there.

The second option, if the warden stayed until dark, would be to go in and kill them both.

Or, option three, he could wait out the warden and move in on Henricks after the officer left.

He mulled over all three and decided killing a cop was never part of his plan. He believed he could do it, but it would make him public enemy number one. He had people all over cheering him for killing the other wolf-killer. The world would hate him for killing a police officer.

Covington felt strongly he was never going to be identified as the person who'd killed the man in Okanogan. And if he played his cards right, he could be in the house, kill Henricks, and be back out, and no one would ever know he was the killer.

Killing a cop was something entirely different. From what he had seen and heard, law enforcement never gave up on hunting down someone who'd murdered a fellow officer. And when they found them, it never ended well for the cop-killer.

His options changed as he sat contemplating them. Covington was watching the house when a tall man with dark hair and wearing a tan coat walked to the brown pickup, got in, started it up, drove down Henricks' driveway, and turned onto the county road.

*　*　*

Luke spent more time talking with James Henricks than he had planned. The man's story about losing his two hounds to the pack of wolves was compelling, for sure.

As he left Henricks' driveway, he thought about what he might do if it had been Jack that had been attacked and killed by the wolves. He felt his hands tensing on the steering wheel just thinking about it. It must have been horrible for Henricks to find the two dogs that had been part of his life since they were eight weeks old ravaged by the pack of wolves.

Luke could definitely see himself wanting some sort of revenge if he had been in Henricks' shoes. Still, the law was the law. He didn't cite Henricks for anything but told him he may ultimately have to charge him with killing the endangered wolf. Luke told him he was going to explain the situation to his boss to see if there was anything he could do.

"That other officer, Hargraves, said I had a right to protect my livestock from the wolves," Henricks said after Luke told him he would try to help. "Those hounds were more than just animals to me; they were my only family."

Luke was thinking about the conversation he'd had with Henricks as he drove down the county road. Just by chance, he glanced up an overgrown two-track road and saw something out of place. He stopped his truck, backed up to get a better look, and spotted a shiny black rig parked about forty yards up the little road.

He parked his truck and walked in to where a black Lincoln Navigator was parked. He wrote down the license plate numbers and checked the doors. They were locked. Luke looked inside, cupping his hands around his eyes up against the glass to see better, and spotted a photo sitting on the center console. It was too dark to see the image clearly, so Luke pulled his flashlight off his utility belt and shined it through the window.

"Oh boy," Luke said when the light hit the photo. It was the exact photo he'd been looking at on Henricks' computer monitor just an hour before. It was the photo of Henricks, yellow happy face and all, with the dead, dark gray wolf. The wolf that had been the patriarch of the pack that had killed his two hounds.

Luke hustled back to his truck, jumped in, and radioed dispatch.

"This is Wildlife 148. I have a potential situation here. Need backup ASAP."

"Roger that, Wildlife 148. I'll contact Kittitas County and get someone coming your way immediately."

Luke gave the dispatcher his location and asked her to have the Kittitas deputy sheriff call him on his cell. He rattled off his phone number.

"Also, can you run this plate?" Luke asked and read the numbers off.

"Roger that."

Luke drove back to Henricks' place and was about to pull in the driveway when his cell phone rang.

"Yeah, this is McCain," Luke said.

"Hey, Luke, it's Hernandez. You got something serious going on up there?"

Alivia Hernandez was a long-time Kittitas County sheriff's deputy. Luke had worked with her several times before and was always impressed with her smarts and professionalism.

"Yeah, you on your way?"

"Rolling with lungs and lights," Hernandez said.

Luke had to think about that for a half second. He had never heard that one before. He explained as quickly as he could about James Henricks shooting the wolf and posting the photo on the dark web.

"I think this is the guy who shot that man up in Okanogan, and he's here to kill Henricks because he shot that wolf."

"I'm ten minutes away," Hernandez said.

Luke turned his headlights off and drove slowly up the driveway.

"I'm going to go check on Henricks, so I'll be out of my rig," Luke said. "Don't shoot me when you get here."

"I would never do that, McCain," Hernandez joked. "Too much paperwork."

Luke hung up, parked the rig well short of Henricks' house, grabbed his trusty Remington 870 pump shotgun, and started for the house. He stayed close to the fence and then crossed over the driveway to get behind the shed that sat just down from the bigger shop building.

Henricks had the porch light on, and Luke could see there was a light on in the front room as well, but other than that, it was darker than the inside of an old boot. His eyes were adjusting to the darkness, but it was still hard to see anything but a black curtain of trees behind Henricks' house. Luke searched through the darkness but saw nothing that told him someone was stalking the house.

* * *

Covington watched the game warden's brown truck disappear down the road and around the bend. The sun had set, and dusk was quickly descending. He shivered from the November cold in the growing darkness. And he shivered from the prospect of what he was about to do.

He wanted to go now, but the plan was for complete darkness, so he waited another ten minutes until he was shaking so badly he had to move. His fingers were numb, and so were his toes. Nighttime at his cabin at the lake hadn't been this cold. Or maybe it was, and he hadn't noticed. Especially after a few shots of Scotch.

He stood and was surprised that he was wobbly. He needed to get things under control if he was going to be successful. Covington pulled the Ruger out of the back of his pocket and held it in front of him.

He could tell by the glow on the grass that the front porch lights were on. But in the back of the house, it was still virtually pitch black. Only a sliver of light could be seen in the kitchen window between drawn curtains. There was a back door, but he guessed that no one out in these parts ever came to the back door. He would need to go knock on the front door and be prepared when Henricks came to answer it.

Knock, knock, knock, the door would open, and Covington would blast the wolf-killer right in the forehead. That was the plan.

No time like the present, so he walked around the side of the house and up onto the porch. He knocked lightly and waited.

Three seconds later, a voice inside said, "Come on in!"

This was interesting, Covington thought. What should he do? He could wait for Henricks to come to the door, or he could go into the house. He decided to go in. He turned the doorknob, pushed the door open slowly, pistol at the ready, and moved in.

Seeing no one in the hall, Covington closed the door behind him and moved slowly forward.

He never saw or heard the brown truck pull back into the driveway behind him.

Chapter 30

James Henricks had taken Luke's warning to heart, and as soon as the game warden left, he went to his bedroom to throw a few clothes and necessities into a duffel. He had a buddy who lived in Vancouver, and he knew he could shack up with him, at least for a night or two.

He planned on throwing out a bale of hay for the horses, and with a full 150-gallon heated stock tank, there should be enough water for two or three days.

The chickens, well, they would just have to fend for themselves. He'd throw a couple scoops of grain out in the yard in the dark, and they'd have plenty for the next day.

He was at his gun safe, pulling a Glock 45 pistol out to throw in the bag, when there was a knock on the front door.

Henricks thought about it for a couple seconds and then figured it had to be the game warden returning to tell him something. So, he yelled, "Come on in!"

He waited to hear Luke say something, but there was nothing. He heard the front door close and some soft footsteps. Henricks had watched in the movies where someone in a house said "hello" when they thought they heard something, or when someone was hiding. Every time he saw it happen, he thought how stupid the people were. He wanted to say hello but resisted the urge.

The Glock was loaded, as were all his guns in the safe, to save time if a coyote or a raccoon was in the chicken coop. So, the gun was ready if he needed it. Instead of saying something, or even moving, he waited and listened.

The old hardwood floors of the ranch house told him someone was coming his way. The occasional and almost imperceptible creek or crack told him where the person was.

Henricks waited just inside his bedroom door, and in a few seconds a man slowly stepped through into the poorly lit room. The man had a revolver in his hand, but he wasn't ready to use it. Henricks thought for an instant about shooting the guy. Instead, like he'd seen a thousand times on TV, he hit the man in the back of the head with the butt of the pistol.

Unfortunately, it didn't work like it does on TV. When he struck the man on the head, it knocked the pistol out of his own hand. And more importantly, the man didn't fall out cold onto the floor. He staggered and started to turn, raising the pistol to shoot.

That was all Henricks needed to see. He was out of there. He flew down the hall and heard the blast of the pistol and a bullet whiz by his head. Then he was out the front door, down the steps, and running toward the shop. He had a loaded .22 rifle leaning in a corner by the door there, just in case a varmint decided to cause a ruckus.

He never saw Luke coming around the other side of the shop.

* * *

Luke heard the pistol shot inside Henricks' house and went as quickly and safely as possible in the dark toward the house. He suspected there was a killer around, and he might be in there with Henricks. Luke was still thirty yards from the front door when it flew open and Henricks came out like his tail was on fire. Luke almost hollered at him, but five seconds later, a second man carrying a revolver came out the door.

The man was aiming the pistol at the fleeing Henricks, so with no other thought in his head than to protect the running man, Luke pulled up and fired a load of buckshot at the man with the gun on the porch.

He hadn't aimed, he'd just pulled up and shot, figuring some of the buckshot would hit the man and slow him down. And it did. The guy went backwards into the house like someone had pulled him from behind.

Luke jacked another shell into the pump gun, this one carrying a rifled slug, and watched for a minute to see if the man with the gun returned. He didn't, so Luke turned his attention to Henricks. He wanted to make sure that he hadn't been shot and otherwise was okay.

*　*　*

Henricks flew out the door and ran as fast as his legs would carry him. He'd been a running back in high school, and a pretty good one at that, and he was sure he was running as fast as he ever had run before.

He was almost to the edge of the shop when a shot went off to his left. He ducked and chanced a quick look in the direction of the shot and saw, in the little light there was from the front porch light, the game warden aiming a shotgun at his house.

When he got to the shop, he went through the door, found the little .22 rifle, and waited. A minute later, he heard footsteps outside the shop door and Luke's voice say, "Hey, Jim, you okay in there?"

"I'm okay," Henricks said as he opened the shop door and looked at Luke. "That guy scared the shit outta me. Luckily, he's not a great shot. Did you kill him?"

"Don't think so," Luke said as he held up the shotgun. "I'm shooting buckshot, and I believe I hit him, but it would take a one-in-a-thousand shot to kill him."

After a minute, Henricks said, "How did you know to come back here?"

"I saw his rig parked on a little two-track down the road and thought he might be coming to pay you a visit. I tried to get back here quick enough to get you outta there."

"Almost," Henricks said. "What now?"

"I have backup coming," Luke said. "They can clear the house."

Luke pulled out his phone and dialed Hernandez. She should be close.

"You find the guy?" she asked after one ring.

"Sort of," Luke said. "Listen, I need you to pull in behind that black Lincoln SUV and watch for him. If he's trying to get out of here, he'll go for his vehicle."

Luke told her where the Navigator was parked, described the man the best he could from the quick look he'd had of him on the porch, and told her he was probably wounded. She found the little road into the vehicle almost immediately.

"I'm here," she said.

"Okay, be alert and be careful. This guy has killed at least one person and tried for another just now. He's armed."

"Roger that," Hernandez said.

"And call for more backup," Luke said. "We're going to need them."

"Already on their way," Hernandez said.

*   *   *

Covington couldn't believe Henricks had gotten the jump on him. He'd been stunned by the whack on the back of the head, but he hadn't lost his balance totally. He'd tried to turn and shoot, but the guy was quick. He'd taken a snapshot down the hall, saw dust from the sheetrock wall explode just above Henricks' head and watched as he was scrambling out the door.

His head hurt, so he put his hand back there, felt a large pop-knot and sticky liquid matted in his hair. He was bleeding, but at the moment, that didn't matter. He ran to the door, saw Henricks running through the yard, and was just about to shoot at him again when, wham, something hit him in the leg, arm, and shoulder. The bullets, or whatever hit him, did so with enough energy to push him back into the house.

What to do now? He had to get back to his vehicle and get the hell out of there. Covington had no idea who had shot him, but it wasn't Henricks because he'd still been running away when the bullets hit him. Had the game warden returned? Didn't matter. He had to get out of the house now.

Covington ran to the kitchen, opened the back door, and stumbled outside. His leg and arm were burning, and his shoulder and head were pounding. He looked down and saw that his pantleg was already soaked in blood. That wasn't good. He needed to get to his car as quickly as possible.

He hobbled back to where he'd been sitting when he'd spotted the game warden's truck in the driveway. From there, he followed the little trail he had come in on from his vehicle. If he could get to the Lincoln, he would be okay, he thought.

As he got close to the bramble patch, the last hurdle before he would get to his rig, he paused to catch his breath. He was light-headed, probably because he was so out of shape, but also possibly from the loss of blood. As he stood and rested, he heard a female voice over by where he had left his car.

"Roger that," the voice said. "Get Roberts and Vasquez up to the house and send Howard here to me."

Somewhere out there in the night, he heard sirens. It was the law. They had found his vehicle. They were waiting for him.

*　*　*

Luke was tempted to go into Henricks' house, but the sirens he heard in the distance were getting closer, and they were coming fast. He could wait two minutes for the other officers to arrive.

He and Henricks were standing around the side of the shop, Luke with his shotgun trained on the front door, when his phone rang again.

"What's happening?" Luke asked.

"Two deputies will be there in a minute," Hernandez said. "Also got an ID on the owner of the Navigator. Registered to a Peter Covington. Fifty-four-year-old Caucasian. Five foot ten, one hundred and ninety-two pounds. Has a Seattle address."

"Sounds like the man I just shot at," Luke said. "I'm waiting for your deputies to help clear the house. My guess is the guy went out the back door, but if I hit him hard enough with the buckshot, he might still be in there somewhere."

"Roberts and Vasquez are the two deputies coming your way."

"Roger that," Luke said. "Haven't seen or heard anything over your way?"

"Not a thing," Hernandez said.

"Stay vigilant," Luke said.

"I will," Hernandez said. "I have a deputy coming to help here too. He'll be here in a minute."

"Be careful," Luke said and clicked off.

"Ever heard of a man named Peter Covington?" Luke asked.

Henricks thought about it for a minute. "Name sounds familiar, but I can't say as I know who he is."

"That's his rig parked down the road, and by the description I just got from the deputy, it sounds like the guy who was trying to kill you."

Henricks was shaking his head. "All because I killed a wolf?"

"I guess so," Luke said.

Just then, two Kittitas County Sheriff's SUVs appeared around the corner on the county road and swung into Henricks' driveway.

Luke pulled out his badge and held it up in the headlights for the deputies to see as they drove in.

"McCain?" the deputy named Roberts asked.

"Yep, and this is Jim Henricks. This is his place."

Luke gave the two deputies a quick rundown on what had happened.

"My guess is Covington is gone, but let's be careful. I'm pretty sure he's hit. How bad, I don't know."

Luke told Henricks to go sit in his truck while they checked the house.

The two Kittitas deputies went in first, followed by Luke. He now had his service pistol in his hand, as the shotgun could be tough to maneuver in a tight situation. They split up and cleared each room, looking in closets and under the one and only bed in the house.

"Back door is open," Vasquez, the other deputy, said. "And there's blood on the floor."

Luke and Roberts went to the kitchen.

"He's definitely hit," Roberts said.

"We'll need to get some more people out here," Vasquez said.

If Luke had been there by himself, he would have immediately gone into tracker mode and started after Covington. But the attempted murder of Jim Henricks immediately became the jurisdiction of the Kittitas County Sheriff's Office, and since they were on site, they were calling the shots.

Luke walked back to his truck. Henricks climbed out.

"Find anything?" Henricks asked.

"Blood and an open back door," Luke said. "He's out there somewhere."

In the distance, they heard the howl of a lone wolf.

CHAPTER 31

Covington knelt in the grass and listened. He could still hear the female cop talking on the radio occasionally. His shoulder throbbed, and the fiery pain in his arm was getting worse. Even with all that, he was more worried about the wound in his leg. It wasn't nearly as painful as the other two, but the bleeding would not stop.

He remembered reading somewhere that a wound that bled could be stopped by taking a belt and pulling it tight above the wound. He unbuckled his belt, pulled it out through the loops on his pants and wrapped it around his leg. He pulled the belt tight around his leg, but there was no hole for the buckle peg because the belt was made for his waist, not his thigh. It was too big for that part of his leg.

Hearing the woman cop talk again, Covington decided he needed to move. He held the end of the belt with one hand, trying to keep it tight on his thigh, and took off back toward the house. He knew he couldn't go back there, but he had to get far enough away from the woman at his car to start a loop up and around to get back to the county road.

He hobbled away as quickly as he could without making too much noise.

Covington had grown up in the big city and was not an outdoorsy kind of guy. He loved sitting in his chair at his cabin overlooking Cle Elum Lake, but about the only time he was outdoors was when he spent time sitting on the cabin's deck or on the dock on the water below.

"Okay," Covington said to himself as he pushed on, holding the belt tight. "You're a smart guy. You can do this."

He tripped and fell twice over a rock or tree root sitting above ground level. Each time he landed in a heap, making his wounds hurt worse. When he fell, he lost his grip on the belt, and the blood would start up again.

Then he remembered the knife. He never carried a knife but had put a small pen knife in his coat pocket with the binoculars. He could punch a hole in the leather belt with the knife blade to make the belt fit tightly on his thigh.

He pulled the belt tight, put his finger on the spot where he thought the hole should be, and started to work on it. It took a while, but he finally pushed the point of the thin blade through the leather. He turned the thickest part of the blade in circles in the leather to make the hole wider. Then he put the belt around his leg, pulled it tight, and fit the buckle peg through the hole. It didn't totally stop the bleeding, but it stemmed the flow to drops.

Covington sat back. It felt like a major victory. Now he could concentrate on which direction he needed to go. Walking through the dark woods, with the falling and stumbling, and trying to deal with the pain of his wounds, had gotten him off-track. He stood, looked around, and had no idea which way to go.

*　*　*

Because he had shot Covington, Luke couldn't just up and go home. There were questions to be answered and reports by the sheriff's deputies to be filled out. He didn't want to leave anyway, but he felt helpless as the now five different deputies were buzzing around trying to decide what to do while awaiting the arrival of the sheriff himself.

Luke called Sara.

"Hey, where are you?" she asked as she answered the phone.

"Long story," Luke said. He'd been in a couple of different shootings in the past, and while she wasn't ever happy to hear about them, as an FBI agent, she understood it was part of the job. "I'm up above Ellensburg. I've shot at a man trying to kill a man I had come up to interview. I'm fine, but I have to stay here until the sheriff says I can go."

"Did you kill the guy?"

"No, he's wounded and on the run."

"And you aren't going after him? That's not like you."

"I would, but the Kittitas Sheriff's Office is in charge. If they ask me to help with the search, I'll help, I guess."

"Too bad you don't have Jack with you," Sara said. "He'd track the guy for you, wouldn't he?"

"I expect so," Luke said, but the thought of Jack out there tracking someone with the wolves who killed Henricks' hounds in the vicinity didn't sit quite right. Especially after hearing one howl earlier. But he didn't tell Sara that.

"Any ID on the man you shot?"

"Yeah, some guy from Seattle. Might be a vengeance thing. The gentleman I was interviewing killed a gray wolf, and this guy may have been here to seek revenge for the wolf."

"That's weird," Sara said nonchalantly. She'd been around several of Luke's investigations over the years, and many others on her own. She never seemed surprised by what he told her. "Let me know what's happening and when you'll be home."

"I will," Luke said.

"I heard it was supposed to start snowing up that way sometime tonight," Sara said almost as an afterthought.

"Hasn't yet," Luke said. "But it is cold and feels like it could snow."

She told him to be safe, that she loved him, and said goodbye.

* * *

A half hour later, the Kittitas County sheriff showed up and called everyone together. After Luke gave the officers a quick recap of what had happened in the house and the driveway, Deputy Roberts gave an assessment of the current situation.

"The suspect, who we believe is a man by the name of Peter Covington, has been on the run for fifty-seven minutes. He is wounded, but we are unsure how badly. And he is armed. Deputy Hernandez has been at the suspect's vehicle from the first moments after he fled the house, and he has not returned to his car. So, he is still out there somewhere."

The sheriff, who was short, maybe five foot six and a fit hundred and forty pounds, struck an air of authority. His shirt under his jacket was crisp and pressed. Both the shirt and the jacket looked like they had been tailored specifically to fit his small frame.

After thanking his deputy for the assessment, the sheriff said, "We have tracking dogs on the way. But they won't be here for another hour or so. I'm not comfortable sending a bunch of you out there just willy-nilly in the dark without the aid of the dogs, especially with a big snowstorm coming in."

Word of the snowstorm was a surprise to Luke. Sara had mentioned it, but now the sheriff made it sound like it was going to be a major event. If he had just taken off after Covington right away, he might already have the man in custody. Not much he could do about that now.

Luke walked over to the sheriff, whose name was Bob Smith, and said, "I'd be glad to go see if I can find this guy, sheriff. It'd be good to get on his trail before the snow starts falling and covering his tracks."

"Officer McCain," Smith said, looking up at Luke, who had him by almost a foot in height, "I'm sure you'd like to get out there and take the credit for finding this man. You kind of started this whole mess, so why don't you just sit this one out and let my deputies clean it up for you."

There was an obvious arrogance in the man's tone that Luke didn't like. But he just smiled and didn't say anything. He'd been around Smith before and was not impressed with his leadership skills.

"That was rude," Henricks said after Luke walked over and sat down. "Actually, I'm the one who started this whole deal."

"Don't worry about him," Luke said. "He couldn't organize a three-car parade. My guess is Covington will be long gone or possibly dead by the time he gets his manhunt put together."

Three minutes later, the snow started to fall.

*　*　*

Covington had fallen again. He was cold, tired, and just wanted to be back at his cabin, sitting in his overstuffed chair, sipping on a tumbler of Scotch. The freezing temperatures had numbed the pain of his wounds, but the leg with the belt around it was throbbing like crazy. Twice, he had loosened the belt to let blood flow to his foot. With very little blood getting to his toes, they hurt so badly in the cold he hoped they would just fall off.

He knew he needed to keep moving. The problem was he had no idea where he was going. As Covington stood and tried to see something that might help direct him, the temperature changed. It was like it warmed ten degrees in the snap of the fingers. A second later, he felt a snowflake hit his cheek. Then there were more, and in a minute, he was in a beautiful scene from a Christmas card, with snow falling all around him in the forest.

The white snow lightened the woods, but it also created a curtain of flakes, making it even more difficult to see where he was going. He thought about just holing up under a tree until the snow stopped, but he was sure the law would be coming after him.

He spotted what looked like a little trail going slightly downhill. It was a game trail, but since he had never spent any time in the woods, Covington didn't know it. The trail was collecting snow quicker than the surrounding vegetation, which made it stand out somewhat.

He shuffled over to the trail and started walking slowly down it. He stopped a moment later because he thought he heard a hissing sound. But as he listened, he realized what he was hearing were the snowflakes settling on the trees and brush and the ground.

He had been limping down the trail for what he thought was an hour, but in reality was maybe ten or fifteen minutes, when he heard another sound. He froze. Covington listened hard, but all he heard was the snow falling all around him.

Two more steps, and he heard the sound again. This time, he was sure the source of the noise was behind him. He turned and couldn't believe his eyes. There, on the very trail he was walking, was the most beautiful wolf he had ever seen. The animal had gleaming gold eyes set in a dark gray face. Its fur was almost black, streaked with gray. Covington smiled. The animal was here in the wild because of him.

He started talking softly to the wolf.

"Hello, beautiful," Covington said. "Are you here to help me?"

He took a step toward the wolf. He wanted to pet it and show it how much he cared for it and all the other wolves in the world.

The wolf turned a lip up and started to growl—a low, deep growl.

"It's okay," Covington said, reaching out his hand on his good arm. "I won't hurt you. I love you."

The wolf stopped growling.

"See," Covington said softly, taking another step toward the wolf. "I'm kind and good, not like those men who want to kill you."

Then he heard another sound to his right. He looked, and there was a second wolf. This one lighter gray but with the same glowing eyes.

There was another growl to his left. Covington looked and saw a third wolf. It was almost jet black in the white snow background.

"It's okay," Covington said again, although there was a shaky nervousness in his voice now. "I won't hurt you."

Two more wolves appeared out of the trees. He was now pretty much surrounded.

He couldn't run because of his leg and other injuries, and he knew he shouldn't, but he started backing up to try to get down the trail.

The first wolf that had appeared took a step toward him, and again the lip curled and the low growl returned.

Covington reached into his pocket and pulled the revolver out. The last thing he wanted to do was shoot one of these beautiful beasts. In fact, he couldn't shoot one. But maybe if he fired a shot into the air, it would scare them away.

The wolf on his right took a step toward him, and it too snarled and started to growl.

"Please, please, don't make me do this," Covington said, looking at the circle of wolves as he cocked the hammer on the revolver. "I'm your brother. I love you all."

The wolf on the left took a growling step, and the other wolves did the same. Covington pulled the trigger.

CHAPTER 32

Everyone standing around at Henricks' place heard the shot. Deputies Hernandez and Howard at Covington's SUV heard it too.

They all chatted about it for a minute. Hernandez radioed the sheriff, but the never-decisive Bob Smith didn't know what to do.

Two minutes later, from out of the snow, they heard the most eerie sound any of them had ever heard. Not one but several wolves started howling. They howled for three minutes or more. It was mournful and sad.

Later, almost everyone there said it caused the hair on the back of their necks to stand on end and gave them goosebumps.

"Those are the same exact howls I heard from that pack after they killed my hounds," Henricks said to Luke. "I think it's their way of telling the world that they've made a kill. I bet they got him."

"I was kind of thinking the same thing," Luke said as he was retrieving his backpack and shotgun from his truck.

He pulled his winter coat on, threw the backpack over his shoulders, and headed for the back of the house.

"Where are you going, McCain?" Smith barked.

"I'm going to find out what the hell is happening out there," Luke said. "I might not have say over your investigation of Covington, but I do have the authority to see if there's been more wolves killed. Call my boss, call the governor. I don't care. I'm going."

He marched past three deputies who were all smiling and went around Henricks' house. As he feared, the snow had covered any tracks, but Luke figured Covington had tried to get to his car first, so that is the direction he headed.

When he got near where Covington's Navigator was parked, Luke heard Hernandez chatting with another deputy.

"Hey, Hernandez," Luke yelled. "Don't shoot. I'm coming in."

He struggled through a bunch of brambles and popped out to see Hernandez smiling at him.

"I knew you were coming," she said. "Got a text from one of the deputies up at the house. Said you told Smith off pretty good and were headed this way."

Hernandez was a dark-haired, dark-eyed Latina in her early forties. She was short and stocky, but she looked slimmer than the last time Luke had seen her.

"Who the hell voted him into office anyway?" Luke asked.

Hernandez just shrugged her shoulders. "You want me to come with you?" she asked.

"If you won't get into trouble, and if you can keep up," Luke said with a smile.

"I'm jogging twenty miles a week now," Hernandez said. "I can probably run you into the ground."

Running on a flat road or on a treadmill was way different than hiking up and down hills, over logs, and through brush, but Luke didn't say anything about that. What he did say was, "Let's go."

"Which way was the shot?" Luke asked as they started walking.

"That way," Hernandez said, pointing to the northwest.

The second Luke heard the shot while he was standing in Henricks' driveway, he mentally marked the direction it had come from. Between his mark and Hernandez's, they were able to roughly triangulate where the shot had been fired. Nearly fifteen minutes into their search, Luke spotted red blood soaking up through the snow.

"Looks like he was losing a lot of blood," Luke said.

"But just here, nowhere else?" Hernandez asked and then answered her own question. "Maybe he had it bandaged or had a tourniquet on it."

"Maybe," Luke said. "The snow has almost covered his tracks, but I can see he's on this game trail."

"Looks like he's dragging a leg," Hernandez said as she inspected the tracks further.

They had walked another quarter mile when Luke stopped and said, "Oh-oh."

"What?" Hernandez asked.

"Wolf tracks," Luke said. "And they're on top of Covington's tracks. They're following him."

"That's not good," Hernandez said and pulled her service pistol. "Is that scattergun of yours loaded?"

Luke nodded as he knelt and inspected the tracks more closely.

"There's at least three wolves, maybe more," he said.

"Aw geez," Hernandez said. "Would they attack a person?"

"They might if they smell blood. And Covington is definitely bleeding."

* * *

Snow was quickly filling in the wolf tracks on top of Covington's tracks, but Luke could see them well enough to move along at a cautious pace. Drops of blood weren't as obvious as the tracks, but still, Luke would notice one here and there soaking up through the snow as they slowly tracked Covington.

"This is really eerie," Hernandez whispered as she trailed closely behind Luke. "I feel like something is watching us."

"Something or someone?" Luke whispered back.

"I don't know, but it is creepy," Hernandez said.

"Just keep your eyes open and be ready," Luke said.

"Ready for what?"

"Covington, wolves, just be ready."

They kept moving, following the tracks. Big, wet snowflakes hit them in the face, and Hernandez was wiping melted snow droplets off her eyelashes every few seconds.

Their footsteps were virtually silent as they crept along in the fresh snow. They moved as one, like a big ghost floating through the snow and trees.

Luke stopped suddenly, and because she was looking behind her, Hernandez walked right into Luke's back.

"What?" she whispered as she backed up a half-step.

"I heard something running up ahead," Luke said.

"That's not good," Hernandez whispered, adjusting her service pistol in her right hand. "I'd love to see a wolf someday, but not today."

"Whatever it was, it was running away from us," Luke said. "Could have been a deer or an elk."

"I'm not buying that." Hernandez hissed. "It was the wolves, right?"

Luke didn't answer. He brought his shotgun up and started walking slowly ahead.

They walked another twenty yards, and Luke stopped again. This time, Hernandez was watching him and stopped at the same time.

"There's something up ahead," Luke said. "Looks like a person lying in the snow."

Hernandez stepped up next to Luke, wiped the water droplets off her eyelashes one more time, and said, "Ah, man."

When they got to Covington's body, Luke was surprised. There was plenty of blood in the snow, but the wolves hadn't touched him.

"They didn't attack him?" Hernandez asked after looking at Covington's untouched body. "So, what killed him?"

Luke stepped closer for a better look. "Looks like a single bullet to the head," he said.

"He killed himself?" Hernandez asked.

"I think so," Luke said. "Small caliber, probably a .22, just like the man who he is suspected of killing up in Okanogan. The revolver is right there next to him."

Luke was looking around and could see wolf tracks everywhere.

"But why would he do that?" Hernandez asked.

"It looks like the wolves had him surrounded, and figuring they were going to attack him, he decided a bullet to the head would be a quicker death than being eaten alive by the wolves."

"I would too," Hernandez said with a shudder. "But he's got the pistol. Why not go down fighting?"

"He was a wolf lover. He was out to kill the men who were killing the wolves. I guess he figured he would rather die than be known as a wolf killer."

Hernandez just shook her head. Then she pulled the radio mic off her shoulder and called it in.

Seventeen minutes later, Deputies Roberts, Vasquez, and Howard found them standing next to Covington's dead body lying in the snow.

"Where's Smith?" Luke asked when they arrived.

"He got into his rig and took off as soon as Hernandez called it in," Roberts said.

"I'm sure I'll hear about it," Luke said.

"No more than I will," Hernandez said. "I may be on desk duty for a year—that is, if I still have a job."

"Tell Smith you were the one who found the body so that he can save face with his adoring public," Luke said. "Write it up and don't even mention me. Say I was off looking for the wolves when you found the body."

Hernandez didn't say anything, but Luke knew that's probably how she would write it up in her report. He had her back, and she had his.

"We'll need to get the coroner out here," Hernandez said. "We should probably tape off the area, and let's flag the trail back to the dead guy's car."

Luke watched as the senior deputy took control of the situation.

"You got this, Deputy Hernandez," Luke said. "So, I'm going to head back to my truck and get home to see if I still have a wife and dog."

"You are dismissed, Officer McCain," Hernandez said with a smile. Then she said, "Thanks, Luke."

Luke just gave her a little wave and headed back through the woods. In all the excitement, he hadn't even noticed it had stopped snowing at some point. So much for the big snowstorm Smith was touting.

When he arrived at Henricks' house, there were two deputies still there, and they, along with Henricks, were sitting in the front room drinking coffee.

"Did the wolves get him?" Henricks asked as Luke walked into the house.

"In a way they did," Luke said. Then he told them all about tracking the man who had come to kill Henricks and finding his dead body, surrounded by wolf tracks, with a self-inflicted gunshot wound to the head.

After talking with the men for a few more minutes, Luke said so long and headed to his truck. He had just reached the pickup and was about to open the door when the wolves started howling again. They were higher up on the hill, but the eerie howls were just as mournful and hair-raising as they had been earlier.

Luke stood and looked up at the mountain behind Henricks' house for a minute, then he climbed into his truck, started the engine, turned the heater up, put the rig in gear, and drove down the driveway, headed for home.

225

CHAPTER 33

Luke hadn't gotten home until close to midnight, and after giving Sara a blow-by-blow account of what had happened in and around Henricks' place, the two didn't get to bed until after one. So, Luke was still asleep when his phone started buzzing on the nightstand at 9:05.

He sat up, looked at Sara's side of the bed, found it empty, and picked up the phone. He glanced at the screen. It was Deputy Bill Williams.

"Hey, Bill," Luke said sleepily as he sat up on the edge of the bed.

"Hey, sleeping beauty. Did I wake you?"

"As a matter of fact, you did. I had a long and interesting day yesterday."

"So I heard," Williams said. "I just got off the phone with Deputy Hernandez in Ellensburg."

"What's up?" Luke asked.

"Couple things," Williams said. "We got the forensics back on the bullet they took out of Rafe Gibson. Okanogan sheriff says it's a match to the bullet that killed the guy up there."

Luke was still waking up, and it took him a few seconds to process the information.

"But Gibson didn't kill any wolves," Luke said. "Or I don't think he did."

"Hernandez is running the gun they found next to the guy you ran down last night, but everyone is thinking it's the gun that killed the guy in Okanogan. So that would mean he likely killed Gibson too."

"That's strange," Luke said.

"And that would also mean that Zach Taylor didn't have anything to do with Gibson's death," Williams said.

Still in a just-woke-up fog, Luke had to think about what Williams had just said. Zach Taylor? Then it came to him. Taylor was the guy who Jim Kingsbury had seen shoot the elk yesterday morning. Was it really just yesterday?

"Did you talk to Taylor's ex-wife?" Luke asked.

"Yes," Williams said. "But she didn't have much to tell me other than her ex is a deadbeat."

"Yeah, I got that," Luke said. "She had no idea how to reach him?"

"Gave me his cell number, which I think you have as well. I've called it, but get no answer."

"Okay," Luke said, scratching his head. "Well, thanks, Bill. I'll try to figure out how to catch up with Taylor." Then he yawned.

"Geez," Williams said. "I really did wake you, didn't I?"

"It was a long day yesterday," Luke said and hung up.

About that time, Jack padded into the bedroom.

"Hey there," Luke said to Jack. The big yellow dog put his

head in Luke's lap and received the obligatory scratch behind the ears.

While he was petting Jack, Luke listened for Sara. He heard nothing. She had probably been at work for an hour. She should have gotten him up before she left, but he was glad she hadn't.

Before heading to the shower, Luke called his captain and gave him a full rundown on what had happened at Henricks' place.

"Funny," Captain Davis said. "I just got the report from Kittitas County, and it doesn't quite match what you just told me."

"You know the sheriff up there," Luke said, remembering what he had told Hernandez about the report. "He's all about the credit for his department. It doesn't matter to me, and Deputy Hernandez might have been in hot water with him if she didn't say she found the body."

There was a long pause, and then Davis said, "Well, I'm okay with it. Although it wouldn't hurt for us to get a little credit too."

"Hold on to that thought," Luke said. "I think I'm about to bust a couple of guys for poaching three cow elk yesterday morning."

"Busy day yesterday," Davis said. "Let me know how it works out."

Luke said he would. Then he almost asked about how he should handle Henricks and the poached wolf, but let it go.

"Talk to you later," Luke said and clicked off.

"Okay, boy," Luke said to Jack. "Let's get going."

Seeing Luke headed to the shower, Jack lay down on a throw rug and fell fast asleep.

*　*　*

On the road a half hour later, with Jack in his favorite spot in the back seat, Luke thought about how he might catch up to Zach Taylor. The poachers had killed three elk but left one in the meadow that Luke had brought to town. That meant there were two elk that needed to be taken care of. Two big animals, like cow elk, are not easy to butcher, so Luke called around to the different butcher shops in the area to see if Taylor had brought any animals in to them.

Butchers are required by law to take down hunting license and tag information when they receive a game animal. None of the shops said they had taken in anything from anyone by the name of Taylor.

"If you do get an elk, or two, in from him, give me a call, please," Luke said to each of the butchers he called.

Before he'd called the butcher shops, Luke had looked up Taylor to see if he had drawn a cow elk tag. There was no Zachory Taylor listed as holding a special draw tag for a cow elk up in the Bald Mountain unit or anywhere in Washington State.

"Who else do we know that is a butcher?" Luke said to Jack.

He got no reply.

Then he remembered that the brother of Max Tucker was a butcher. And Tucker knew Gibson well enough to know he owned a blue Dodge Ram. And if they worked at the same truck place, Tucker certainly must have known Zach Taylor.

Luke pulled off the road, grabbed his phone, and found the number for Charlie Zimmerman, Max Tucker's nosey neighbor.

"Yeah, hello?" a scratchy voice said after about five rings.

"Mr. Zimmerman, this is Luke McCain, the game warden who has been over there talking to your neighbor a couple of times."

"Oh, sure," Zimmerman said.

"Listen, I know you don't pay much attention to what Mr. Tucker is doing next door, but you didn't happen to see him bring home a cow elk yesterday, did you?"

"There's two of them hanging in the tree in the backyard right now," the old man said. "Tucker and some other man skinned them yesterday afternoon."

"Is Mr. Tucker home?" Luke asked.

"I don't see him in the yard, but that old gold-colored Ford of his is in the driveway. There's an older blue pickup parked there too."

"Okay," Luke said. "Thanks for your help."

"Want me to keep an eye on them for you?" Zimmerman asked.

"No, that's okay," Luke said. "Like I said before, I think Tucker could have a temper, and there's no reason to kick that hornet's nest. I'll be by there in a bit."

Luke thanked Zimmerman again and called Stan Hargraves.

"Hey, Luke," Hargraves said. "That was quite a deal up there in Thorp, huh?"

It didn't surprise Luke that the word had gotten around about what had happened at James Henricks' place.

"Yeah, it was," Luke said.

"And those wolves didn't touch the guy after he shot himself?" Hargraves asked.

"Not that I could see," Luke said. "Listen, I think I have a line on a couple guys who may have poached three cow elk yesterday morning up on Bald Mountain. Any chance you can meet me at an address in west Yakima? I think they have two of the elk there."

"I was just headed up into the Ahtanum," Hargraves said. "But give me the address, and I can meet you there."

"I'll text it to you," Luke said and ended the call.

* * *

Little had changed in the mobile home park. Some residents had Thanksgiving decorations hanging in the window, and a couple had Christmas lights up, even though Christmas was still over six weeks away. Even more still had Halloween decorations in the window, with withering carved pumpkins on the porch, long past October 31.

Luke called Hargraves and said, "I'm waiting at the entrance of the mobile home park."

"I'll be there in three minutes," Hargraves said. He was there in two.

When he pulled in behind Luke, both men got out of their vehicles and met at the back of Luke's truck.

"It sounds like the man who owns the house, Max Tucker, and another guy by the name of Zach Taylor are in the house," Luke explained. "Or they may be in the backyard. I'll go up and knock on the front door, and you can sneak around into the back to make sure no one bolts."

They had done this dozens of times before when making contact at personal residences.

Hargraves just nodded and said, "Lead the way," before walking back to his truck.

Luke drove around the little lane and pulled up in front of Tucker's house. There were no Halloween, Thanksgiving, or Christmas decorations in the window. He stopped his truck squarely behind the blue Dodge Ram, a pickup that Luke was now convinced had been Rafe Gibson's. He looked at the license plate. The number was the same Jim Kingsbury had seen the morning before up near Bald Mountain.

Hargraves pulled in behind Luke, got out, and waved at a little old man sitting on the front porch of the next house over.

"That's Charlie Zimmerman," Luke said as he was walking up the drive to Tucker's house. "Nice old guy, lived here for forty-one years."

Hargraves chuckled.

Luke stepped up onto the old, indoor-outdoor, carpet-covered porch and knocked through the screenless screen door.

He heard footsteps, and a minute later the door swung open.

"Well, if it isn't the game warden," Tucker said, a little too loudly. "What you here to get after me for now?"

Luke could hear footsteps heading to the back door.

"No sense running, Taylor!" Luke yelled. "We have the back covered."

It was wasted breath, as the man was already out the back door. But he didn't go far. Luke had Tucker come with him, and they walked around the house. There, they found Taylor lying face down in the grass, not far from the two skinned elk carcasses, with

Hargrave's knee in his back. Hargraves was putting handcuffs on Taylor's wrists.

"I'm getting too old for this crap," Hargraves said as he stood up, working his right shoulder in a circle.

"Did ya have to tackle him?" Luke asked with a smile on his face.

"Yes," Hargraves said. "And I think I pulled something."

"You shoulda just shot him," Luke said. "That's what I would've done."

"You've already reached your suspect shooting limit this week," Hargraves said as he helped Zach Taylor to his feet.

"I guess I have at that," Luke said as he put cuffs on Tucker.

CHAPTER 34

Two weeks after the shooting at Henricks' place in Thorp, and the arrest of Max Tucker and Zach Taylor for poaching three cow elk, Luke was driving through Naches. He spotted Jim Kingsbury's truck parked at the diner, so he pulled in.

It had been a busy couple of weeks with follow-up interviews and paperwork on the investigation into Peter Covington's death. It was determined that Luke shooting the man to protect James Henricks had been justified. And the Kittitas County coroner confirmed that Covington had taken his own life with the same pistol that was used to kill Arthur Miller in Okanogan and Rafe Gibson. It was never determined where Gibson had been killed.

Luke had talked to Bob Davis about Henricks shooting one of the wolves that had killed his two hounds after he'd had to scare them off his place a few times.

"Hargraves went up there and talked to him earlier and told him he had the right to protect his property and livestock," Luke explained.

He might have forgotten to tell Davis about how Henricks had gone hunting for the wolves and didn't shoot them in the actual act of killing the dogs.

"I think that's justified," Davis said. "Just let Joe Ames know. He'll probably want to see the carcass."

"Already called him," Luke said.

He had put the wolf in the department's cold storage unit and called Ames the day after the shooting at Henricks' place.

An energetic reporter with *The Seattle Times* had done a deep dive on Covington after his strange death on the east slopes of the Cascade Mountains. She found that the man, either through his personal financing or through five different corporations he owned, had donated nearly two million dollars to seven different environmental groups that were suing everyone they could think of to keep the wolves on the state's endangered species list.

The story said Covington had put up tens of thousands of dollars as rewards for the identification and conviction of any person who illegally killed a wolf in Washington State. The reporter was unable to find any payouts for any of the rewards offered.

The reporter did discover that Covington had a large house overlooking Cle Elum Lake, and much to the displeasure of Covington's girlfriend, his last will and testament specified that the lake house and his mansion in Seattle were to be sold with all the proceeds going to the World Wildlife Federation, with specific instructions to use the money for wolves and wolf habitat. The rest of Covington's estate was to be divided equally and donated to the Save a Wolf organization, the Shadowland Foundation, and the Wolf Conservation Center.

After the will was read, his girlfriend immediately hired an attorney to fight for her fair share of Covington's estate, claiming she had been his constant companion for the last nine years. She conveniently omitted the fact that she never accompanied him to the lake house, where he spent nearly five months out of the year. During those months, she traveled abroad with a "friend" named Salvador Espinoza.

It was specified in Covington's will that "the bitch"—he explicitly told his attorney to use those words—was to receive only the 2025 Lincoln Navigator and the 2025 Audi RS E-Tron GT sports car. The girlfriend sold the Navigator to the first used car dealer who came to the impoundment lot in Ellensburg. Then, she and Espinoza drove the Audi to Los Angeles, vowing never to return.

* * *

Three days after it was verified that Covington had killed Artie Miller up in Okanogan, Deke Price wandered into the Okanogan County Sheriff's Office and confessed to being the operator of the website on the dark web that showed photos of poached wolves taken by members of what became known as the Renegades.

Before he went to the sheriff's office, Price had scrubbed his computers of any photos or information that would identify any of the poachers and told the detectives who interviewed him that he never knew anyone's identity. He was just the facilitator, he told them, and once a photo was posted on the site, with the faces blocked out, he immediately destroyed it.

Two days later, two FBI agents showed up on Price's doorstep, escorted him back to the sheriff's office, in handcuffs, and grilled him with questions about the Renegades for five hours. Because he truly knew nothing, he was unable to tell them much.

"Who hacked your site?" one of the FBI agents asked.

"I tried to find out," Price said. "I worked for days trying to figure out who hacked into the site, copied the photos, and posted them all over the place. Whoever it was, they were on a different level than me."

The agents asked Price the same questions nine different ways, but they always got the same answers.

"Listen," Price finally said. "I don't know who the members were, or who hacked the site. I'll gladly take a polygraph test to prove I'm telling the truth."

Finally, the agents escorted Price back to his apartment, unlocked the handcuffs, and let him go.

Price waited an hour, then drove to Trey Creech's house and told him everything that was said.

"So, they don't know I was in the photo with Artie?" Trey asked.

"No, and I wouldn't say another word about it. Ever," Price said. And they didn't.

*   *   *

Luke looked through the café windows and spotted Kingsbury at his favorite booth. He was surprised to see Frank Dugdale, the man with three first names, sitting across from Kingsbury. The two men were in an animated conversation.

Arguing like an old married couple, Luke thought to himself as he jumped out of his truck and headed for the door. He had good news for Kingsbury regarding the bonus points he desperately wanted and felt it was best to give him the news in person.

Max Tucker and Zachory Taylor had pled guilty to killing the three cow elk without the proper tags, and each was fined over a thousand dollars for the poaching infractions. The elk and their rifles had been confiscated. Tucker also lost his hunting license for three years because of his previous poaching violations.

Luke never heard if Taylor's wife had him arrested for stealing the plates off her Chevy Tahoe.

"What are you boys arguing about now?" Luke asked as he slid in next to Dugdale. He wanted to have a front-on view of the shirt Kingsbury was wearing today.

"Putting maggots in your mouth to keep them warm," Dugdale said. "That's an old wives' tale. Nobody ever did that."

"Some of the old boys who fished for whitefish around here did it all the time," Kingsbury said. "Isn't that right, Luke?"

"I think so," Luke said. "But I'd sure want to know where the maggots came from before I did it."

Then he turned to Dugdale and said, "What's become of your lady friend?"

"Aw, I found out she was just after my money," Dugdale said, which sent Kingsbury into a laughing fit.

"You don't have any money," he finally said, coughing and wheezing.

"I got more than you," Dugdale said.

"Never said you didn't," Kingsbury said. "But that gal must have been blind to think you have much."

Luke could see this going on for a while, so he jumped in. "Listen, I have good news for you, Jim. I just found out that you are getting double the reward bonus points for turning in those two guys for shooting the elk up on Bald Mountain."

Kingsbury just smiled, looked at Dugdale, and said, "I told ya! You shoulda dumped that woman and gone elk hunting with me that day."

Then he turned to Luke and said, "Hot dang! Thanks, Luke. Can I buy you a slice of pumpkin pie?"

Luke thought about it for only half a second. Tomorrow was Thanksgiving, and he would get plenty of pumpkin pie, but enjoying a piece with these two characters was worth it.

"I'd love some pie," Luke said. "Thanks."

He looked at Kingsbury's shirt. In bold, sans-serif, white type on a black t-shirt, it read: WHAT DOESN'T KILL YOU WILL MAKE YOU STRONGER. Then, in smaller letters, it read: EXCEPT FOR WOLVES, WOLVES WILL KILL YOU.

Luke chuckled at the shirt and thought about the last few weeks and everything he'd been through.

"Now," Kingsbury said, interrupting Luke's thoughts. "Tell us about what happened up there in the mountains above Thorp. We heard you shot some rich dude with your shotgun."

"Yeah, okay," Luke said. "But can I finish my pie first?"

Acknowledgements

Special thanks to my wife, Terri, and sons, Kyle and Kevin, for reading along and encouraging me as I wrote this book. I know they may be partial, but it makes it so much easier to soldier on when you know someone is excited to know how the story ends.

And thanks to my brother, Doug Phillips, for his assistance on some technical stuff, including his guidance on the quickly changing world of AI. By the way, I have not used artificial intelligence in the writing of any of my books and never will. Like them or not, every word on the preceding pages came out of this simple brain of mine, which has never been, and never will be, compared to a computer.

Thanks also to superfan Alta Conrad, who volunteered again to proofread this book to help make sure it is as mistake-free as possible. I appreciate it greatly!

About the Author

Rob is an award-winning outdoor writer and author of the bestselling and critically acclaimed Luke McCain mystery series set in the wilderness of Eastern Washington and featuring a fish & wildlife officer and his yellow Lab, Jack.

Rob and his wife, Terri, live in Yakima, Washington with their very spoiled Labrador retriever.

www.ingramcontent.com/pod-product-compliance
Lightning Source LLC
Chambersburg PA
CBHW060711190726
48289CB00002B/629